City of the Dead

A Claire DeWitt Mystery

Sara Gran

W F HOWES LTD

This large print edition published in 2011 by
W F Howes Ltd
Unit 4, Rearsby Business Park, Gaddesby Lane,
Rearsby, Leicester LE7 4YH

1 3 5 7 9 10 8 6 4 2

First published in the United Kingdom in 2011
by Faber and Faber Ltd.

A CIP catalogue record for this book is available
from the British Library

ISBN 978 1 40749 064 9

Typeset by Palimpsest Book Production Limited,
Falkirk, Stirlingshire
Printed and bound in Great Britain
by MPG Books Ltd, Bodmin, Cornwall

MIX
Paper from
responsible sources
FSC® C018575

LP

CHAPTER 1

'It's my uncle,' the man said on the phone. 'He's lost. We lost him in the storm.'

'Lost?' I said. 'You mean, he drowned?'

'No,' the man said, distressed. '*Lost*. I mean, yeah, he probably drowned. Probably dead. I haven't heard from him or anything. I can't imagine how he could still be alive.'

'So what's the mystery?' I said.

A crow flew overhead as we talked. I was in Northern California, near Santa Rosa. I sat at a picnic table by a clump of redwoods. A blue jay squawked nearby. Crows used to be bad omens, but now they were so common that it was hard to say.

Omens change. Signs shifts. Nothing is permanent.

That night I dreamed I was back in New Orleans. I hadn't been there in ten years. But now, in my dream, it was during the flood. I sat on a rooftop in the cool, dark night. Moonlight reflected off the water around me. It was quiet. Everyone was gone.

Across the street a man sat on another rooftop in a straight-backed chair. The man flickered in

1

and out of focus like an old piece of film, burned through in spots from light. He was fifty or sixty, white, pale, just on this side of short, with salt-and-pepper hair and bushy eyebrows. He wore a three-piece black suit with a high collar and a black tie. He scowled.

The man looked at me sternly.

'If I told you the truth plainly,' the man said, 'you would not understand.' His voice was scratchy and warped, like an old record. But I could still make out the tinge of a French accent. 'If life gave you answers outright, they would be meaningless. Each detective must take her clues and solve her mysteries for herself. No one can solve your mystery for you; a book cannot tell you the way.'

Now I recognized the man; it was, of course, Jacques Silette, the great French detective. The words were from his one and only book, *Détection*.

I looked around and in the black night I saw a light shimmering in the distance. As the light got closer I saw that it was a rowboat with a lantern attached to the bow.

I thought it had come to rescue us. But it was empty.

'No one will save you,' Silette said from his rooftop. 'No one will come. You are alone in your search; no friend, no lover, no God from above will come to your aid. Your mysteries are yours alone.'

Silette faded in and out, flickering in the moonlight.

'All I can do is leave you clues,' he said. 'And hope that you will not only solve your mysteries, but choose carefully the clues you leave behind. Make your choices wisely, *ma'moiselle*. The mysteries you leave will last for lifetimes after you are gone.

'Remember: you are the only hope for those that come after you.'

I woke up coughing, spitting water out of my mouth.

That morning I talked to my doctor about the dream. Then I called the man back. I took the case.

CHAPTER 2

January 2, 2007

The client already knows the solution to his mystery. But he doesn't want to know. He doesn't hire a detective to solve his mystery. He hires a detective to prove that his mystery can't be solved.

A cab dropped me off at Napoleon House in the French Quarter. The client was already there. I sat across the table from him and listened to him pretend he wanted me to solve his mystery. He didn't know he was pretending. They never do.

My client was Leon Salvatore: male, late forties, graying and shaggy, with something that could have been a beard or maybe the leftovers of a few weeks without shaving. He looked like an old hippie who was never really a hippie at all. He wore jeans and a T-shirt that said CAMERON PARISH CRAWFISH FESTIVAL 2005 above a picture of a smiling red crawfish throwing himself into a kettle.

That would be their last crawfish festival for a while.

4

Leon ordered a beer. I got a Pimm's Cup and a bowl of jambalaya.

'So,' I began. 'The last time you saw your uncle was . . .'

'Saw him?' Leon said. '*Saw* him?' I had an image of him sawing his uncle in half. 'Well, I don't know. Maybe a few months before.'

'So,' I began again, 'when was the last time you spoke to him? Or, you know, can otherwise pinpoint his location in time and space and so on.'

'Oh, okay,' Leon said agreeably. 'I talked to him on the phone Sunday, the night before the storm hit. He was home, and he said he was going to stay home.'

'Which was . . . ?'

'Just a few blocks from here. Vic lived on lower Bourbon. He was going to stay there. I tried to tell him, you know, this is not a good idea. I offered to come get him, to take him with us. I went to my girlfriend's, *former* girlfriend's, house in Abita Springs. *That* was a fucking mistake, but at least we were able to leave pretty easily. So I called Vic on Sunday to see if he'd changed his mind. I talked to him Friday and then again Saturday and again on Sunday. I tried to convince him to evacuate. Obviously, that didn't work. By Monday the phones were down and . . .'

The rest of his sentence was obvious and he didn't say it out loud.

'So,' Leon went on with his story. 'You know. It

5

was a while before I was worried. It was a few days before we could get out of Abita Springs. We were safe up there, but we didn't have any power or water or anything and not a lot of food, so we left when they had the roads cleared. Cleared of the big stuff. It still took us about ten hours to get to Memphis—we had to clear shit off the road every few miles. So, first we went to Memphis for a while, maybe seven days, but that was really crowded and all we could get was this tiny hotel room out near Graceland. And it was full of, you know, Superdome people, and they were really angry, and, you know. It was kind of scary. So then we flew to, hmm, Austin. Right. We have some friends out there and we stayed in a trailer on their place for a while. Then they had some friends coming and we had to go, so we went to stay with some friends in Tampa for a few weeks. Then we went back to Abita Springs for a while. Then—'

The waiter brought our drinks and my food. He set everything down on the table carefully, just so, and I could tell it was the first day he'd ever waited tables.

'Anyway,' Leon said when the waiter left. 'What was I saying?'

'Your uncle,' I reminded him.

'Right,' he said. 'Vic. So it was a while before I realized he was, you know, missing. I mean *missing* missing. Disappeared, not just, uh, misplaced. See, I knew he didn't have phone service, and I figured he lost his cell phone or it never started working again or whatever, so I wasn't surprised not to hear from him for a while. Not for a few days. I figured he probably wouldn't go to the Superdome or the Convention Center. They were forcing people to go, but he was a smart guy and I figured he'd avoid that. And he had, you know, connections. He wasn't just some guy.'

He wasn't. I hadn't known Vic Willing, but I knew who he was. Vic Willing had been an assistant district attorney for the New Orleans prosecutors' office for more than twenty years. He was fifty-six at the time of the storm. He prosecuted murderers and rapists and drug dealers. Like most New Orleans prosecutors, he didn't do it very well. But he did it better than the other prosecutors in his office. He was known as a square-dealing, decently intelligent DA who probably could have actually won cases had he been someplace else—someplace where the cops and the DAs were on speaking terms, someplace where there were less than three or four murders a week, someplace where the prosecutors had secretaries and their own copy machines and government-issued phones.

I'd seen him in court, but I'd never spoken to him. Vic was from a rich neighborhood Uptown, and most of the lawyers from his world – and there were plenty of them – went into something way more lucrative. On any given day in court, Vic would be wearing the most expensive suit in the place. If anyone minded, they kept it to themselves. New Orleans was a little like England: people were comfortable with class distinctions.

Vic had disappeared sometime after August 28, 2005. His French Quarter apartment didn't flood. The whole neighborhood suffered only wind damage and minor flooding from a burst water pipe under the wax museum. He had plenty of food and water available from the dozens of restaurants nearby, some of which stayed open, all of which were broken in to and left open. He even had a small backup generator in his building – not uncommon in New Orleans, where power outages were at least monthly and more often weekly, depending on the time of year and your neighborhood. Leon had looked for Vic, and Vic's friends had looked for Vic, and even the cops had looked for Vic. They had found nothing.

He'd vanished.

'Now, by the *next* Saturday,' Leon continued, 'after they'd cleaned out the city, I started to worry. I mean, *really* worry. Because he should have been able to get to a phone by then. There were bulletin boards you could check. Places online you could check for missing people. So I started with the bulletin boards, the phone calls, all that. I called all the evacuee centers, the nursing homes, the hospitals. Nothing.'

'Any leads?' I asked.

Leon shook his head. 'No. No sign of him. I

8

followed up every 'Elderly' or 'Middle-Aged White Male' I came across. And there were *a lot* of them. You know, some people just lost it. Especially older folks – a lot of them couldn't take the strain and just cracked, mentally. A lot of people didn't know who the hell they were anymore. Thank God for the Internet. You know, hospitals put pictures of old people up, hoping someone would claim them. Young people too. Especially anyone who was, you know, disabled, or ill, or mentally ill to begin with.' He paused. 'It was kind of like a lost and found. But for people.'

We were quiet for a minute. The sun came out for the first time all day. It lit up Leon's face just enough to show his scars and then went back behind a cloud. He was scarred under the surface, scars you wouldn't see unless you'd trained your eyes to see.

Leon frowned and continued. 'Anyway. So I did all that. I called hospitals, nursing homes, I went through all the aid groups, everyone. Nothing. No sign of him. I tried the coroner's office here in the city, thinking maybe they had him. Nothing. That's more or less where I gave up. And then I called you.'

'So,' I said. 'What do you think happened?'

'I don't know,' Leon said. 'I mean, the storm – there were some people you just never saw again. It wasn't like a war, where someone comes and knocks on the door and tells you that your loved one is deceased or whatever. There was no organization or anything like that. People just disappeared.'

We looked at each other.

'How tall was he?' I asked.

'Tall?' Leon said. 'Tall? About six feet?' That's what people say when they don't know how tall a man is. For a woman the answer is five-five. In any case, he was probably close to that, and the water was nowhere near that high in the Quarter. If he'd drowned, he would have had to try pretty hard to do it.

'Is it possible he went to help?' I asked. 'Went out on one of the rescue boats?'

'Well, sure,' Leon said. 'It's *possible*. I guess he could have drowned someplace else. I guess he could have gone *toward* the water, trying to help, but you know, I don't think so. Vic wasn't exactly that type. Not that he was a bad guy,' Leon qualified. 'I mean, he was nice and everything. But swimming around helping people, getting dirty – I don't really see him doing that. He wore these buckskin shoes in the summer and if someone stepped on them, you know, he wasn't happy. So, no, I don't see that. Anyway. He could have been out somewhere, looking for food or whatever, just walking, and he could have been drowned that way. You hear about these walls of water – it's hard to know exactly what happened where. But it's unlikely. So, you know. That's pretty much all I can say.'

We looked at each other for a minute. I shivered. The air was forty degrees and gray, hovering next

10

to snow. This being the South, it was unlikely it would ever quite get there.

'Tell me about your uncle,' I said.

'He was a lawyer,' Leon said. 'You know that.'

'Yes,' I said. 'I know that. What was he like as a person?'

'Huh,' Leon said, as if thinking about it for the first time. 'Well. You know. He seemed nice. We weren't really close. We used to all get together over the years for Thanksgiving and Christmas, birthdays, funerals, whatever. After my mom passed on, I was Vic's only family here in town, so I tried to check in with him every once in a while. Probably not as often as I should have. But he was busy. Work kept him real busy and he had this big social life – he went to balls and that kind of thing, all that rich-person stuff. He was in a lot of clubs, a lot of Mardi Gras stuff. Hmm. He'd lived in New Orleans all his life. I think you know all this.'

'Where's the rest of the family?' I asked.

'Well. My parents are gone. They're gone for a long time now. Vic was my mother's brother. My sisters, one is in New York and one is in L.A. They're great. On my father's side there's still a lot of people here in the city, but that's another family. They saw Vic at holidays and stuff like that, but they weren't close. And Vic, he never had kids. He dated, you know, but nothing ever developed. I don't think he wanted it to develop. I think he liked living alone.'

11

'So as far as *that* family goes, your mother's family, it was just the two of you?'

Leon nodded. 'Here in the city, yes. Just us two. It was just my mother and Vic. They had some cousins, but they were older and they're all gone now.'

'Did you love your uncle?' I asked.

'Well,' Leon said, frowning. 'He was my uncle.'

''Cause you know,' I said. 'This kind of investigation is going to be a lot of money and a lot of time and you might not like what you find out. So if you didn't love him, you might want to rethink this while you can. It's a big thing, and there's no going back.'

Leon paused for a minute before he answered. I finished my jambalaya. The waiter came and took my bowl and spoon and napkin just as slowly and carefully as he had given them to me.

'Vic left me everything,' Leon finally said. 'He didn't have to do that. He had this property – little pieces of land all over the city. He'd inherited it all from his father. I knew there'd been some money there but I didn't know there was that much. It probably would have gone to me no matter what. There was no one else. But Vic, he went to a lawyer and made a will. He made sure I got everything and knew where it was and all that.' He paused again and frowned. 'I thought I would be okay. Until I started cleaning out the apartment. *His* apartment. And then I realized it

12

wasn't right. It wasn't right to leave him like this. I guess I feel like I owe him. Like maybe I owe it to him to find out what happened. Personally – well, he's my uncle. It's not like I *didn't* love him. It's not that I *don't* like him or anything like that. I just. Well. You know.'

'I know,' I said.

'You know what it says in the Bible,' Leon said with resignation. '*Look out for thine uncle as you would thineself.* Or whatever.'

'I don't think that's in the Bible,' I said. 'But it's a nice thought.'

Leon shrugged.

'Oh, and there's one more thing,' he said. 'A kind of important thing. Even though I don't really think it's true.'

'What's that?' I asked.

'There's someone who says he saw him.'

'*Saw* him?' I asked.

'This crazy guy,' Leon said. 'Jackson. I mean, I don't think that's his real name, but that's what people call him. And I don't think he's that crazy, either, but he's, you know, a street person. He hangs out in Jackson Square. Homeless guy. Used to be a musician, I think. I don't really know. Anyway, I saw him when I came back in town and we stopped to talk for a few minutes. And he said he had seen Vic. He knew that Vic was my uncle. Jackson said he saw Vic down near the Convention Center. On Thursday.'

'Thursday,' I said. '*After* the big flood?'

'So he says,' Leon said doubtfully. 'He said they stopped and talked and Vic gave him a few dollars.'

'Thursday,' I said. 'So that would mean he was still alive after the worst of the flood. No wall of water or anything like that.'

'Well, yes, that's what it would mean,' Leon said. He shrugged. 'I don't know. Jackson's a nice guy but, you know. I'm not sure he has a firm grasp on the day of the week.'

We sat quietly for a minute.

'Can I ask you a question?' Leon said.

'Yes,' I said. 'Ask.'

'How old are you?'

'Forty-two,' I said. I was thirty-five. But no one trusts a woman under forty. I'd started being forty when I was twenty-nine.

'Wow,' Leon said. 'Sorry. Just, you know. You look really young. Wow. Do you do something, or—?'

'Water,' I said. 'I drink a lot of water. Eat a lot of fresh fruit. And I do a lot of yoga.' I'd never done yoga. I rarely drank water. 'It really helps with the collagen.'

'And I heard you were in the hospital, maybe,' Leon said hesitantly. 'That there was some issue regarding—'

'Oh, no,' I said. '*That*. No. Not a hospital. It's crazy how rumors spread. That was like a retreat I did. Like an ashram?' I'd never been to an ashram. I'd had something like a nervous breakdown and had ended up in the hospital. 'Now can I ask you something?'

'Okay,' Leon said agreeably. 'Sure.'

'Why me?' I asked. ''Cause you know I'm one of the most expensive detectives in the world. And with travel expenses and everything. And the rumors.'

Leon frowned and sighed. 'Well, I asked around, and people said you were the best.'

'That's true,' I said. 'I am.'

'So what do we do now?' Leon asked. 'I don't really know how this is supposed to work. Do you need to talk to his friends or anything like that?'

'No,' I said. 'Not yet.'

'Do you want to talk to the police?' Leon asked. 'I mean, they did try, so—'

'No,' I said.

'Do you want a list of suspects? 'Cause you know, as a lawyer, he made a lot of enemies, so I figured—'

'No thanks,' I said. 'No. I'm not that kind of detective.'

'So. What are you going to do?'

'I'm going to wait,' I said. 'I'm going to wait, and see what happens.'

Leon frowned.

'Oh,' he said. 'Oh.'

When the waiter brought the bill he dropped it on the floor next to the table, and when he picked it up a rumpled, dirty little piece of paper was

15

stuck to the fake leather wallet. It was a business card. I picked it up. On the card was a poorly drawn picture of a bird flying over rooftops.

NINTH WARD CONSTRUCTION, it said. WE CAN DO IT!

Underneath was an address in the Lower Ninth Ward and a phone number. It wasn't constructing anything now.

I turned it over. A name was written in ballpoint pen on the back. Underneath was a message: *Frank. Call me I can help!*

I put the card carefully in my wallet and put it in my purse.

The first clue.

CHAPTER 3

In my room that night I looked over the file I'd started on Vic Willing. On the inside front cover of the file I'd taped a picture of Vic I'd printed out from the Bar Association website. Vic was fifty-six, male, white, formerly blond, now silver-haired, five-ten—which was taller in New Orleans than in, say, San Francisco or New York— fit enough, good-looking enough, blue-eyed, and wearing an expensive tie. I suspected that he always wore expensive ties.

Also in his file I had his last three credit card statements, banking records for six months, e-mails from his easy-to-hack e-mail account, and medical records. Vic had high blood pressure and high cholesterol, common enough, especially here. Elevated PSA levels could have meant something, but his prostate health hardly mattered now.

As for his shopping, well, his ties *were* expensive, a hundred bucks a pop. So were his hats, his suits, his shoes—even his underwear was silk. He went to expensive restaurants and hotel bars a few nights a week, probably to meet with other lawyers. His e-mails were just as predictable, concerning work, meetings, and occasional social events with friends. He wasn't married and never had been. The society columns occasionally showed him at fundraisers, where he went with friends or friends' wives or other lawyers. I figured he was gay.

A few days ago I'd sent out e-mails to detectives I knew and lawyers I knew and people I knew from New Orleans. It turned out plenty of people I knew knew Vic Willing, had met him or spoken to him or knew someone who had. Their answers were in the file.

A prince, most people said. A really good guy. *Really* good. Generous. Always had time for you, at least a little, considering how valuable his time was. There was the time he bailed his adversary, the defense lawyer Hal Sherman, out of OPP, the notorious Orleans Parish Prison. There was the pro bono consulting work he did on the Shimmel case, on his own time, and there was the job he'd gotten for Harry Terrebone when he got out of rehab and no one else would touch him. He even volunteered, when time allowed, mentoring the young men of New Orleans and encouraging them to abandon their murderous ways. Stay in school, kids. Don't use drugs. Murder is bad. Et cetera.

He was my go-to guy at the DA's office, one retired NOPD cop wrote in an e-mail. *The only one you could deal with. You know what* they're *like. But Vic was different. You could really talk to him.* The cops and the DAs in New Orleans had a long-running

18

feud. It was like the Hatfields and the McCoys. Except when the bullets went flying, it was everyone else who got shot.

Rumors of bribes and corruption hounded the DA's office. Those kinds of accusations were commonplace in any law enforcement bureau – after all, even the most honest agents of the law made mistakes, and people who really did commit crimes didn't like to admit it. And all departments had their bad apples. But in New Orleans most of the apples were bad and most of the accusations were true. Bribery and corruption were everyday business here.

But none of the accusations tainted Vic Willing. *An honest lawyer*, another detective I knew wrote. *If there is such a thing.*

If I were a cop I'd look at Leon for offing Vic. But I was no cop. Leon could probably kill someone if circumstances called for it – most people could. But I didn't see Leon having the organizational talents he would have needed to pull this off.

Vic's banking records were long but dull. A lot of deposits and a lot of withdrawals. He made a semi-decent income at the district attorney's office, but his fancy ties were financed by inheritances. His father, Tolliver Willing, had invested well in real estate and left all of his holdings to his only son, Vic. Leon's mother, Vivian – Vic's sister – had married a musician and was largely cut out of the family fortunes for her bad judgment. Wisely, Vic hadn't sold any of the properties he'd inherited, and was still collecting rent on five residential buildings in the Garden District and the French Quarter when he died. Now they were all Leon's. They were all high and dry and their value had doubled in the past few years. Real estate values had been rising quickly before the storm, and even faster since, now that there was so little real estate left.

I looked at Vic's cases, or what I'd been able to find in the past few days. I'd make a more detailed review later if I needed to. Vic was a prosecutor. Like most New Orleans prosecutors, he won plenty of small cases and lost almost all the big ones. It was nearly impossible to get witnesses to testify in cases of big drug deals or murder because the witnesses knew that, conviction or no, they'd be killed for testifying. No major drug dealer acted alone. Even if the accused was sentenced and locked up – unlikely – one of his compatriots would settle the score. Further, the police department was renowned around the world for its incompetence and its inability to work with other agencies, as was the DA's office. Between the two of them big cases just didn't work. New Orleans' labyrinthine legal system, based on the Napoleonic Code, didn't help matters. Put it all together and New Orleans had both the highest murder rate and one of the lowest conviction rates in the country.

Of 161 murders in New Orleans in the past year,

only one murderer had been successfully prosecuted and convicted. Talk about unlucky – 160 of your pals go free and you go to Angola.

'No, I never ask, "Why me?"' Silette said in his last interview, after his daughter, Belle, had disappeared. 'Because every day of my life before, I had asked, "Why not me?" Now it all makes perfect sense that I should be as miserable as everybody else.'

I got everything back in the file and put away in a dresser drawer. From my suitcase I took a little muslin pouch that had five I Ching coins inside. I threw the coins on the bed. Constance Darling, my teacher, taught me the five-coin method long ago.

Hexagram 25. I looked it up in the old, tattered paperback she'd given me, one of five books I'd packed for the trip: the five-coin *I Ching Manual*; Silette's *Détection; Poison Orchids of Siberia: A Visionary Interpretation*; a book on the witchcraft practices of Northern Mexico; and a paperback novel to read on the plane.

> Hexagram 25: Snake on the mountain. The snake swallows his own tail and is never satiated. When the queen weeps, the rice weeps with her. A good man feeds rice to the snake, and at last he is full. A home without rice is a home without joy.

I picked up the phone and called Leon.

'I'd like to see where Vic lived,' I said. 'Can we do that tomorrow?'

'Well, no,' Leon said. 'I'm helping this guy I know gut his house in Mid-City. But we could do it the next day. Sure. Great.'

'Great,' I said.

'Great,' Leon said. 'And hey. Listen. Could we make a time limit for phone calls? Maybe, you know, ten or eleven?'

I looked at the clock. It was 1:11 A. M.

'Sorry,' I said. 'But no. I don't think that will work.'

When I got off the phone with Leon I called Frank from Ninth Ward Construction. I dialed the number from the card I'd found in Napoleon House.

We can do it! I can help!

Maybe we can. Maybe he could.

The number was disconnected.

From my purse I dug out a magnifying glass and looked more closely at the photo of Vic I'd taped to the file. In plain sight his tie had little green dots on it. Under the magnifying glass I saw it was an animal of some kind. I got a stronger magnifying glass.

The dots were little green parrots, hundreds of them.

Case #113, I wrote across the top of the file. *The Case of the Green Parrot.*

CHAPTER 4

'There are no innocent victims,' wrote Jacques Silette. 'The victim selects his role as carefully and unconsciously as the policeman, the detective, the client, or the villain. Each chooses his role and then forgets this, sometimes for many lifetimes, until one comes along who can remind him. This time you may be the villain or the victim. The next time your roles may switch.

'It is only a role. Try to remember.'

Silette wrote one book, *Détection*, in 1959. Jacques Silette was a genius. So I thought. So a few thousand others around the world thought too. Most people thought he was a liar or an idiot or a fraud or had never heard of him at all. I could forgive the people who'd never heard of him. I wasn't sure about the rest.

Silette's own history was murky. He wasn't especially secretive, just bored by things he already knew. He spent nearly all of his life in Paris. He was born sometime between 1900 and 1910 and became a detective sometime between 1930 and 1940. What is known is that by 1945 he'd solved the famous robbery of the Banque Française and recovered the rarer-than-rare first edition of Vidocq's memoir that had been missing since 1929. We American dicks have it easy, with dozens of murders a day to choose from. The French have to settle for book heists and bank robberies.

I'd moved to New Orleans in 1994 to work for Constance Darling, the detective. She was a former student of Silette's; student, friend, collaborator, lover. I left New Orleans when she was murdered nearly three years later. Constance had spent the late fifties and early sixties in Paris with Silette and then, for reasons I didn't know, abruptly broke it off and moved back to New Orleans. When she left, Silette took up with another student, this one even younger than Constance. For a genius, he was pretty happy, or so it seemed. But his happiness wouldn't last. It never does.

'Happiness is the temporary result of denying the knowledge one already has,' Silette wrote. 'Once one knows what one knows – once one knows the solution to his mysteries – happiness is besides the point. But in rare cases, something much better can bloom.'

But nothing better bloomed for Silette. On a trip to the United States in 1973, Silette returned to his hotel room in New York City after giving a lecture to find his young wife, Marie, only twenty-four years old, drugged unconscious. Their daughter, Belle, was gone. Only two years old, Belle was Silette's only child, and he adored her. A few years later Marie, who had never been entirely stable, died from what the doctors called 'unknown causes': grief.

No one ever saw Belle again. Silette never solved his own greatest mystery. He never found the smallest clue, not the hint of a solution. The great detective went on, but not for long. By 1980 he too was dead, his heart broken, chipped away from every direction – daughter gone, wife gone, work practically forgotten by the few who had ever remembered to begin with.

Constance told me all this late at night over coffee at her kitchen table in New Orleans, in her big house in the Garden District. Constance wasn't much for emotional displays, but she had tears in her eyes as she told me about losing the people she'd loved. Silette had enemies, she told me. Criminals he'd put away, rival detectives, philosophers and psychoanalysts who resented his theories.

'When a person disappears,' Silette wrote in *Détection*, 'the detective must look at what she took with her when she left – not only the material items, but what is gone without her; what she carries with her to the underworld; what words will go unspoken; what no longer exists if she is made to disappear.'

Twenty-odd years after he wrote *Détection*, in his

last interview, Silette was asked his own question: What had disappeared when his daughter vanished?

'My happiness,' he answered. Silette never spoke publicly again.

CHAPTER 5

On my second day in New Orleans I still needed to get a car. I'd planned to do it the day before, but I'd missed my flight from San Francisco to New Orleans and had had to book a later one. I'd gotten to the airport with plenty of time, but I got pulled aside and searched by the TSA folks and asked some questions. Never take a case involving people who can put you on the no-fly list.

'The detective will never be thanked for revealing the truth,' Silette wrote. 'He will be despised, doubted, abhorred, spat upon. There will be no parades, no flowers, no medals for him. His only reward will be the awful, unbearable truth itself. If that is not enough, he is in the wrong line of work, and must rethink his calling altogether.'

In a car rental place by the Convention Center I tried to rent a car. I ended up renting a truck. A big white pickup truck with four wheels across the back, in case I needed to veer off-road and up a mountain to run over some wild game, maybe, or dip into a valley to scout out a source of fire. I'm sure it happens all the time in Gretna.

'This our most popular model,' the woman at the counter recited in a monotone Louisiana accent. 'Everybody want the truck.'

'But *I* don't want a truck,' I said to the woman. '*I* want a car.'

'We outta cars,' she said, not looking at me. 'We only got the truck. You want it?'

At home in San Francisco I drove a two-door Mercedes coupe from 1978. It would fit on the back of the truck with room to spare.

'No,' I said. 'But I'll take it.'

In my big fat truck I put on WWOZ and drove in a spiral through the city. The damage started about fifteen blocks away from the 'sliver by the river,' as people now called the high ground by the Mississippi. That was the oldest part of the city, and the part most likely to be visited by tourists. The sliver was like New Orleans always was. An average tourist visiting the city wouldn't notice much difference. I saw a few collapsed porches, the occasional missing roof, a few abandoned cars turned into garbage dumps. Some of it was storm damage and some of it, no doubt, was just damage.

Past the high and dry sliver was an intermediate zone, the areas where the water only visited, leaving quickly and never coming too high. Services were obviously spotty: most street lights were dark and trash was piled high. Some houses were crumbling down toward death, some were on their way up toward rehab. Signs with letters missing told the story: lots of OTELS and HOT BO LED CRA FISH and AWN SH PS. In the intermediate zone I started to see the marks spray-painted on houses: circles with X's through them, numbers and letters in the hollows of the X. Some of the spray paintings were obvious – *1 dead, 2 cats, 3 live* – but some were mysterious, cryptic: *1x3. TC5.*

Maybe they'd borrowed the letters from the signs; maybe if someone put them back in, all could be repaired.

After a few more blocks I saw the first apartment complexes without walls, furnished rooms exposed, like a dollhouse. Here was a bedroom, there a kitchen, here someone's living room frozen in time. Mixed in were block after block of little wood shotguns, every fourth or fifth house collapsed in a pile of rubble, houses tilted this way or that, ready to give up and tumble down at any minute. Whole blocks of housing projects stood boarded up and empty, some because of the flood, some closed for years.

People were few and far between. I saw some cleaning their houses or walking toward the functioning strips of the city. I saw more sitting on porches, doing what people do when they're overwhelmed. Just trying to think of where to begin was enough to make you sit back down and not get up. But the main occupants of the intermediate zone were drug dealers and their customers. The boys coming in and out of abandoned shotguns and cottages openly carried weapons in their waistbands, barely concealed under oversize jeans and big sweatshirts and thin, billowy white T-shirts. There was no secret to what they were doing.

Their customers were relatively diverse, many of them white, many black, a few Latino, a good number in big pickups with four wheels across the rear like mine, almost all with Texas plates. I didn't know if that meant they were from Texas, here to capitalize on the rebuilding, or if they were locals who bought cars while they were evacuated in Houston, or if people registered their cars in Texas because of Louisiana's sky-high insurance rates. I figured you could get pretty much all the basics here; cocaine in various forms, heroin, maybe meth, possibly pot, although that could be a separate, indoor industry.

The dealers were not diverse. They were all young men between thirteen and twenty-five, all black, and all wearing white T-shirts or white undershirts and huge jeans that hung down to display fancy boxer shorts, sometimes two pairs. Some wore parkas or large hooded sweatshirts to protect from the cold. Most had gold caps on some or all of their teeth. Most had their hair done in twists or braids of one kind or another that ranged from four to six inches long, although a minority wore neat, longer dreadlocks. They were as similar as Wall Street brokers in gray flannel suits or white-coated doctors in a hospital or Marines in uniform – and like those other people in uniform, their sameness subdued something in them, made them forget a piece of themselves. Something that should have been in their eyes wasn't there.

I drove up toward the lake, through Broadmoor and Mid-City to Lakeview. The streets got quieter until the quiet was a roar, eerie and deafening. Here the buildings had a ring around them where the water peaked and sat for a few days before receding. With each block the yellowish-brown water line was higher and higher. It went from the stairs to above the porch to the windows to above the windows, and then there was nothing for it leave a mark on except the trees.

The damage didn't end. It seemed like it should be over, and then on the next block it was worse: buildings missing walls, houses pushed by the force of the water into other houses, cars on top of cars, blocks of houses half collapsed, boats on sidewalks, parking lots of cars covered with the chalky white dust the dirty water left. It had been more than a year since the storm. But on some blocks it was as if nothing had happened since then; literally nothing, not even a breeze or a rainfall or a bird or even a breath.

I drove back down Carrolton. Near the highway I found a flooded, abandoned strip mall. I pulled into the parking lot, and it was hard to imagine that it was ever much less dreary than it was now, with its dollar store and discount beauty supply store and fast food chicken joint and payday loan office and check casher. At each corner of the parking lot was the concrete base of what used to be a streetlight, probably broken long before the storm.

Since I'd been in New Orleans I'd noticed that nearly every car I saw was like mine: a big, shiny new oversize pickup or four-by-four in white or silver, the offspring of drowned cars and FEMA checks and hysteria. But each car or truck had at least one scar: a crushed fender, smashed head- or taillight, a deeply dented side panel or hood or door. People still drove like they were in an emergency: weaving in and out of lanes, driving fast, stopping faster, still trying to outrun the storm. My unblemished truck stuck out like a sore thumb.

If there was anyone within half a mile, I hadn't seen them. I checked my seat belt and tightened it up a bit. Then I started up the truck and drove around the parking lot in figure eights and then in circles, building up a tiny bit of speed with each turn, staying under thirty miles an hour so I wouldn't set off the airbags. I made one more loop and didn't turn and drove right into the base of the streetlight in the corner of the parking lot. Instead of bracing myself I softened every part of my body, and when the truck hit the concrete it was like riding a wave as it broke. I heard a satisfying crush of steel and glass.

The car set off an alarm to let everyone know

it had hurt itself. I turned it off and got out of the car to see the damage. A chunk of concrete had crumbled off the lamppost base, leaving the dead wiring poking out like bones and veins. On the car there was a dent as big as a deer in the front fender, surrounded by a constellation of little mini-dents and bumps and scrapes.

Now I looked normal. Or as much as I ever would.

I drove back down to a gas station on Magazine Street and Washington for some water and snacks for my hotel room. I parked outside the lot on Washington. When I got out with my water and nuts and Chick-o-Sticks, two boys were leaning on the driver's side door of my truck. The boys were about eighteen, wearing the standard uniform of oversize jeans and black hooded zip-front sweatshirts. One had his sleeves pushed up and I saw tattoos on his forearms and hands, number-letter combinations that I knew stood for neighborhoods and gangs and housing projects but looked as random as the markings on the houses: 3MP, 7WB.

The taller boy had short hair and a beautiful face with big, sad, liquid brown eyes. The shorter boy had neat dreadlocks just past his shoulders, and dark skin. His face would have been gentle and friendly if he'd let it. But he was trying hard to make it mean, although he couldn't quite pull it off. Under his sweatshirt the boy with dreadlocks

33

had on a white T-shirt with a photo of another teenage boy on it, hands thrown up in the mudras of neighborhood codes and gang symbols. The picture was framed in a printed frame made of thousand-dollar bills.KWAME 'PEANUT' SINCLAIR, it said. 1990–2006. LOVE U 4-EVER.

'Excuse me,' I said. 'My truck.'

The boy with dreadlocks smiled like the cat who'd swallowed the canary, and stepped away. He tried to look mean but he just looked goofy. A funny, goofy kid with a nine-millimeter under his billowy white shirt.

The taller one didn't step away. He stayed where he was and looked at me and didn't smile.

I stood and looked at him. He was about my size and much, much stronger. Under his baggy clothes I could see the outline of a young, strong body. But if he could generate the energy to throw a punch, I'd be shocked. He looked like he was sleep-walking.

I figured he was looking for someone to take his life. I didn't want it.

Me and the boy looked at each other.

'You oughta thank him,' Dreadlock Boy said, eyes bright, with an accent so thick I could barely understand him.

Suicide Boy and I looked at each other. The gray sky hung low above us.

'Yeah?' I asked. 'Why's that?'

'He guardin' your truck for you,' Dreadlock Boy said.

Suicide Boy looked at me. *End it,* his eyes said. *Do it. Now.*

I didn't say anything. I knew that look.

'It's true,' Dreadlock Boy insisted. 'He put a blessing on it for you. Now it's like, consecreted.'

I figured he meant *consecrAted,* but *consecrEted* was pretty good too. A secretion that consecrates. I looked at my truck. There was a puddle under the front tire. The tire was wet. I figured Suicide Boy had peed on it. *Consecreted* it was.

Dreadlock Boy smiled. Suicide Boy didn't. He kept looking at me, hoping today might be the day he'd be put out of his misery.

It wasn't. Not as far as I was concerned.

'Hey,' Dreadlock Boy said. 'What those tattoos mean?' I have a dozen or so tattoos, but he could see only two: *T* on my left wrist and *K* on my right.

'I don't remember,' I said. 'I was drunk.'

I walked around the truck to the passenger side and unlocked the car and got in. While I did, Suicide Boy finally pushed him-self off the driver's side door and stepped away. I climbed into the driver's seat and started the truck and pulled out without looking at the two boys again, letting the small event die a natural death.

In my rearview mirror I saw the boys standing on the street. Dreadlock Boy was laughing. Suicide Boy wasn't.

*　　*　　*

35

As I drove back downtown I called a crime reporter I knew at the *Times Picayune* to see if he knew anything about Vic Willing.

'Hey!' I said. 'Jimmy! It's Claire DeWitt.'

He laughed. 'Oh my God. Seriously, who is this?'

'Claire,' I said. 'Jimmy, it's Claire. I'm in the city.'

'No, seriously,' he said. 'Come on. Who is this?'

'Really,' I insisted, wondering if I was right. 'It's me. DeWitt.'

'Oh my God,' he said. 'For real? Seriously. You're actually calling me? On the phone? This is actually Claire DeWitt?'

'Yes,' I said, less sure than ever that I was, in fact, Claire DeWitt. 'It's me. Listen, I know we didn't quite—'

'Oh my *God*,' he said again. 'This is rich. This is truly fucking rich. Claire DeWitt. Oh my fucking God.'

'Yeah, so I was thinking, I could really use your—'

'Oh, no. No. Absolutely not. I don't even know why I'm talking to you. No. I'm sorry, but no. I really shouldn't even be talking to you. You know that, don't you? In fact, I'm not talking to you. Goodbye.'

He hung up.

It went better than I expected.

CHAPTER 6

My hotel was guaranteed to come with free wireless. FREE WI-FI, their website said. When I reserved my room, I double-checked.

'You have wireless, right?' I'd asked.

'Absolutely,' the clerk assured me. 'All of our rooms come equipped with free wireless Internet.'

The Internet service hadn't worked for more than three minutes at a time since I'd been there.

'It's *cocks*,' the clerk told me. At first I thought he was describing the men behind the broken wireless service. Later I find out he was talking about Cox, the Internet service provider. 'They're really difficult to deal with. *Cox*. They just screw you.'

After a few false starts the next morning I found a coffee shop on Frenchman Street that had wireless – not through their own service, which was similarly screwed by Cox, but from the bicycle shop next door.

'Cox *loves* them,' the girl in the coffee shop told me bitterly as she made my espresso. 'Cox *always* fixes their stuff first.'

★　　★　　★

I had plans to meet Leon at Vic's apartment at three. I got there at two-thirty and parked the truck across the street and watched. Vic's place was on lower Bourbon Street, near the edge of the Quarter, an old Spanish-style apartment complex from the early 1800s. The block was quiet; the noise and crowds and vomit of upper Bourbon, a few blocks away, didn't reach here. I'd forgotten that in New Orleans every block was its own world; *block by block* was how locals described their city, good and bad. This block was a quiet one, entirely residential on the face of it, although you could bet at least a few illegal enterprises lurked behind the Spanish exteriors. Even the clip-clop of the horse-drawn carriage tours sounded far away. The street was picked up and the sidewalks swept clean.

I walked up and down the street and back to Vic's building. Through the gate I saw a court-yard dominated by a pool. Around the pool were a few metal tables with chairs, and bougainvillea and bamboo grew around the perimeter. On a sunny day it was probably nice. Today it was cold and empty. At three-twenty Leon showed up. I met him by the gate and he let us in. Vic's apartment was on the second floor.

Houses are like people, only less annoying. To take them in you start with the big and work your way down to the small. First I walked through the apartment, looking, with Leon trailing behind. It was swank. Antique furniture, spotlessly clean aside from seventeen months' worth of dust, everything tasteful and neat and magazine-ready. Newish appliances in the kitchen and a hole where the refrigerator had been. Leon told me that's as far as he'd gotten in cleaning out the place. Thank God. Losing the refrigerator was bad enough.

There was a bedroom, an office, a living room, a dining room, and the kitchen. The office was the only room that had any personality. The personality was 'I work a lot.' Neat stacks of papers were piled on the desk. I flipped through them. Money stuff and work stuff, none of it interesting.

I walked through the whole place. Then I did it again, only more slowly, and then again, slower still. Nothing happened. In the kitchen were two sets of dishes, one for special occasions and one for every day. I asked Leon what happened to all the food.

'Well, they made us throw out the fridge,' he said. 'And the rest of it . . .' He frowned. 'I don't know. I guess he ate out a lot.'

'No soup?' I asked. 'No crackers?' Everyone has a can of soup in the cabinets somewhere. Everyone has a can of something they thought they would want and then didn't want but won't throw away because it's perfectly good food.

Leon shrugged.

I went through the apartment again. In the bathroom cabinets I found a variety of prescription drugs dating back to 1995, including a pretty recent and nearly full bottle of Vicodin, which I stuck in my purse along with some penicillin and an almost-empty bottle of Valium. All three were prescribed by a DDS.

'Nothing interesting in here,' I told Leon, swallowing a Valium. He sat on the sofa and turned on the TV, ignoring me.

It isn't enough to open drawers and look in closets and open the medicine chest. Everyone knows that you'll do that. Everyone knows that someday, someone will look in their medicine chest. Everyone knows that someday, someone will look in the locked desk drawer, the safe, the box under the bed. I'd look through all Vic's hiding spots, but I knew all I'd find there is what *he* thought was important. And people are usually wrong about what's important. If I wanted to find out what was really important I needed to look for the places he forgot about. What was so familiar that he didn't think to hide it? What slipped into the cracks of the house – in between the sofa cushions, behind the refrigerator? What had he left in the sink? What was next to the bed? Why these books? Out of millions of books in the world, why did Vic choose to keep these here in his office? The less books a person had, the less the books had to say. Not enough of a sample to observe patterns. One cookbook out of five books meant much less than twenty out of a hundred.

But Vic was easy. There were two cases, fiction and non-, almost all hardcovers. I skimmed the bookshelves. Most of Dickens, all of Flaubert and

Zola, all of Poe, and the complete Mark Twain, all in decent editions. I pulled a copy of *Thérèse Raquin* off the shelf. Its cloth cover stuck to *Nana* on one side and *Germinal* on the other. I cracked the book open and it creaked. Vic hadn't read any of them. A decorator or bookseller had stocked the shelves for him.

In the nonfiction case Vic Willing had a manual for his computer, a manual for his car, and about a hundred books about New Orleans. These looked like someone had actually read them. They were roughly organized by topic: cookbooks, history, politics, architecture. At the end were about ten books on Mardi Gras Indians, also known as Black Indians or Indian gangs.

The Indians were groups of people – mostly black, mostly men – in New Orleans who on Mardi Gras and Saint Joseph's Day and other mysterious occasions got together to play music and dance and chant in their own strange language. They were not Native Americans. Some Indians, like Bo Dollis, were such good musicians that they went professional. In America no one knew who they were, but in Europe and Asia – and in their own neighborhoods in New Orleans – they were stars. The Indians organized themselves into tribes with names like the Wild Magnolias and the White Hawks. Within the tribe were ceremonial, ritualized rankings and jobs and positions. The Spy Boy from each tribe would go ahead and arrange or avoid encounters with other tribes, the Witch

Doctor was the spiritual leader of the tribe, and the Big Chief was, obviously, the Big Chief. On holidays they dressed up in costumes that were somewhat Indian but more Vegas: sequined, beaded, and feathered.

I'd been fascinated by the Indians when I lived there, but never understood them. Constance had Indian friends, but she wouldn't introduce me.

'They're touchy,' she explained. 'Complicated.'

I'd seen Indian practice, far away from the tourists and months away from Mardi Gras, just a group of men together in a dirty park in New Orleans, chanting and playing instruments. It was ten years ago. I'd just got the news that Constance had been killed, and I was driving around the city for no reason at all, taking in what I could before I left. Without her there was no reason to stay. I was near Shakespeare Park when I heard their drumming, and I circled into the park, hoping to catch a glimpse of them.

The men huddled together, some with cowbells and blocks and tambourines, tapping out a beat as they sang. One man stood in the center, his eyes rolled up to heaven, whites shaking under the pink of his eyelids, calling out a chant.

But then the men saw me watching and the practice broke up. The chanting died down, and the men each went in a different direction, and by the time I got out of my car it was as if no one had been there at all.

Most of what the men chanted was in their own Indian language, but a few words were in English.
Sister Constance,
Sister Constance,
You left us all too soon . . .

Apparently Vic had been fascinated by the Indians too, or at least interested. I got a chair and looked on top of the bookshelf. Nothing. As long as I was up there I looked around the room. Nothing but dust.

Under the sideboard was the safe. I craned my head and looked under the desk. There was the combination, scotch-taped to the underside: 8-18-85. I looked at the serial number on the safe. It was the date he bought it.

Inside was another disappointment. A crappy .22 revolver that was practically frozen from rust and less than a grand in cash. I left it open for Leon.

I settled down at Vic's desk. There were some papers on the desk, not filed yet, and I went through those first. Nothing interesting. I turned on the computer. It was nearly empty. Weather, TV schedule, more weather, and sites for three different Mardi Gras krewes. His e-mail was boring and work-related or boring and personal. He was invited to a lot of dinner parties. He didn't go to many.

That was it for the office. I asked Leon if I could use the house keys for a minute. He looked confused but said yes.

I took the keys and left the house and walked down to the corner. Then I stopped, turned, and walked back. Nice block, lots of cute houses, swanky apartment buildings like Vic's, gardens with bougainvillea and banana trees, lots of bright fresh paint. His building didn't have parking, so likely Vic would often have to park a block or more away. Every day Vic would walk down this block, see these gardens, and those cute houses, and then get to his house. His house stood up well by comparison. It was as nice as any in the neighborhood.

I let myself in. Stopped and chatted with a few imaginary people by the pool. I looked at the concrete floor of the courtyard. No bullet marks.

I said goodbye to my imaginary neighbors and climbed the stairs. I opened the door to the house and put the keys on the little antique table placed by the door for just that reason. I looked at Leon, who'd turned on the TV.

'Shoot me,' I said.

Leon lifted up his hand into the shape of a gun and shot me. I fell back. I rolled over and looked at the floor where I'd fallen. Nothing. No gunshot, no stab marks, no blood.

'Can you do me a favor?' I asked.

Leon looked unsure. 'Of course. Sure. It depends.'

'Can you go outside and ring the doorbell?'

Leon looked relieved and went outside. I sat on the sofa. He rang the doorbell. I didn't answer. He rang it again. I flipped through channels on

44

TV. Leon rang the doorbell again. This time I stood up, walked to the door, and answered.

'Oh my God,' I said. 'It's you.'

Leon smiled, getting into the swing of things. Everybody loves a mystery.

'And I have a gun,' he said.

'You're threatening me,' I said. I took a few steps back.

'Yes,' Leon said. 'I'm making threats with the gun. *Real* threats with a *real* gun.'

I thought for a moment. Leon kept his gun hand fixed on me.

'He would have turned,' I said. 'And run toward his gun.'

I turned toward the office.

'Bang,' Leon said behind me.

'Bang,' I repeated. I crouched down and looked at the floor. No bullets, no scars.

'Do you have a metal detector?' I asked Leon.

'Ah, no,' Leon said.

Sometimes I don't get people. For people like Leon it was always someone else's job to bring the metal detector or the magnifying glass or pony up the fingerprint dust. In any case, it was unlikely Vic was shot in the house. No blood, no bullets, nothing out of place.

I left and walked around the block again and thought about nothing. When I came back my mind was fresh. I opened the door and started again. Leon was sitting on the sofa watching *Love Connection*.

45

'You kept the cable on?' I asked.

'No,' Leon said. 'Just the power. They just never shut it off.'

I put my keys and some imaginary mail down on the little antique table by the door. I took off my boots and went to the bathroom. I went to the kitchen and pretended to look for something to eat. With my imaginary snack, I went back to the living room.

That was when I saw it. Something in the living room was off. I stood and looked at the room for a few minutes before I saw what it was.

It was the furniture. The furniture arrangement was off. In a traditional-swanky place like Vic's, the living room should have been symmetrical. But it wasn't.

The sofa was good and centered. One wing chair sat off to the side at a proportionate distance. But the other wing chair was off, a good two feet away from where it should have been.

'Did you move this chair?' I asked Leon.

'Uh, no,' he said. 'Was I supposed to?'

I picked up the chair and checked the rug underneath it. The dents were deep. This chair lived here.

I sat in the chair. If Leon looked straight ahead he saw the TV. But if *I* looked straight ahead I saw the bedroom.

No. Not the bedroom. The bedroom window. I looked around, changed position. There was nothing to see from this chair except the bedroom window.

I got up and went to the bedroom window. It had a little terrace that faced Bourbon Street. It was just big enough for two or three people to stand on. Next to it, coming up from the street, was a live oak tree. In the corner of the tiny terrace was a dead, potted bottle palm.

I stepped through the window to the terrace. I stood still and quiet and closed my eyes. It was cold, and at first I shivered, but I breathed slowly until I wasn't shivering anymore and I was just there.

I heard cars far away. Sirens. Three blocks from here a Dalmatian-Lab mix barked, twice. I heard children crying. Bass-heavy rap shaking a car. The pop of a gun on North Rampart Street. The everyday sounds of the city.

There was a clue here. I could feel it, like vertigo or a sun spot.

Clues are the most misunderstood part of detection. Novice detectives think it's about *finding* clues. But detective work is about *recognizing* clues.

Clues are everywhere. But only some can see.

I took a deep breath through my nose. I smelled food from the restaurant next door, smoke from a fireplace nearby, death, dirt from the potted plant – and something else. I breathed in again. Something grainy and earthy and good but musty, musky.

I opened my eyes. I went to the corner of the terrace and pushed aside the dead palm. Behind it was a wooden bird feeder. Underneath was a little pile of black earth. I took a pinch of the earth and sniffed it.

This was what I'd smelled. Decomposed sunflower seeds. The feeder had fallen off of the live oak tree next to it.

'Erk.'

I looked up. In the tree, two or three feet away from me, was a small green parrot. He was about eight inches tall and a brilliant jungle green, with a creamy white beak. Under his wings two blue feathers peeked out, one on each side. His little feet gripped the branch, and he swayed slightly, as if he were drunk. But his eyes were sharp and sober.

The bird cocked his head and looked at me.

'Erk?' he said.

We looked at each other.

'Restaurant's closed, buddy,' I said. 'Time to get a job.'

But the bird didn't move. He only looked at me with his funny little head moving from side to side. He looked like a clown with fat little clown pants on.

Each clue you find is like a new pair of eyes. Now I looked around the street, and in the trees nearby I saw more birds: finches, pigeons, a female cardinal, a grackle on the ground by the door to the building. I hadn't seen them before. But they were there.

I went back inside.

'He fed birds,' I said to Leon. Leon was still on

the sofa. *Love Connection* had morphed into *Family Feud*.

Leon made a little face of disgust. People in New Orleans have a thing about birds.

'Oh. I forgot about that,' he said. 'Those parrots. I think they've got some program going on to get rid of them. They're an inverted species or whatever you call it.'

'Invasive,' I said. 'So are we.'

'Yeah. They eat crops,' Leon said.

'Unlike us,' I said.

He frowned. 'They're dirty,' he said. 'They spread disease.' I looked at him.

'They're from—' he began, then stopped. 'They live in—'

'I heard some of 'em are communists,' I said. 'Watch out. Do you mind if I take fingerprints?'

'Fingerprints?' Leon said, confused. 'They have fingers?'

'Uh, no,' I said. 'Well, maybe. But not from the parrots. From the house.'

'Oh,' he said. 'I guess not. Knock yourself out.'

From my bag I found a black leatherette case about the size of a composition book. I put the case on the coffee table and took out a small glass jar of black powder, a camelhair brush, and a little book of sticky plastic pages, each page backed with stiff white paper.

First I needed a control print: Vic Willing's. I could probably find one online – in most states lawyers had to leave their prints on file with some regulating body or other – but there was no Internet service nearby and it would be a hassle in any case, so instead I found Vic's toothbrush and hairbrush. Carrying them with my fingernails, I brought them back to the coffee table and dusted them with the black powder. Prints bloomed under the powder like roses. I tore off a few sheets from the book of sticky paper. Carefully I peeled the clear sticky stuff from the white backing and pressed it to the handle of the hairbrush, and then spread it back across the white backing. There were a bunch of smudges and one perfect print. I did the same on the toothbrush. I got another perfect print.

Next I took prints from some spots around the house a visitor was likely to touch, labeling them as I went. The doorknobs. The refrigerator. The safe. The television – you'd be surprised how many murderers put the TV on before or after they kill someone. And the bird feeder. I put all my little papers in an envelope and stuck them in my purse.

I had a feeling there was more to the apartment than I'd seen. Vic had held secrets here. People bury things in their houses, things they can't get rid of but can't take with them. They aren't physical but they exist all the same. All houses are haunted. Some by the past or the future, some by the present.

I went to the bedroom and turned off the lights and lay down in Vic's bed. The sheets were crisp and possibly ironed and not very comfortable. I let my breathing slow down and my mind drain until I was almost asleep.

Almost immediately I sat up and got out of bed. What I'd felt wasn't rest or peace. It was struggle.

Vic was at war with himself. But so are most of us. It was ugly. But it wasn't much of a clue.

I asked Leon if I could hold on to the keys so I could come back and look for more clues if I needed to.

He said no.

'It's just that I only have one set,' he said, shuffling in place a little. 'It's not that I don't trust you,' he clarified.

'It's just that you don't trust me,' I said.

He hemmed and hawed a little before I let him off the hook.

'It's okay,' I lied. 'You will.'

'I'm sure,' he said. 'I will.'

He was lying too.

CHAPTER 7

Constance Darling was an unconventional teacher. She would drive me out to the swamps on a moonless night and leave me there to find my way home by the wind and the stars. She'd toss a newspaper clipping about a murder that took place in Manhattan in 1973 on my desk and tell me to solve it. She taught me to read fingerprints like tea leaves and eyes like maps. She taught me how to smell trouble literally and figuratively. She sent me to lamas and tulkus, to swamis and psychics. Like most detectives, she kept a police scanner in the kitchen, and if we weren't busy we'd go to crime scenes and solve the crimes before the NOPD even showed up. Not that they wanted our help. Most of the time they ignored us. But Constance was always right.

'There are two kinds of detectives,' Constance told me a long time ago. We were in her library in her home in the Garden District. 'The first are those that decide to be a detective. The second are those that have no choice at all.'

We all get the call a little differently, she explained. For some of us it's a dream, sometimes an omen, sometimes one of those big famous life-changing moments – near-death experience, heart attack, loss of a loved one. When it's over you know you've got to do what's been in your heart all along and hang up your shingle as a PI. Whether you're fifteen or fifty, once the call comes to solve mysteries, eventually you'll have to give in.

Constance was a detective since the day she was born. I like to think I was too, even though I had a long, bumpy road between my first bottle of fingerprint dust and my PI union card. But then again, so have most of us.

I was eleven or twelve when someone gave my best friend Tracy the Official Cynthia Silverton Girl Detective Fingerprinting Kit. Something happened to us when we saw that kit; a déjà vu, a thrill of recognition even though we'd never felt it before. With our other best friend, Kelly, we spent weeks fingerprinting every surface of my parents' big, crumbling mansion in Brooklyn, even the south wing, which was supposed to be sealed shut because of the hole in the roof. Kelly lived with her parents in a cramped apartment nearby; Tracy lived in the projects across the street with her father. My house was much better for exploring.

Breaking in to the south wing was our first taste of crime, detection's twin sister.

Tracy, a born criminal, somehow broke open the lock that had been rusted shut for years. We each took a sharp breath when we got the door open

53

and saw the sun streaming in on the broken wood floor, the rotting furniture still in place. Pigeons had moved in, and when I jimmied open the door the birds didn't fly away but looked at us: *What are you doing in our house?* My parents had given us the same look minutes before as we raced through the parlor, where they read a ouija board with their 'adviser,' Dr Oliver. *Money coming soon,* Dr Oliver promised, as always. *I see a windfall any day now.*

But in the south wing my parents, and the whole rest of the world, were miles away. We trod carefully and kept quiet. We didn't know the words for it, but we each felt it – a drop in pressure, a smell, a shudder in the *nadis*, the opening of an inner door.

There was a mystery here.

I put the fingerprinting kit down and carefully, gingerly testing each floor board before we put our weight on it, we crept around the room. The pigeons watched and cooed as we peeked under sheets draped over old furniture, carefully opened doors to closets full of chipped china and disintegrating linens. As far as I could tell it was like the rest of my parents' house, full of old things and dust.

But it was Tracy who knew better. It was Tracy who had the courage to creep around the edges, avoiding the rotted middle of the floor. It was Tracy who found the old dumbwaiter at the far side of the room. Tracy who somehow opened the rusted latch, Tracy who pulled up the old rope, unused for decades. And Tracy who found the mystery.

A copy of Silette's *Détection*, sitting on the tray of the dumb-waiter, waiting for us.

Three years later Tracy disappeared. Kelly and I were the last people we knew of to see her, alive or dead. No one saw Tracy or heard from her again.

Wherever she went, whatever happened to her, she took our copy of *Détection* with her.

CHAPTER 8

Back in my hotel I put on all the lights in the bathroom, the brightest spot in the place. Then I lay a cleanish pillowcase over a piece of wood I'd found on the street and put the wood over the sink, making a table. On the left side of the table I put a clean sample of Vic's fingerprints, nearly complete, from his house. Next to it, on the right, I put a random print I'd taken from the house. I looked at them both under my magnifying glass. It was a match. I changed the second print and looked again. Another match. Again – a match. Again – this time *not* a match. But I was pretty sure it was Vic's left hand – it was the same size and had the same low Whirl of Esteem. I made a note on it and put it aside. Another print – a match. Another – a match.

After fifteen prints I came across one that wasn't a match to either hand. It was big and probably male. UNKNOWN MAN, I labeled it.

I went through the rest of the prints. I found a few more, but most were smeared and degraded. Those people had, likely, visited Vic's house, but not for long and not lately. They'd touched the front door and that was about it. Unknown Man had been in the refrigerator. He'd been in all the kitchen cabinets. He'd been in the bathroom and the bedrooms. Unknown Man had put his hand on the bookshelf. His index finger touched the spine of *Nana*.

Unknown Man had fed the birds.

There was a knock on my door. It was the clerk from the front desk.

When I'd checked in to my hotel on Frenchman Street I'd opened the door and stepped inside and tripped over the bed. From the bed I found a light switch and flicked it on. I was also in reaching distance of the TV, the closet door, the bathroom door, and the dresser.

I'd gone to see the clerk at the desk again. He was a young man, white, in his twenties, and looked like a college student or dropout. He wore a rag wool sweater and shorts and socks and sandals. I guessed, from the looks of him, that *Dude, he liked to party.*

'Hey,' I said. 'Hi. My room's a little small.'

The clerk looked at me blankly.

'Your room?'

'Yeah. Yeah. My room. I checked in yesterday. Room—' I looked at my key. '108.'

The clerk shook his head slowly. He looked at me like he was worried about what might happen if he made me angry. 'Uh, I don't know, *ma'am*. I think that room is taken.'

'Yeah,' I explained. 'It is taken. It's taken by me. I was wondering if maybe you have a bigger room available?'

He looked at me long and hard and finally a spark of recognition lit in his eyes and spread through his face.

'Riiight,' he said, with a little smile. 'I remember you. Room 108, right?'

'Right,' I said. I gave up on the room and moved on to my next query. 'Do you like to party?'

I opened the door and let him in. He looked around. 'Dude. This room is small.'

'Yeah,' I said. 'Someone should do something about that. You got it?'

He handed me a large white envelope with the hotel's logo printed on the corner. I shut the door. I'd paid him up front. I sat on the bed and opened the envelope and smelled the weed. It was shake, probably Mexican, but not half bad. Although if there's any weed that's more than half bad, I haven't met it yet. I put it aside for later and went back to the fingerprints. The next step was scanning them to see who they belonged to.

There was a phone book in my room. It was from 2005.

I asked the clerk at the desk for a phone book. He gave me the same one.

I looked at him.

'That's it,' he said. 'They haven't made a new one.'

We looked at each other.

'It might be kind of out of date,' he said.

In the phone book I found a list of copy places. I stuck the mystery prints in my purse and drove over to the closest spot, on Elysian Fields. I'd scan the prints into the computer, fake some credentials for myself, unlock some passwords, and compare the prints to the databases.

At the copy joint there was a note on the door.

Back in fifeteen minutes

I waited fifeteen minutes. I waited twenty-five. No one came back. I checked the phone book and went to the next place, up in the Central Business District. The young man behind the counter didn't know what a scanner was, although if I wanted to come back when the manager was available, which might be later or tomorrow or never ever ever, perhaps she would be able to advise me. The third place was closed. There was a big bright sign in the window that said OPEN, but they were closed. The fourth place from the phone book was falling down and moldy, with piles of trash in front, obviously unopened since the storm and unlikely to scan anything anytime soon. I went back to the first place, which was now open. But their power was off.

'Might as well go get a cup of coffee and relax,' the man behind the counter said. 'It's gonna be a while.'

I went to the coffee shop. The power was out there too. I got a glass of water. I did not relax. When the power went back on I went back to the copy shop.

Finally I scanned the prints from Vic Willing's house. After a few twists and turns I managed to run it through the local cop's database.

Unknown Man was very, very known to the police: Andray Fairview, unfortunate owner of a misspelled name, a short adult record, and a long juvenile one – supposedly sealed but easy enough to access if you're Claire DeWitt, world's greatest private eye. Current resident of Orleans Parish Prison, being held on possession charges, trial date forthcoming. He'd been arrested yesterday afternoon – just my luck.

I printed out everything I could find on Andray Fairview, the long, sad public record of his life. Andray Fairview, this is going down on your permanent record. I skimmed the papers as they printed. Andray's mother was the county and his father was the state. Lots of arrests, most of them for possession with intent to sell, some for theft, a few for assault, plenty for carrying a concealed weapon. Almost no school record, and what there was was pitiful. Two murder charges, both dropped. I figured I'd rectify that soon enough.

As I was jogging the pages into a rectangle and sticking them into a folder I saw a picture of Andray Fairview and dropped the papers.

It was the boy who'd peed on my truck. Suicide
Boy.

'There are no coincidences,' Silette wrote. 'Only
mysteries that haven't been solved, clues that
haven't been placed. Most are blind to the
language of the bird overheard, the leaf in our
path, the phonographic record stuck in a groove,
the unknown caller on the phone. They don't
see the omens. They don't know how to read the
signs.
  'To them life is like a book with blank pages. But
to the detective, it is an illuminated manuscript
of mysteries.'

CHAPTER 9

*D*étection was long out of print now and hard to find at any price. I bought copies whenever I came across them in thrift shops or used bookstores that didn't know what they had. I'd packed one with me for the trip to New Orleans. I was superstitious about going anywhere without it, even though I knew most of it by heart now.

Détection was maddening. The book is notoriously difficult – sometimes nonsensical, always contradictory, repeating the bad news and never repeating the good, never telling you what you want to hear, always just out of reach.

That was how I knew it was true.

The copy Tracy found in my parents' house was the first U.S. version, a cheap yellow paperback with a picture of Silette on the cover, scowling in a black suit. The publisher, strangely, had decided to market it as part of a crime series. *A real look in the* EXCITING *world of France's top criminologist!* Nothing could be further from the truth. Not unless by 'EXCITING' you meant 'exciting to finally glean a shadow of meaning after years of study.' That kind of exciting.

Once you've read Silette there's no going back, people say. Something in you is changed, and you won't be your old self ever again. No matter how you may want to forget what you've read, you never can.

Once you know the truth, there are no second chances. No do-overs, no changing your mind, no turning back. The door shuts behind you, and locks.

Over the next few months after finding the book in the dumb-waiter, Kelly and Tracy and I took turns with *Détection*, passing it around until we nearly had it memorized. We read the little yellow paperback until the spine cracked and the brittle brown pages crumbled in the corners and the covers fell off the book.

We understood almost none of it. That didn't stop us from loving it.

Détection was a door to another world; a world where, even if we didn't understand things, we were sure they could be understood. A world where people paid attention, where they listened, where they looked for clues. A world where mysteries could be solved. Or so we thought.

By the time we realized we were wrong, that we had misunderstood everything, it was too late. Silette had already branded us. For better or worse, we were not the same girls anymore.

CHAPTER 10

After a few wrong turns I made it to the College of New Orleans in Broadmoor. It had been badly flooded. I remembered where the criminology department was, but when I got there it was closed, and not looking too good. I peered in through a window and saw dim sunlight streaming in: the roof was missing.

A handwritten sign taped to the door said FOR CRIMINOLOGY, LIT, AND OCCUPATIONAL THERAPY CLASSES GO TO DOUBLEWIDE HALL. An arrow pointed straight ahead.

I walked around the building. Behind it was a series of trailers, some connected to each other, some independent. When I got closer I saw a banner hung across the front of the first one: DOUBLEWIDE HALL.

I opened the door to Doublewide Hall. The whole trailer shook when I shut the door behind me. Inside were a few desks piled with banker's boxes and one desk with a blond girl at it. A little sign taped to the girl's desk said RECEPTION.

'Hi,' the blond girl said, fakely friendly. She was alert and cute and about twenty-one. That wasn't her fault. For all I knew there was a heart of pure evil behind that cheerful blond façade.

'Can I help you?'

'Yes,' I said. 'Is Mick Pendell around? I was in the neighborhood and thought—'

'Do you have an appointment?' the blonde asked.

'No,' I said. 'You can just tell him Claire DeWitt is here to see him.'

The blonde made a sad face. 'I'm sorry. I really can't put anyone through without an appointment.'

'You don't have to put me through,' I said. 'You don't have to put me through anything. Just call him.'

'I'm sorry. He really can't see anyone without an appoint—'

'Can you just tell him I'm here?'

'I wish I—'

'Can you just tell him?'

'I really—'

'Tell him.'

'I—'

'Tell him.'

'We—'

'Tell him. Tell him. Please. Just tell him.'

'*Okay,*' she finally said. She didn't try to hide her hatred. I didn't blame her. She picked up the phone and dialed. She muttered a long apology and then hissed *'Claire DeWitt'* as if it were a curse. That's the usual pronunciation. The person

65

on the other end muttered something back. She thanked him and smiled and hung up.

'He says he'd love to see you,' she said brightly. *'With an appointment.* How's—'

'I don't think so,' I said. 'I don't think that's going to work.'

I reached into my purse and found a notepad and a pen. 'How about if I leave Mr Pendell a note. Would you please pass that along to him?'

'Absolutely,' she said. 'I would love to.'

You're dead, I wrote on the paper.

I folded it in half and gave it to the girl. She took the paper with a frozen smile and kept her eyes on her computer screen, unblinking, until I left.

On my way back downtown my phone rang.

'Claire?'

'Yeah?'

'Claire, it's Mike. Mike Yablonsky. How you been?'

'Hungry,' I said. 'Thin. Starving. Since you haven't paid me the five hundred you owe me, I got nothing to eat, Mike. I'm starving here.'

'I'm sure,' he said. 'And I'm sure it looks good on you, Claire. Listen, I got your e-mail. About Vic Willing. Who hired you for that one?'

'The nephew,' I said. 'The guy disappeared in the storm. You knew him?'

Mike was a cop when I lived here. Now he was a PI. He had Constance to thank for that. He

66

wasn't an educated guy but he was smart, and he had the knack. I trusted him. As much as I trusted anyone, at least.

'Yeah,' Mike said. 'He hired me a few times. And I saw him around, you know, court, those PBA fundraisers, shit like that.'

I was way uptown on Claiborne. In front of me on the street was a big white cherry picker, the kind of truck with a big hydraulic arm that could lift someone up twenty or thirty feet in the air to fix a phone pole or wash a window. The truck pulled over by a nexus of power lines on the next corner. I pulled over across the street. I could drive and talk on the phone at the same time. But I wouldn't do either well.

'And?' I said.

'And,' Mike said. 'I don't know.'

'You don't know what?'

Two men in white jumpsuits got out of the cherry picker truck, looked up at the pole where the power lines met, and conferred. I looked around. The power seemed to be working fine here.

'I don't know,' Mike said. 'I mean, I'm not saying he was a bad guy.'

'Of course not,' I said. I figured that was exactly what he was saying. 'But?'

'I mean, he was a good guy,' Mike said defensively. 'Always good to me, at least.'

'But?' I said.

The men got back into the truck. One hopped

into the cherry picker part. The other got behind the controls.

'But something about him,' Mike said. 'Nothing he said. Nothing he did, either. But it was like – like sometimes a cloud would pass over him.'

'A cloud?' I said.

'A black cloud,' Mike said. 'There was something going on there.'

'Like what?' I said.

'Like I got no fucking idea,' Mike said.

That was all he had to say about Vic. He invited me to come out and have dinner with the family in Metairie. I said I would if time allowed. I wouldn't.

A black cloud. I'd felt it in Vic's bedroom, just for a second.

I watched the men in the cherry picker for a few more minutes. I couldn't figure out what they were doing.

I left.

'The detective thinks he is investigating a murder or a missing girl,' Silette wrote. 'But truly he is investigating something else altogether, something he cannot grasp hold of directly. Satisfaction will be rare. Uncertainty will be your natural state. Sureness will always elude you. The detective will always circle around what he wants, never seeing it whole.

'We do not go on despite this. We go on because of it.'

CHAPTER 11

That night I lay in bed and read more about Andray Fairview. He'd been arrested yesterday afternoon, rousted with five other boys for loitering. It must have been just an hour or two after he'd peed on my truck. A search revealed – surprise! – one nine-millimeter semi-automatic handgun, one small bag of what appeared to be crack cocaine, one large bag of what appeared to be marijuana, both pending further testing, and unnamed drug paraphernalia. No cash was mentioned, which would hurt the case but, I was willing to bet, had enriched the cops. My guess was that this was more like a uniformed mugging than a real arrest. Andray would be out in a few days at the longest.

Andray was eighteen, African American, and a native New Orleanean. Father unknown, mother missing since leaving Andray at a hospital three years after giving him a misspelled name and a crack addiction at birth. Andray had officially aged out of foster care six months ago but hadn't actually had a foster placement for six years. Instead he'd been assigned to the St Joseph's

Service Center Home in St Roch – which had closed in 2002. No one noticed that he had no placement after that. He had a record longer than my hotel room, but I didn't see anything more interesting than I'd seen at first glance: more possession, more assault. It didn't take much to rack up those charges, especially if you were black and poor and male. I guessed I'd done a lot more assaulting and carrying and narcotic using and distributing than Andray, but my jacket was less than half as long. Then again, I'd rarely used a nine-millimeter or an AK-47 in my assaulting, like Andray had.

He'd been arrested for murder twice. Both arrests ended in a release after sixty days. That was the usual down here. The locals called it a sixty-day homicide or a misdemeanor murder or a 701–701 being the code that said the cops had sixty days to charge the suspect or let him go. Sixty days was a long time to put a murder charge together. Sixty days was a long time to put the Constitution on hold. But not long enough for this town. More than ninety percent of people arrested for murder in New Orleans were released in sixty days.

But a 701 was no cakewalk for the guy they arrested, either. A homicide suspect in New Orleans was more likely to be murdered himself than tried in court. The cops might as well have painted a target on the kids they held, guilty or not, for sixty days before they put them back out on the street.

Any contact with the cops was grounds for the death penalty, and the judges and juries on the street didn't need sixty days to make a case stick.

People kill each other everywhere. The difference was that in New Orleans, no one tried to stop them. The cops blamed the DA and the DA blamed the cops. The schools blamed the parents and the parents blamed the schools. White people blamed black people and black people blamed white people. In the meantime, everyone went on killing each other.

I put the official records aside and looked at the fingerprints again. Like most criminals, Andray had a strong Robber's Swirl and a short Temper Curve. I wasn't surprised he was in jail. Vic had an overdeveloped Line of Denial and a small scar where his Conscience Whorl should have been. Typical lawyer. But both men had a strong and well-defined Heart Center in their thumbs. I didn't expect that.

Constance taught me the esoteric art of reading fingerprints long ago. There were only a few people left who really knew how to do it, and none here in the States. Some were in Europe, most were in India. When Constance died I had to continue my study from books and intuition.

'Never be afraid to learn from the ether,' Constance told me.

'That's where knowledge lives before someone hunts it, kills it, and mounts it in a book.'

★ ★ ★

I figured I had it solved. Andray Fairview broke in to Vic's house, found him at home, took some food, and took Vic too. Andray probably planned to take Vic to an ATM for a withdrawal. When he found out they were all down, he killed Vic and ditched him in the floodwaters. It wasn't a perfect crime, but it was a damn good one. Given that teenagers are rarely criminal masterminds, I figured the case would be over in a few days. The case of Vic Willing was as good as closed.

Or so I thought until I fell asleep that night.

CHAPTER 12

I walked down a long street that used to be in a city. Now it was deserted, covered with white ash and dried gray mud. Brown plants died along the side of the road. Ruins of cars and houses sat still and broken on either side of the street. The air smelled sweet and sickening, like organic decay.

I saw something at the end of the street – a house or a truck or a large animal. When I got there I saw it was a tank, the old-fashioned kind with a long barrel.

Out from the top popped Vic Willing.

Mardi Gras beads hung from the tank's barrel. *Send to Tom Benson,* someone had written along one side. *George Bush's Lunch Box* was written on the other.

On Vic's shoulder was a green parrot, the kind I'd seen in front of his apartment.

'It's the end of the road,' Vic said. His voice was different from what I'd imagined: grainier, better, more southern.

'Yeah,' I said. 'I see that.'

'There used to be a city here,' he said.

'That was a long time ago,' I said carefully, weighing my words in my hands.

He nodded.

'She told me to tell you,' Vic said. 'Remind you.'

'Remind me what?'

'There are no maps here,' he said.

'Then how do I find my way?' I asked.

Vic smiled at me. 'Follow the clues,' he said. 'You already missed one. Here.'

He tossed something at me. It somersaulted through the slow, thick air to my hand. I caught it. It was a copy of *Détection*. The book fell open to page 108. I couldn't read the text.

'She told me to tell you,' Vic said. 'Believe nothing. Question everything.'

'What?' I said. 'Who?'

But Vic just turned his tank around and drove off, chug-a-chug, down the street.

'She told me to tell you,' I heard him call from the tank. 'Follow the clues. Believe nothing. Question everything. That's the only direction you need.'

When I woke up I rushed to my copy of *Détection* and opened it to 108.

'You cannot follow another's footsteps to the truth,' Silette wrote. 'A hand can point a way. But the hand is not the teaching. The finger that points the way is not the way. The mystery is a pathless land, and each detective must cut her own trail through a cruel territory.

'Believe nothing. Question everything. Follow only the clues.'

I knew the case of Vic Willing wasn't over yet.

CHAPTER 13

The waiting room off Orleans Parish Prison, famously known as OPP, smelled like fear and disinfectant. Most of the other people in the waiting room were mothers and lawyers. Across the room from me was the boy with dreadlocks who'd been with Andray when he'd peed on my truck. He didn't recognize me. He flipped through the pages of a *telenovela* someone had left in the waiting room. In the corner of the room two other boys, both white, leaned forward in their chairs, elbows on their knees. They wore big but short pants with long white socks and white undershirts and baseball hats on sideways. They scowled and tried to look frightening. They succeeded in looking a little frightening.

After waiting an hour and watching other people come and go, I went up to the guard.

'I think you forgot me,' I said. I gave him my name.

'I ain't forget you,' he said defensively. 'You ain't on the list.'

'I put my name on the list when I got here,' I said.

'It ain't here now,' the guard said.

We put my name back on the list. I had to start all over again. It would be at least half an hour before I was called. I went outside for some air.

The two white boys were sitting on the steps, smoking. They looked at me. I looked at them. One was brunette, average build. The other was a redhead and rail-thin. Both had tattoos on their arms like the other boys I'd seen – numbers, letters, codes, memorials. The redhead also had a rosary tattooed around his neck.

There are no coincidences. Only clues you've been too blind to see, doors you haven't found the key to open.

'For the detective whose eyes have truly been opened,' Silette wrote, 'the solution to every mystery is never more than inches away.'

I went over to the boys and sat next to them, inches away.

'Hi,' I said. 'I'm Claire DeWitt. I'm a private eye from Brooklyn, New York.'

They sat up and looked at me. No matter how far downhill it goes into yuppiedom, Brooklyn always impresses people. Between that and the PI business I had a good introduction to anyone under the age of forty who'd ever owned a hip-hop album.

'I'm here working on a case,' I said. 'A *very important* case.'

The boys nodded, and tried to look dependable and upright.

77

'And what I need to know,' I said, 'is if either of you has ever seen this man.'

I took out my picture of Vic Willing and showed it to them.

They looked at the picture. When they did, something happened to the redhead. It was like a door shut across his face and locked tight. He didn't blink. He didn't wrinkle his forehead or move his eyes or any of the other normal things someone would do looking at a photograph. Instead he locked up, like a car that'd run out of oil.

The brunette boy looked at the photo and shook his head.

'Uh-uh,' he said. 'Sorry.' He was telling the truth.

The redhead shook his head. 'Sorry,' he muttered.

He was lying. I looked at him. He started to look nervous. His foot tapped. Suddenly he stood up.

'Fuck this shit,' he said angrily to the other boy, throwing his cigarette on the ground. The brunette looked confused. 'This is *bullshit*,' said the redhead. 'Waiting here all fucking day to see that nigga. He ain't even *come* visit me when I was in Charity, not once. *Fuck* this.'

He turned and walked away without looking at me. The brunette boy, confused, trailed behind him.

The truth may have been inches away. But I still wasn't close enough to grasp it.

I went back inside and read a book I'd brought with me on Mexican witchcraft. When my name was called I went through two metal detectors, both of which missed every piece of metal I had on me, and ended up in a square room that had the same smell and more lawyers and less mothers. A guard pointed to a round table near the middle, where Andray Fairview sat waiting for me where a guard had left him.

I sat in the plastic chair across from him. He didn't look up.

'Hi,' I said. He looked up, saw me, and looked back down. I didn't know if he recognized me or not. I doubted it.

His eyes were big and pale brown, the whites streaked with red and pink. Under the neckline of a thin T-shirt a gunshot scar blossomed on his chest. His eyes were fixed down on the linoleum floor, and his breathing was long and shallow. He sat slumped in his chair as if it took all of his energy to stay sitting up.

'I'm Claire DeWitt,' I said. 'I'm a private investigator.'

That usually gets a good response. Everyone loves a mystery. But Andray just looked up and lifted his eyebrows and then let them fall back down, gradually, to his occipital ridge. If he recognized me, he gave no sign of it.

'I found your fingerprints in someone's house,' I said. 'A man named Vic Willing.'

I gave Andray time to respond. He didn't say

anything. But under the affected blankness on his face I saw something else – fear, maybe, or just loathing. He didn't like me, I saw that. But I couldn't quite make out if he was scared of me too.

Andray had two sharp wrinkles going from the top of his nose to above his eyebrows. Above that three thin creases were etched horizontally across his forehead. He had a lot on his mind for an eighteen-year-old kid. Either he was smart or anxious or both.

Usually I can read people. Most are easy. A hand to the face means they're lying, an extra blink gives away nervousness, a raised eyebrow signifies surprise. But Andray wasn't easy. All the clues were there, but I couldn't put them together in a way that made sense.

I knew one thing. He wasn't happy to see me.

And whatever he knew about Vic Willing, I wouldn't get it easy.

On his arms he had a series of tattoos, most of them coded references to neighborhoods, housing projects, gang affiliations, and sundry other historical markers, in bold gothic print. One tattoo stood out. It was on the back of his right hand. In fancified, delicate script, it said LALI.

'Who's Lali?' I asked.

'No one,' he said. It was the first time he'd spoken to me: his voice was deep and his accent was heavy. 'No one' came out as one short, hostile word: *no-un*.

'No one,' I repeated. 'I got some tattoos like that too.'

He ignored my attempt at a joke. For a split second, I saw something in his face. It was a question, asking for something. *Save me*, it said. Or maybe *Kill me*.

'She your girlfriend?' I asked.

He looked away again and didn't say anything.

'Vic Willing disappeared sometime during the storm,' I said. 'I'm trying to find out what happened to him.' I'd noticed that when people in New Orleans said 'the storm' they didn't mean the literal storm, which only lasted a few hours. They mean the whole week, the time between when evacuations began and when they ended seven or eight days later.

Andray didn't say anything.

'Can you tell me where you were?' I asked. 'During the storm?'

'Convention Center,' he mumbled.

'Let's start earlier than that,' I said. 'Let's start with Friday night. The Friday before the storm. What'd you do that Friday night?'

He took a deep breath and sat up a little and looked at me directly for the first time.

'Friday night,' he said. 'Friday night was just normal. *Sunday* night, that's when it started. We went down to the Superdome. We got out of there *fast*. They didn't want to let no one out, but we found a way.'

'*We?*' I said.

81

Andray nodded. 'Me and Terrell,' he said.

'Who's Terrell?' I asked.

Andray looked like he was surprised I didn't know Terrell. It wasn't unreasonable in New Orleans, where everyone knows each other.

'No one,' Andray said, blinking. 'A guy I know. You ain't know him. It was me, him, and Trey. Trey, he gone, so you ain't getting no alibi from him. So then I start looking for my girlfriend, Lali. Ever since the storm she don't want nothing to do with me, but then she was my girlfriend. So I go to this house where she's at and I get her. Then, me and Terrell and Lali and Trey, we go looking for my mother.'

'You find her?' I asked. I hadn't known he still knew his mother. That wasn't in the file.

He shook his head, and came to life, which in this case meant getting angry.

'So then I went down to the Superdome, to look for her,' Andray went on. 'By then, they had people in the Convention Center too. So we went over there and, you know, that was some fucked-up shit. So me and my friend Peanut – he dead so don't waste your time looking for him – we go off and we got a car for everyone to get out of town in. And so me, Terrell, Peanut, Pee Wee, Lali, Peanut's little sister, her kids, Pee Wee's girl, *her* kids – we all drove out to Houston. Drove right up to the Astrodome, and those mothafuckas turned us down. Said we weren't authorized or some shit like that. But then these other people, they saw us get turned away. And they took us back to their own house, their own house where they lived, and they made us dinner, found us a place to stay, all that. Nelson, was their name. Tom and Mary Nelson. So, you know,' he said, in case I was wondering, 'they got some good people out there too.'

'What day was that?' I asked.

Andray shrugged. 'I lost count,' he said. 'One day just bleed right into the next.'

I changed tracks again.

'How did you know Vic Willing?' I asked.

'I did the pool in his building a few times,' Andray said. 'Pool place. They sent me to him.'

I'd seen on his sheet that last year Andray had hooked up with a nonprofit called Southern Defense. They sent him to an employer called Supirior Pools, Inc. – *sic* – the pool place in question. He did about ten jobs for them before he stopped showing up.

'Yet your prints were all over the apartment,' I said.

'I went in sometimes,' Andray said. He seemed insulted that I would think otherwise. 'You know, use the bathroom, have a drink. He all right. He give me a drink, something to eat, stuff like that.'

'What'd you drink?' I asked.

'Water,' he said, without skipping a beat.

'What'd you eat?'

'Sandwich.'

'What kind?'

83

He shrugged.

'Huh,' I said. 'So what'd you guys talk about?'

Andray shrugged again. 'Shit.'

'Sorry,' I said, leaning forward. 'I should have been more specific. What did you talk about? When he was giving you water and mystery sandwiches, what did you talk about?'

Andray shrugged again. 'Just talked.'

'Sorry,' I said, leaning back. 'My fault. I don't think I'm making myself clear. See, I think you probably *weren't* close personal friends with Vic Willing. I think you probably *killed* Vic Willing, and I think at the very least you looted his house. So I'm giving you the chance to defend the extremely unlikely possibility that you and Vic Willing actually had a *relationship* by explaining to me what the basis of that relationship was by telling me *what you talked about when you talked to Vic Willing.*'

Andray looked at me.

'Birds,' he said defensively. The lines on his face deepened, and he scowled. 'We talked about birds.'

'Birds?' I said.

'Yeah,' Andray said. 'He fed these birds. Made a big fucking mess on the terrace. Seeds everywhere and bird shit and shit like that. He pay me extra to clean it up for him when I did the pool. I thought birds were, I don't know, like rats. Dirty. No good. But, you know. Once you watch them they're like – I don't know. They're cool. They're just, you know—' He shrugged.

84

'Birds?' I suggested.

'Yeah,' Andray said. 'Just birds. He showed 'em to me, you know, all the different kinds and stuff.'

'Vic did?' I said skeptically. 'Vic told you about the different kinds of birds?'

'Look,' Andray said angrily, reaching into his back pocket. 'He gave me this. A book. To show me the different kinds.'

He handed me a small paperback book. With a chill I saw the familiar blackbird on the cover of the slim paperback.

Détection, by Jacques Silette. On the cover of this edition, the U.K. paperback, was a blackbird in flight.

'The mystery is not solved by the use of finger-prints or suspects or the identification of weapons,' Silette wrote. 'These things serve only to trigger the detective's memory. The detective and the client, the victim and the criminal – all already know the solution to the mystery.

'They need only to remember it, and recognize it when it appears.'

CHAPTER 14

I went out to breakfast at the Clover Grill the next morning. Over eggs and grits I looked over Andray's file again. He'd shut down after showing me his copy of *Détection* and I'd left soon after.

I didn't know where he'd gotten that book. I doubted Vic Willing gave it to him to show him the different kinds of birds, since it was not, in fact, about birds.

Then how had he gotten it? And why did he carry it in his pocket? When I'd asked him he'd gone back to monosyllabic non-responses. *I dunno. Nothin'. No reason.*

Détection, I wrote in my file. *Andray. Why?*

I went back to his record. He'd been removed from one foster home for suspected sexual abuse by the foster father and another for suspicion of neglect by the foster mother. After that he'd been ripe for picking by the gangs that ruled New Orleans.

In other cities there were programs and missions and social workers just waiting for a malleable lump of humanity like Andray to fall into their

86

lap. They'd train him to be obedient to a boss and a wife instead of a pimp or a gang leader. That was objectionable on its own terms, but at least he'd have a chance. But there weren't enough of those programs in New Orleans in any case, and most of the few that had existed had closed since the storm. If he could find a program, he'd have to compete for a spot with twenty other kids, all of them probably a better risk than he was.

And besides, I was pretty sure early death was a job benefit for Andray.

When I came back from breakfast Mick Pendell was waiting in the lobby of my hotel for me. He sat stiffly on a rigid high-backed chair, flipping through *Detective's Quarterly*. He looked like he was waiting to see a doctor about an unusual lump.

I hadn't seen Mick in nearly ten years. I recognized his tattoos before I recognized his face, especially the little star near his eye on his left temple. I felt a rush of something I couldn't name – nostalgia, maybe, maybe happiness.

I put a lid on it.

'Well, gee,' I said coldly. 'It's my lucky fucking day.'

Mick heard my voice and jumped up. He looked good. He'd gone a little gray around the edges but he carried it well. He wore an old black sweater over a T-shirt, and black jeans, all of it faded and rumpled and not too clean. He had his sweater pushed up, and I saw that his arms were now completely covered in traditional Japanese tattoos: water, flowers, black swirls. On his knuckles were rune marks and around his wrists were words: HATE on the left and LOVE on the right.

If you ask me, if you can't remember which is which, maybe you ought to stay home.

'But unfortunately,' I said, 'you didn't make an appointment. So. You know. Bye.'

Mick laughed as if I were joking.

'Claire,' he said, smiling wide, his voice deep and aged. 'Claire. Oh my God. I am *so happy to see you.*'

I didn't need to be a private dick to know he was lying. No one has ever been happy to see me. Not unless I owed them money. Even that didn't always fly.

I looked at him.

'I'm sorry I couldn't see you,' Mick said, putting his hands in and out of his pockets. 'I'm sorry about the appointment thing. I just—'

'You just had better things to do,' I finished for him. 'As do I.'

I turned to walk through the courtyard to my room. Mick followed.

'It's just—' he began.

I walked faster. He caught up to me.

'It's just—' he said again.

We'd reached my room. I took out my key and opened the door.

'Sorry,' I said. 'I would invite you. It's *just* that,

you know, I want you to go away.' I waved my fingers. 'Go.'

'Claire,' Mick said, trying to catch my eye. 'Claire. I'm sorry about the appointment thing.'

'No, you're not,' I said. 'You came here because you want something. And whatever it is, you're not getting it. So you can go now.'

'Oh, come ON!' Mick cried, maneuvering between me and the door. 'I was in with a student! I—'

'You're lying,' I said. 'Next you're going to tell me you value our friendship and that you think of me often and you're so sorry we lost touch and then you're going to ask for whatever it was you were going to ask me for. So you might as well just ask and get it over with.'

'I *do* value—' he began.

'Look at the time!' I cried, looking at my watchless wrist. 'It's all gone. There's none left.'

Mick sighed. 'Yeah, okay,' he said, dropping his fake smile. 'Listen. I *do* need your help.'

'Oh-h-h,' I said slowly. 'You need my help. What a fucking surprise. I never would have guessed. I am totally fucking—'

'Okay,' he said softly. 'Okay.'

We didn't say anything for another long minute. We each shivered.

'I'm cold,' Mick said. 'Come on.' I looked at him again. Now that he wasn't trying so hard I saw that he was tired. He looked older than I'd expected him to be. If I was thirty-five that made

89

him forty-ish. He looked ten years older than that.

I opened the door and didn't stop Mick from coming in behind me. There was a heater along the baseboard of one wall and I cranked it up. I put down my bag and took off my coat and sat on the bed, curling my feet under me. From the ashtray on the dresser I took half a leftover joint and lit it up, inhaling deeply.

Mick sat on the end of the bed. He took the joint when I passed it to him and smoked a little before handing it back to me.

'I heard you went to see Andray Fairview in OPP yesterday,' he said.

I blinked. Out of all the things Mick had possibly wanted, I hadn't expected anything to do with Vic or Andray.

'That was fast,' I said.

'I'm in this *group*,' Mick explained, as if he knew how ridiculous it was. 'Southern Defense. We provide legal services to people who otherwise would get none. People like Andray.'

'You *volunteer*?' I said. 'Mick, that's fucking *incredible* of you. You deserve a *fucking medal*. Don't for a minute think that I'm not impressed, because—'

'Believe it or not, Claire, I'm not trying to impress you,' he said bitterly. 'I—'

'I choose not to believe it,' I said. 'But what do you do? Don't they get public defenders?'

Mick lay back on the bed and smoked a little

more weed. He sighed again. 'Of course they get one *on paper*,' he began.

'Stop sighing,' I said. 'It's annoying.'

He took another big inhale but this time stifled the sigh and exhaled silently. 'Yeah. So they get a defender on paper, but there aren't really any here. So this group, Southern Defense, they're supposed to help by giving them defenders. But they don't have enough defenders either. They've got fourteen but they're all totally overextended. So they recruited people like me, criminologists—'

'Professors of criminology,' I corrected him. Mick used to be a PI but gave it up to teach and donate his time to nonprofits like this. I hadn't forgiven him for it yet, and I didn't plan on doing so anytime soon. Teaching was a waste. School was the worst possible place to learn anything, or so it seemed to me from my brief time there. If he really wanted to help people he ought to be out there solving mysteries.

'Whatever,' he said, muting another a sigh and rolling his eyes. 'There's a bunch of us who are like the second string, who can't serve in court but can give advice and hook people up with resources or whatever. So I was working with Andray on this bullshit charge he's in there for now, and then today he mentions to me that a crazy white lady came to accuse him of murder. And, well—'

'And I'm still the first crazy white lady you think

of,' I finished for him. 'That is practically fucking *moving*, Mick. Really. It's almost touching.'

Mick sat up.

'Listen,' he said. 'Claire. Andray Fairview did not kill Vic Willing.'

'How do you know?' I asked.

'I know him,' Mick insisted. 'He did *not* kill Vic Willing.'

He sounded anxious. He hoped he was telling the truth, but he was far from sure.

It doesn't matter what people want to hear. It doesn't matter if people like you. It doesn't matter if the whole world thinks you're crazy. It doesn't matter whose heart you break. What matters is the truth.

I lay back on the bed and looked at the ceiling. Mick lay next to me and tried to catch my eye. We lay next to each other and passed the joint back and forth. A carriage trotted down Frenchman Street. Two drunks argued as they walked past the hotel, slurred words indecipherable.

'Are you going to tell the cops?' Mick asked after a while.

'No,' I said. 'I won't do anything until I'm sure he did it. Even then, I'll probably leave it up to the client.'

'He's a good kid,' Mick said. 'If you get to know him, you'll like him.'

'I don't like anyone,' I said. 'Especially kids. And especially good ones.'

'He's different,' Mick said.

'No one's different,' I said. 'Except worse. That kind of different.'

He rolled over onto his side and looked at me. He was starting to wrinkle around his temples, lines spreading out through his tattoo. But he still looked good. I didn't say anything.

'You know me,' Mick said finally. 'Give him a chance, okay?'

I sat up on the bed and pretended to be interested in my fingernails and didn't say anything.

I didn't know when Mick and I had stopped being friends. We'd both been apprenticed to Constance, him before me. We were never rivals; we were more like brother and sister.

But Constance took a whole world with her when she died. In the world she left behind, we were just two people who used to know each other. To her we were two other people, a better Claire and a better Mick. For all practical purposes they'd died along with Constance. As far as I knew no one missed them.

No one except me.

'Okay,' I said. 'I'll look into it. I'm not making any promises. But I'll look into it a little more.'

'Shit,' Mick said, sitting up. 'Thank you, Claire. I mean it. Thanks.' But he wasn't smiling. He just looked a little less miserable.

'*But*,' I said. 'You're helping. And you are *not* doing the fun stuff.'

Mick nodded. He knew what I was talking about. Financial records, case files, evidence – if we found

93

any – all of it would have to be sifted through. It was boring work, and he was good at it.

'Fine,' I said. 'Now tell me what you know about Vic Willing.'

Mick shrugged. 'People said he was a good guy. I met him a few times. Never worked on a case he prosecuted, but you get to know people. He was one of these *guys*, you know, a real New Orleans character. Talked a lot, had a loud voice, went to Galatoire's and places like that. Wore seersucker suits. Sort of super-confident in that way that rich people are, sometimes. Very white-guy alpha male. Charming. You know the type.'

I shrugged. I didn't know if I knew the type.

We talked about Vic some more. Mick didn't have anything interesting to say. Then we went over Andray's alibi, slim as it was. I asked Mick about the people Andray had spent the week of the storm with, or said he did.

'Huh,' Mick said, frowning. 'Huh. Trey's gone, not dead, I don't think, but I don't know where. Peanut is no longer with us, unfortunately: definitely dead. Terrell . . . well, he's around, but I'm not sure – he's not really such a hot alibi. He's kind of, you know, in the life. Lali, she might be okay.'

He told me where to find Lali. Turn right at the abandoned gas station. Left at the fallen-down house. Watch yourself on the next corner; it's hot these days.

'I heard you were in the hospital,' Mick said. 'You okay?'

94

'Yeah,' I said. 'No. I don't know why everyone thinks that. I went to a spa for a while. That's all.'

I asked Mick if he knew why Andray would have a copy of *Détection*.

'Andray?' Mick said. '*Détection*? The Silette book?'

'Yeah,' I said. 'The Silette book.'

Mick wasn't into *Détection*. He took what Constance had to offer but wasn't interested in what was behind it. To him it was just a crazy book, one of many crazy books Constance and I had passed back and forth. Mick thought books were just books.

He shook his head. 'I can't even begin to imagine,' he said. 'I'm not even sure how well Andray can read. I mean, he can get by, but that's a hard book.'

I sat up and told Mick to leave. He asked if he could take me to lunch the next day and I said yes. Then he left.

I remembered what he used to smell like, woodsy and sweaty. I rolled over on the bed to the spot where he'd been.

He didn't smell like that anymore. Now he smelled like pot and plaster dust and smoke and mold. Like sadness. Like New Orleans.

CHAPTER 15

A few months ago, after a hard case, I'd gone on a fast to purify myself from its ill effects. I stopped eating. I stopped sleeping. I did not stop using drugs. A week went by, then two, then a month. After fourteen days I could see the codes in grocery receipts and billboards. After thirty days I could read clues in the wind, see signs in the clouds. But on the thirty-second day I collapsed a few blocks from my apartment in Chinatown. The ER doctor in the Chinese Hospital sat on the side of my bed and looked at my chart. He made notes in Chinese. I'm not Chinese and he didn't know I could read what he wrote. *Affectless. Listless.*

'Dr Chang says you're his patient,' he said. The doctor was young and looked pretty listless himself. But Chang's name gets you special treatment around here, and he pretended to be interested in me.

I nodded. I was studying the patterns of the fabric of the sheets. There were fractals in the warp, quadratic equations in the weave.

'Chang says you're a detective,' he said. 'You solve mysteries.'

I nodded. I moved my gaze to the water in the plastic cup by my bed. When I moved the water shook, rippling the quantum particles in all directions of time. I had known of this before but had never seen it with my own eyes. I could see all kinds of things now I couldn't see before; things I'd only read about, things I'd dreamed of.

'If you want to kill yourself,' the doctor said wearily, 'this is, like, the least efficient way possible to do it. And it's going to be really, really unpleasant. Because we will make you eat. We will make you sleep. And you really don't want a feeding tube down your throat.'

'What do they put in those things, anyway?' I asked, suddenly curious. 'Is it, like, ground-up food? Ensure? Glucose? Do you put vitamins in, because—'

'Yeah. It's a solution,' the doctor said.

'A solution,' I repeated. Every mystery has a solution. Maybe that was the solution to this one.

The doctor kept talking but I stopped listening. Some amount of time passed, or appeared to. The doctor wasn't there anymore. My own doctor, Nick Chang, came in. Dr Chang is trained in Traditional Chinese medicine, in Chi Gong, yogic flying, ayurveda, and the teachings of Edgar Cayce. Among other things.

I thought he would understand.

'I can see everything,' I told him. 'I'm not sick. I'm fasting.'

'Fasting you plan ahead of time,' Nick said. 'You just stopped eating.'

'I'm spontaneous,' I said. 'You know that.'

'You have three choices, Claire,' he said, trying to catch my eye. 'Check in to hospital. Get put into hospital. Or come with me.'

I watched as a fly darted by, beating his little wings at exactly 108 beats per second. I read his thoughts, concerned only with bringing home food for his beloved. Flies! How I had misjudged them!

I looked at Nick, at his breath pouring in and out of his nose, his heart pumping, lungs rising and falling. I saw through his skin as his blood cells reproduced and died and reproduced again.

'My car's outside,' he said.

He knew I wanted his car, a snazzy green Karmann Ghia.

'Can I drive?' I asked.

'No,' Nick said. 'Absolutely not.'

I didn't say anything. Time moved, backwards or forward. I wasn't sure.

'This isn't like the other time,' I said. 'It's nothing like that.'

Nick didn't say anything.

Nick drove. We headed north and I didn't notice where we were going until we were halfway across the Golden Gate Bridge. Marin passed by in a green blur. We started seeing the signs near Santa Rosa. SPOT OF MYSTERY, the signs said. One had a photograph of two men, twins, standing in a room. One man's head touched the ceiling while his twin was two feet shy. HOW CAN IT BE? the sign queried.

The Spot of Mystery was one of those places where a house mysteriously slid down a hill and violated all the known laws of physics with its irregular floors and uneven walls and balls rolling uphill – which the tour guide would assure you are absolutely, definitely not optical illusions. Also featured were a small flock of pygmy goats, two hot springs, several large redwoods, and a gift shop. Behind all this were cabins for rent. The place was run by a retired PI from San Francisco named Jake. I'd heard about it for years. I'd never been there before. I'd never needed it before.

'Claire's going to take care of the goats,' Nick told Jake when we arrived. Jake nodded. A young man who may or may not have been Nick's son showed me around and set me up in a cabin. Taking care of the goats was hard work. The main thing was making sure they didn't get too fat. There was a vending machine for goat pellets, and they'd learned to look hungry. The fat goats had to be segregated in a separate pen where visitors couldn't feed them.

That night, after hours of shoveling goat shit, I slept again. A few days later, after more shoveling, fence mending, and goat-scolding, I started eating.

Nick came to see me once or twice a week, adjusting the herbs he brought in for me to take, working on filling in the holes in my aura, discussing my treatment with the late Dr Cayce. At the end of the third week I told him about it.

'It was a girl,' I said. I was sitting up in bed, looking out the window. 'A case. A missing woman. A missing girl. I found her in the bay. She was—'

I didn't finish my sentence.

'You see bodies all the time,' he said.

'She was like me,' I said. 'She looked just like me.'

'So?' Nick said.

'She didn't look like me,' I said. 'She looked like someone I knew.'

'The girl who disappeared?' he said. 'Your friend?'

I nodded.

'But it wasn't her,' he said. 'That was a long time ago.'

'I know that,' I said. 'I know that now.'

'You want to join her,' Nick said.

That wasn't exactly it. But close.

At night everyone at the Spot of Mystery gathered in the main house, behind the cabins, for dinner. I heard people talking about plans, schemes. I kept my nose clean and my head down. People pretended they didn't know who I was. Everyone knew who I was. Somehow word of my trip to the hospital had spread far and wide. Every PI in the country now knew Claire DeWitt was crazy. But most of them had already known that.

I concentrated on the goats. They were good company. They overlooked most of my personality defects and failures, my withdrawal of food from the fatties, and my inability to speak goat. It was strong medicine. After four weeks I couldn't see the signs in the clouds anymore, but I was fattened up myself and well rested and fairly grounded in this reality. In another few weeks I was ready to go back to work. That was when Leon called. I was ready to say no. I wasn't interested in going to New Orleans. I hadn't been there since Constance died.

'Take it,' Nick said on his last visit. He held his hand lightly on my wrist, taking my pulses. 'Take the job. You have to tie up loose ends sometime.'

'I don't have any loose ends,' I said. 'Not with that place.'

'You're lying,' he said.

'I'm not,' I said.

'You don't know you are,' he said. 'But you are.'

I trust Nick.

I took the case.

CHAPTER 16

'No one is innocent,' Silette wrote. 'The only question is, how will you bear your portion of guilt?'
Mick called me the next morning. Andray was out of OPP already. I figured in cops' salaries and guards' salaries and buildings and transportation and sundries it cost about ten grand to keep Andray Fairview off the streets for three days. Mick explained that the NOPD had no drug lab. It had been ruined in the storm. Because of a backlog that pre-dated the storm by years, it would take months to test the drugs from recent arrests elsewhere. It was easier just to release anyone with less than, say, an entire truckload of cocaine.

Over a sushi lunch Mick tried to sell me on Andray's pious innocence again. Mick was the worst type of guilty; the type who wanted to *help*. My guess was that just about now he was discovering what a depressing, useless job it was. Especially in New Orleans, where most people's idea of help was a bigger gun.

It turned out his criminal justice program wasn't Mick's first encounter with Andray Fairview. Mick

102

already knew him from a drop-in center for youth where Mick *also* volunteered.

'Basically,' Mick said, picking at a seaweed salad, 'I only go to make myself feel better. Like I'm doing something. Almost every one of these kids has major post-traumatic stress disorder. They're like vets, basically. They're like people who went through a war. It's not just the storm. That's far from the worst thing that's happened to most of them.'

He stopped and looked at his seaweed for a minute, as if he were wondering how it got there and what it was.

'Anyway,' he went on, still looking suspiciously at the salad, 'I knew Andray from there. He used to come by sometimes and take a shower, get something to eat, get some clean clothes. He's been on his own for a long time. As long as I've been going there, which is five years. These kids – well. The schools are a mess, the city's a mess, their families are gone. Anyway, Andray's different. He's a good kid. He's smart. *Really* smart. He used to sell dope and I can see him doing that again, you know, falling backwards a little, but killing someone – I don't think so. I really don't think so.'

'I'm sure,' I said. 'I'm sure he's a *saint.*'

Mick looked up. 'Claire, I'm telling you . . .'

I took a sip of tea.

'You're telling me a lot of things,' I said. 'You're telling me that you're depressed. You're telling me that you're drowning in guilt. But you haven't told me anything so far that proves Andray Fairview didn't kill Vic Willing. His prints were in Vic's house, he's killed before—'

'You don't know that,' Mick said, weakly trying to fake liberal outrage.

'You don't *want* to know it,' I said. 'But you know it just fine. He was in a gang since he was eleven. What do you think he's done?'

Mick looked at me like he was going to hit me. Then he leaned back into his chair and closed his eyes. I expected him to come back with a witty rejoinder but instead he stayed there, his head against the wall and his eyes closed.

'How about you?' I finally asked, looking at my sushi. The colors were so bright that it looked artificial; pink salmon, red tuna, green wasabi. 'How'd you make out?'

Mick shook his head.

'That good, huh?' I said.

He shook his head and squeezed the top of his nose between his thumb and forefinger, as if his sinuses ached. For the first time I noticed he wasn't wearing his wedding ring. 'I lived in Mid-City, Claire,' Mick said. 'I lost everything.'

'Oh,' I said. 'What about—'

'She left,' Mick said. 'She moved back to Detroit.' He opened his eyes and looked at me. 'Less crime.'

'You're kidding,' I said.

He shook his head. 'Not kidding.'

He closed his eyes and leaned his head against the wall.

Some people, I saw, had drowned right away. And some people were drowning in slow motion, drowning a little bit at a time, and would be drowning for years. And some people, like Mick, had always been drowning. They just hadn't known what to call it until now.

CHAPTER 17

I started the case of Vic Willing again. Under a gray sky in Jackson Square there were three people reading tarot cards and palms, two people handing out leaflets about how to get to heaven or hell, and about five men who met the description Leon had given me of Jackson. This was the man he said had seen Vic Willing the Thursday after the storm. Skinny guy, old, black, missing some teeth, gray and black woolly hair. Usually wore an overcoat and usually carried around one big bag of cans and another big bag of his stuff.

I looked at the potential Jacksons. Two looked mean. One looked crazy. One got up and walked away fast when he caught me looking at him. I didn't see Vic or Leon having a relationship with any of those men. That left one who could be Jackson.

I walked over to him and he smiled and held out a battered paper cup.

'Got any change today?' he asked with a thick southern accent.

'Sure,' I said. I put a five in his cup. He thanked me.

'Are you Jackson?' I asked.

He said he was. I introduced myself and asked if I could sit down with him for a minute. He said yes. I sat down and explained to him who I was and what I wanted from him – an account of when he last saw Vic Willing. He told me more or less what Leon had told me:

'It was Thursday,' Jackson said. 'Down by the Convention Center. The National Guard, they rounded everyone up and brought them over there. They didn't know any better. I mean . . .' He paused for a second. 'You'd think after they realized, they would have stopped.' He shook his head. 'Anyway. The police was rounding everyone up and bringing them there. I was hanging out outside and I see Vic. He didn't know no one else there, I think – I mean, it was a lot of people like me. Not a lot of people like him. So I think he was happy to see me.'

'Maybe he was just glad you were okay,' I said.

Jackson wrinkled his brow, thinking about it. 'Maybe,' he said. 'I mean, Vic wasn't the type, so much, you know, concerned with other people like that. But it did seem like that, so who knows. So anyway, he comes over and says Hey Jackson and I say Hey Vic, I'm glad to see you okay, which I was. As bad as that place was, I was happy to see everyone who was there, 'cause I knew they were alive, at least. So I was happy to see him too.'

'Did he say where he'd been?' I asked.

Jackson thought before he answered. I liked this

guy. He thought more in five minutes than most people did in a week.

'No,' he said. 'No, he did not. At least not that I remember.' He looked at me and I thanked him and then he went on: 'So I asked him if he was okay and he said yes, and he asked if I was okay, did I need anything, and I said no, thank you, because frankly I didn't think he had anything. I mean, money's no good if there's nothing to buy. I didn't understand people stealing TVs and things like that – I mean, you can't eat 'em. All we needed was food and water, and there wasn't any. Whole city cleaned out by then – restaurants, stores, everything. Kids went out, kids who knew how to steal, and they broke in to the stores and restaurants and got water and whatever else they could find and brought it back for the babies and the old folks. Some of those kids didn't eat nothing themselves, not one bite. But that was all done by then. There were people's houses but that's not something I would do. Not going in someone's house. Not at that particular point. Anyway. Vic asked if I was okay and I said yes, and then he asked how I got there and I told him. He was acting real concerned, you know, like he cared. He asked where the water was coming from, what was going on and all that. I told him, as far as I knew, the water was everywhere. And he asked which levees had broke and I told him what I knew, which wasn't much. Rumors were flyin' all over. People were saying crazy things, like people eating dogs and babies and things like that. But some of the craziest things turned out to be true, like people on the rooftops in Lakeview and down in the Ninth Ward, and just about all of Arabi and Chalmette being all wiped out. So, you know, I told Vic that. I told him everything I knew. Then we shook hands and he was off. No, actually, he gave me some money first. I told him I didn't need it. Nothing to buy. But he gave it anyway.'

'So when you saw Vic,' I said. 'You're sure it was Thursday?'

'I am,' Jackson said.

'How are you so sure?' I said.

He looked a little offended. 'How you sure today's Tuesday?' he asked.

'Tuesday?' I said. 'Tuesday? Are you sure? Because I thought it was Wednesday.'

'Tuesday,' Jackson repeated with confidence.

I looked around. A group of chubby tourists were about ten feet away, taking pictures of the Presbytere.

'HEY,' I called out to them. 'Hello.'

They looked around with a little fear and located me as the source of the sound. That did not reassure them. I'd dressed in a hurry and I wasn't at my visual best. I wore boots, jeans, two black sweaters, and a red vintage women's overcoat with an ermine collar that probably should have been retired. I was also suffering from an unfortunate homemade haircut/bleach job that had involved pinking shears. I could see how it didn't inspire confidence.

'What's the day,' I hollered to them. They looked at each other and then turned away. You know how it is in the city. Those fancy slickers could be up to anything with their trick questions and clever tongues.

Jackson and I looked at each other and shook our heads. Tourists.

'The day,' I yelled at them. 'That's all I'm asking.'

Finally one tall brave man in his fifties hollered back. 'January ninth,' he called.

'Thanks. But I meant Tuesday or Wednesday,' I called out.

'Oh,' the man said. 'Tuesday.' He gave me a smile full of pity and turned back to his group. Then he thought better of it and turned back around, smiled again, and came over and handed me a folded-up dollar bill before retreating back to his tribe.

'Bless you,' he said.

'You too,' I said, taking the dollar. The man smiled and left. Jackson looked at my new dollar bill. I put it in my pocket. Jackson frowned.

'Okay. It was Thursday,' I said. Jackson nodded.

'How did you know Vic, anyway?' I asked him.

Jackson shrugged. 'I know everyone around here. And everyone know me too. That's just the way it is. I go all over getting my cans. You see everyone that way.'

I asked him if he remembered anything else and he said no. I asked if I could come back and see him again if I had more questions and he said yes. I gave him twenty dollars and left.

I believed Jackson. Vic Willing had been alive on September first. He hadn't died in the flood.

One cause of death ruled out. Only an infinite number of possibilities to go.

CHAPTER 18

Lali Valentine was the only decent alibi Andray had given me. Ms Valentine's last known address was on Baronne Street in Central City, a few blocks away from the Garden District. This was where Andray was from, right on the other side of St Charles Avenue from the District, like two sides of the same coin. Even the floodwaters seemed to have known the difference, slowing to a trickle by the time they reached St Charles and coming to a gentle stop at Prytania Street.

When I got to Lali's address it was gone. A big pile of lavender painted wood shards lay where the house had stood. In between the shards I could see little bits and pieces of a home: a pink sock, a can of tomato soup, a Lil Wayne CD, a White Hawks record.

Two men were hauling everything out of a house down the block, and I went over and asked them if they knew Lali.

The men were filthy, covered in plaster dust and mold. One of the men took off his dust mask and frowned.

'Lali,' he said. 'Lali. I think she's staying with her cousins on Magnolia Street. I don't know the number. It's a blue house, right across from the projects. You can't miss it 'cause it's, like, folding.'

'Folding?' I said.

'You'll see what I mean,' he said. He went back to work.

I thanked him and went back to my truck, but then I stopped. On the corner was the truck with a cherry picker. In the cherry picker was a man doing something to a transformer – one of the little power boxes on top of a pole, twenty-five or so feet up. In some cities they were underground; in New Orleans they were above ground, wires strung around the city like a cat's cradle.

The man wasn't from Entergy, the idiotically named power company. Their people had blue uniforms. This man was in white. Another man was in the truck, operating the crane.

'Hey,' I said to the man operating the cherry picker. 'Hi.'

He either didn't hear me or pretended not to hear me.

'Hey. Hello.'

No answer. I saw he had earmuffs on, the kind men use when they tear up the sidewalks.

I went back to the man who'd given me directions to Lali. This time his smile was less genuine.

'Excuse me,' I said. 'Sorry to bother you again. But I was wondering. Do you know what those men are doing over there?'

The man shook his head. 'It's funny, I been wondering the same thing. They're not Entergy. And the phone company got nothing to do with the power, and that's what's up there – transformers. So no, I got no idea. What do you think?'

We looked at the men in white and then back at each other.

'I don't know,' I said.

'I don't think it's anything good,' the man said.

'No,' I said. 'Me either.'

I thanked him again and went back to the corner. I watched the man in the cherry picker for a few minutes, but I couldn't quite see what he was doing up there. It looked like he was fixing something. But the power was still off for the whole block. Maybe he was trying to fix it.

Maybe. But no one was trying to fix the power anywhere else. And I doubted that one little transformer was why it was down.

Mysteries never end. But you can't solve them all. Not in one day, at least.

I drove toward the Magnolia Projects. The projects were closed. I didn't know if they'd been closed before or after the storm – like a lot of cities, New Orleans was shutting down its projects and sending people out into the world with Section 8 vouchers. Across the street was a blue shotgun house. The shotgun was missing its back wall. The side walls folded in where the back wall was missing.

On the porch was a young girl of maybe seventeen with a pretty face and black hair in a ponytail. Her legs dangled where stairs used to be. Next to her was a boy about twelve, just as pretty. The girl was smoking a cigarette, or a joint, passing it to the boy, who had a few drags before handing it back.

I parked the truck and got out and walked toward them. The girl watched me and the boy watched a tree on the street. The tree lay on its side, roots sticking out like arms. The girl smoked the cigarette. Up close I saw it was long and thin like a hand-rolled joint, but brown and wrinkled, as if it had been wet. Whatever they were smoking, it smelled sour. It wasn't pot. The girl handed it to the boy, ignoring me.

'Are you Lali?' I asked the girl.

She looked at me.

'Lali?' I asked again.

She nodded.

I gave her my spiel of who I was and what I was doing and what I wanted. She looked down at the ground beneath the porch while I talked. She didn't seem to be listening. They passed the cigarette back and forth.

'I ain't feel good,' she said when I was done. 'I think I'm sick.'

Her accent was so thick I had to translate in my head as she spoke. She looked sick. She looked listless and her hair was dull and broken. If she was in Westchester she'd be on thirty different meds and seeing three kinds of therapists. Here, she got a folding house.

I asked her if she remembered seeing Andray that night.

'I dunno,' she said. She didn't look at me. 'Andray? Shit, I ain't seen him in, I don't know. Long time. During the storm? I see Terrell. That's who I see during the storm. Terrell and Trey. And Peanut too. I seen him.'

I pulled myself up on the porch and sat down next to her.

'Andray might be in trouble,' I said. 'You might be his only alibi.'

She laughed. It sounded like nothing was funny and nothing ever had been.

'*Andray*,' she said. '*That* mothafucka.'

The boy reached into his pants and pulled out a .44 Magnum. I watched him. He didn't point the gun at me or Lali. He pointed it at the tree. Lali seemed not to notice.

'Shit,' she said. 'I ain't remember nothing. That was fucked up. I ain't remember seeing Andray nowhere.'

'I'm not a cop,' I said to her. 'I'm trying to keep Andray out of jail, not put him in.'

I explained the situation to her again. She didn't listen. She took a big hit off her cigarette and exhaled toward my face. It smelled sour and acidic.

'What is that, anyway?' I asked.

The boy shot the tree.

Lali and I both jumped in place. When the shot

116

hit the tree a bunch of living things rushed out of it: squirrels ran in a panic across the street, pigeons flew away in terror. The boy fell back from the blast and a quick smile flashed across his face.

I reached over and grabbed the gun from the boy.

'Fuck,' he said. 'I need that.'

He looked at me. He looked scared. I gave him back his gun.

'Them fuckers was laughing at me,' he said.

'The fuckers in the tree?' I said.

He nodded.

'Maybe,' I said, 'they were just laughing.'

The boy furrowed his brow, weighing the possibilities.

I wrote down my phone number on a piece of paper and handed it to Lali.

'Call me,' I said. 'Please. If you remember anything.'

I gave her and the boy five twenties each. The boy laughed and looked something like happy for a second. Lali folded the bills up tight and put them in her pocket without looking.

I turned to look at her as I got in my car. She saw me looking and took the piece of paper with my name and number on it out of her pocket. Her eyes looked empty. It was like no one was home.

She crumpled the piece of paper into a ball and threw it into the tree. The boy cocked his gun and shot it.

That was it for Andray's alibi. I went back to my truck and drove back to where I'd seen the cherry picker. He was gone, but those things do about forty with a tailwind and I knew he hadn't gone far.

I drove around in wide figure eights, weaving in and out of Dryades Street, now called Oretha Castle Haley Boulevard, the main artery of the neighborhood and near the geographical center of the city. Central City was the heart of the intermediate zone. Dryades used to be a busy commercial street, where blacks and Jews and Asians and everyone else who wasn't white enough for Canal Street shopped. It was hard to believe now. Almost every storefront was shuttered and sealed. The only spots open on the long strip were a credit union, a dirty grocery store, a few art galleries drawn by the cheap rent, daycare joints that looked like nightmares, and places with names like COMMUNITY POWER! and THRIVE! and FOOD ALLIANCE PROGRAM. In front of the latter was a long line, snaking down the block and around the corner, men and women and children trying to be patient. It's hard to be patient when you're hungry. Boys hung out in threes and fours and fives on street corners, people in big trucks like mine stopping to buy what they were selling. Some of the boys laughed, being boys despite it all. Some looked somber and serious, trying to send a message.

Dryades had been named for the nymphs that

lived in trees, sisters to the Muse streets a few blocks downtown. But even the nymphs were gone now, off to the Quarter to have fun, or at least have a drink.

I was on Danneel Street when a Crown Victoria, painted in brilliant electric blue metalflake and raised on double-size wheels, turned a corner behind me. I saw it in my rearview mirror as it came quickly around the corner and slowed down in front of four or five boys working on the corner. A boy leaned out of the car window on the sidewalk side.

In his hands was an AK-47.

By the time I realized what was going on it was too late to do anything about it.

I stepped on the gas as gunfire rang out from behind me. Everyone screamed. In the rearview mirror I watched as everyone ran or ducked or hid. The boys who had been on the corner – the targets, presumably – ran in every direction. No one was hit, as far as I saw – it seemed like an easy shot but in reality the driver was going too fast and the shooter didn't know how to handle his weapon.

I stopped about a block away. I knew I should keep driving away. I didn't. I heard a *ding* as a bullet nicked my fender. But I wasn't a target. The Crown Vic pulled up beside me on the right and quickly passed me, ignoring me and making a right turn.

They weren't running away. They were coming

back for another pass. I looked behind me. The boys who hadn't run too far were coming back to life on the corner, laughing and enjoying their good luck.

I put the truck in reverse. I stopped thinking and backed up to the kids, rolling down my window as I did.

Three of the boys were back on the corner, laughing like you do when you're happy not to be dead. The boys saw me driving backwards down the street and looked at me, confused. One ran off, yelling 'FIVE-OH' as he did, the universal call for cops.

There were two boys left, watching me speed down the street toward them in reverse. I stopped in front of them and put the car back into gear.

One of the boys was Andray Fairview. The other was the kid who'd been to see him in jail, the boy with the dreadlocks. For all I knew *he* was the one who'd peed on my truck.

I rolled down my window.

'They're coming back,' I called to Andray. 'Get in the truck. They're coming back around.'

As soon as the words were out of my mouth the Crown Victoria turned the far corner.

I opened the door to the truck.

'GET IN,' I yelled at Andray. He looked around and saw that all the boys had run away except him and his friend. Andray and the other boy looked at each other. Andray looked at me and back at the boy. In his look was a plea.

Andray wouldn't leave the other boy.

'Both of you!' I screamed. 'NOW!'

I felt cold on the back of my neck. Someone was going to die any second now.

Andray and the other boy ran the few steps to the truck and dove in the passenger window, pulling each other in behind them. I hit the gas and made a screeching left and drove toward St Charles.

The boys panted in a tumbled heap beside me, limbs and trunks tied up in a pile. They pulled themselves apart and sat up. The boy who wasn't Andray pulled a nine millimeter out from his waistband and leaned out the window, gun in hand. I checked the rearview mirror. The Crown Victoria was a good block behind us.

'Get him back in the car,' I said to Andray. 'NOW.'

Andray tugged at his friend's waistband and muttered something to him. The boy came back inside the car.

'Gimme your gun,' I said. The boy made a face like I was crazy. I checked the rearview again; the Crown Victoria was gaining on us. Soon we'd be in the Garden District, the one part of the city where some kind of peace was enforced—but it was only a matter of time before people started shooting each other there too, and today might be the day.

'GIVE IT TO ME!' I screamed.

Andray's eyes opened wide. He took the gun from the boy and gave it to me.

121

'Take the wheel,' I said to Andray. I suppose I should have asked if he knew how to drive, but I didn't. He didn't. He took the wheel nonetheless and replaced my foot on the gas when we switched seats and the truck moved straight-ish-ly forward.

'Move,' I said to his friend, and we switched too, until I was all the way to the right.

Andray tried to drive. I tried to shoot. Carefully, keeping my head low, I steeled myself and as quickly as I could, raised up, leaned out the window, aimed at the Crown Victoria, and shot and kept shooting. As soon as the shots were out I pulled myself back into the truck and covered my head with my arms, and just in time: a bullet hit the side-view mirror, sending shattered plastic and glass on my hair and arms.

But I'd hit my mark. The front tires of the Crown Vic were blown, and fluids were leaking from the underside of the motor. The car skidded out and hit a parked car along the right side of the street. The driver slammed on the brakes and got out of the car, but it was too late. He wasn't catching up with us now. And no way was the shooter good enough to get us from a block away.

In the rearview mirror I saw the driver of the car who'd been following us. At the oldest, he was fourteen. He looked pissed off. But the shooter didn't look upset at all.

No one could be that bad of a shot. He had been less than ten feet away from Andray and his friends.

He was no killer. But he was trying.

When we crossed the border into the Garden District, Andray took his foot off the gas and let the car roll to a stop. I leaned across the other boy and shifted the gear to Park. On the still, empty street, we looked at each other.

We laughed. Almost being killed does strange things to you.

I took the gun I was holding, carefully wiped it down with my T-shirt, and handed it back to Andray's friend.

'Fuck,' he said.

I nodded in agreement.

We all laughed again.

From far away we heard sirens.

'Shit,' Dreadlock Boy said. 'Fuck fuck fuck.'

Warrants, I figured. I switched places with Andray and drove the truck over to Magazine Street. I knew the cops in New Orleans, and if they responded to the shooting at all, it would be a quick drive around the neighborhood. They were unlikely to stop a white woman for – well, for anything really, but especially not in connection with a gang shooting in Central City. I asked Dreadlock Boy where I could drop him. He and Andray looked at each other. Deadlock Boy looked scared. Only then did I understand that Dreadlock Boy had been the target all along.

I'm not the world's greatest private dick for nothing.

First we drove to an empty block in the Irish

123

Channel, where, after a quick stop at a hardware store for a wrench, me and Andray and Dreadlock Boy – who as it turned out was the infamous Terrell – switched the plate off my truck for one we nicked off an old man's Buick. Terrell, a smart boy, removed the side-view mirror from another truck like mine and switched those too. He also, with my permission, picked out a broken two-by-four from a pile of garbage and smashed in the other bumper. No one would think it was the same truck now. Now that he wasn't trying to be frightening, Terrell's good nature shone, and he grinned as he smashed up my truck.

'Should I do the other side?' he asked politely after he'd crushed the right side. 'Or just leave it?'

We decided to just leave it.

The alterations to the car would clear us with the cops. As for the shooters, I didn't know. In most cities I wouldn't have worried about it much – we white ladies are pretty safe if we stick to our own neighborhoods, the beneficiaries of generations of racism whether we want it or not. No one is eager for the problems that come with shooting someone who might make the TV news. But in New Orleans, I was pretty sure that even a white lady getting murdered didn't merit much attention from the cops. A few days ago a white woman had been killed in Bywater, shot in her home while she held her baby daughter in her arms. The rest of the country was in an uproar. In New Orleans it was just another murder.

After we had the truck in order, I drove to a motel on Airline Highway in Metairie. The strip was lined with them, back from when this was the main artery into the city, before Highway 10 came along and ruined everything. Now they were shabby and lonely, some renovated into hooker hotels, some still waiting for things to pick back up, which would surely happen any day now.

Inside the hotel a caved-in ceiling took over half the lobby, leaving off a small mountain of plaster cordoned off with yellow Caution tape.

PARDON OUR APPEARANCE WHILE WE RENOVATE! a sign said.

With a fake ID I booked a room for myself and my son under the name Sylvia Welsch, and gave the key to Terrell.

He looked at me suspiciously.

'Just take it before I change my mind,' I said.

He smiled and thanked me. He and Andray exchanged a complicated handshake and some ghetto language I didn't understand. We left.

An hour later the sun was down and Andray and I were sitting in my truck in an empty parking lot for an abandoned fruit wholesaler, just outside the Quarter by the railroad tracks. It was quiet and smelled like gasoline. We each leaned back in our seat, drained. I put the radio on, low, to WWOZ. We passed a forty-ounce bottle of malt liquor and a blunt back and forth, not saying anything. The forty was Andray's and the weed was mine,

125

although it was at Andray's insistence that we rolled it in a cigar wrapper. We old white ladies like our plain old E-Z Widers.

'You a good shot,' Andray said, grudgingly, after a while.

'I told you,' I said. 'I'm a private eye.' The truth was, it'd been an easy shot. I'd always liked guns, and I was a pretty good shot even before I met Constance. But it was Constance who taught me to shoot with my eyes closed. It was Constance who taught me how to persuade a bullet that you and it were on the same side. It was Constance who told me that the bullet wants to hit its target. You only had to encourage it. We'd find an empty lot somewhere and practice. No one ever stopped us. Back then, in my first months with Constance, I thought New Orleans was paradise.

Andray looked at me. 'Shit,' he said. 'I didn't believe you.'

'I don't blame you,' I said. 'People lie.'

He nodded. 'How you get a job like that?' he asked.

'Well,' I said. 'You have to go to school and study hard. You need really good grades. And then you have to go to college. Meet the right people, all that.'

'Oh,' Andray said. He leaned back in his seat a little.

I laughed. 'I'm kidding,' I said. 'I'm totally kidding. I didn't do any of that shit.'

Andray laughed a little, unsure. 'For real?'

'Yeah, for real,' I said. 'All that stuff is bullshit. I don't know. You just do it.'

He looked at me. 'You didn't go to college and that?'

'Uh, no,' I said. 'I left home when I was seventeen. I didn't even finish high school. Got a cigarette?'

Andray took out a pack of Newport Lights and held the pack out to me. I took one and so did he, and he lit us each up, letting the blunt smolder on the screw-top to the forty.

'Where you from?' he asked, still not sure about me.

'I'm from Brooklyn,' I told him.

Andray almost smiled. *'Brooklyn,'* he said. 'You from *Brooklyn?'*

'Yep.'

'It was like here?' he asked.

'Well, no,' I said. 'At its worst, it was never like here. But close. You know: despair, poverty, murder. My high school was the first in the country to have metal detectors. And a nursery. But less murder. Less guns.'

'Brooklyn,' Andray said, nodding approval. The knowledge seemed to relax him a little. 'That's no joke.'

'Well, it is now,' I said. 'It's all rich people now.'

'That's what this city gonna be like soon,' Andray said, nodding. 'They don't want no black people here no more. White people want it all for themselves.'

I didn't say anything. I didn't know any white people who wanted New Orleans all to themselves. The sad part was that no one seemed to want it at all.

'You ever go back there?' he asked. 'Home?'

'Brooklyn?' I said. 'Rarely.'

'You don't like it now?' Andray asked.

'No,' I said. 'I don't like it at all.'

We sat for a minute. I could tell Andray wanted to ask me something. I sat quietly while he worked up the courage to do it.

'You was there?' he asked finally, looking down at the bottle of beer in his hands. 'In New York? When, you know?'

'Yes,' I said. 'I lived in California already. But I was in New York.'

'You were *there* there?' he asked.

'Nearby,' I said. 'I was in Chinatown. I was working on a case.'

'That's near?' he asked.

'Yeah,' I said. 'And then I went down to the site.'

'Shit,' Andray said. We sat silently for a minute.

'There was a lot of bodies?' he finally asked.

'No,' I said. 'Ashes. A lot of ashes.'

We were quiet for another minute. then Andray asked, 'Were you scared?'

Everyone always asks that. I don't know why.

'Yeah,' I said. 'It was scary. It was a long time before we knew it was over. It seemed like it would keep on happening. Like it was a war. Like it was

128

gonna be a war. And I couldn't get out of the city for a while. There were no flights. I had to rent a car and – well, it's a long story.'

'Oh,' he said.

Then after another minute he said, 'You ever seen a dead body?'

'Yeah,' I said. 'Lots of times.'

Andray wrinkled his brow, deepening the creases on his forehead.

'Ever anyone,' he asked, 'like – like someone you knew?'

I nodded. I thought he wanted to say something but neither of us knew what it was.

After a while he said, 'Water's different. Everyone was like, you know. Still there.'

'Yeah,' I said. I remembered the girl in the bay. She'd drowned trying to go home. Trying to swim. She froze instead. It's an ugly way to die.

'You saw people you knew?' I asked.

He nodded.

'You still see it?' I asked.

He nodded again. 'Not all the time, anymore. But yeah. Sometimes.'

'Yeah,' I said. 'I got things like that.'

'Someone you saw?' he asked.

'Yeah,' I said. 'No. I never saw her. But I see her all the time.'

Andray nodded and we were quiet for a while. We killed the blunt. He took a long, thin paper-rolled joint out of his pocket and lit it and took a drag. It smelled strange and chemical-y. It was the same thing Lali and the boy who shot the tree had been smoking.

'What *is* that?' I asked.

Andray laughed.

'You ain't know this?' I shook my head. 'Called wet. It's like a joint – see, they mix up weed and tobacco, sprinkle in a little dust – you know what that is? Angel dust?'

'Yeah,' I said.

He nodded. 'Okay. So you roll it up and then you dip it in embalming stuff, the stuff they use at funeral parlors.'

'Embalming stuff?' I said incredulously.

Andray laughed and nodded. 'Yeah.' He smoked a little more, and his eyes glistened. 'It's good shit.' He handed the cigarette to me.

I looked at it. Smoking embalming fluid wasn't exactly on my list of things to do in New Orleans. I was tired and the day could fairly be called *over*. Going home and going to bed would be a perfectly reasonable thing to do – perfectly reasonable, and no one could blame me at all.

But the detective's job is not to be perfectly reasonable. The detective's job is to follow the clues wherever they lead. And right now, they were leading toward the strange burning cigarette in Andray's hand.

I took it and smoked a little. Under the pot and tobacco it tasted like cheap cocaine, or nail polish remover. Nothing happened.

The White Hawks came on the radio, an Indian

130

gang that had made some good recordings on and off since the seventies. Andray muttered along with the song, sung in the mysterious-to-me language of the Black Indians.

'You understand that?' I asked Andray when the song was over. 'You know what that means?'

'Kind of,' he said. His lips formed a tiny little smile. 'My uncle, he was in the White Hawks.'

'Shit,' I said. 'Is that him singing?'

He shrugged. 'Maybe. He died a long time ago – 2004, he died. I used to stay with him, sometimes.'

'Where'd he live?' I asked. We handed the joint back and forth.

'Annunciation Street,' Andray said. 'He was real nice. And his girlfriend, Aqualia, she *real* nice. She a real good cook too. I used to stay with him a lot. He worked at Hubig's. You know, the pie place?' I nodded. Hubig's Pies were a packaged, chemical-y, turnover-type snack sold nearly everywhere in New Orleans.

'He was coming home one night,' Andray said, his voice shaking a little. 'And he was . . . he was . . . you know.'

He rolled the window down and spit out it. I didn't say anything.

After a minute or two Andray turned back toward me.

'He used to tell me this thing from the Bible,' Andray said.

'"*Let the dead take care of their own,*" he used to say. "*Let the dead go their own way.*"'

'It's 'Let the dead bury the dead,' I said. 'It's in the Bible.'

Andray wrinkled his brow.

'My uncle, he used to say there was two Bibles,' he said. 'Or one, but it been split in half. He said half's in the book, on paper. But the other half is inside people. You born with it, but it's up to you to find out. You gotta learn to see it for yourself. That's the only way.'

'Smart man,' I said.

'He was,' Andray said, nodding. 'He was that. He knew what was gonna happen too. He always say, 'No revenge. Whatever happens, let it die with me,' he said. '*Let the dead take care their own.* They got their own things to do now. Indians don't settle fights with knives and guns. They settle fights with costumes and songs.' When he died I wanted to, you know. But I knew what he wanted, so.' He shrugged. His hands were tied.

We passed the joint back and forth. The moon hung low in the sky; with each inhale from the joint it seemed to get lower and bigger, until it was right on top of the car. We looked at it.

'You see that?' Andray asked. He smiled.

'Yeah,' I said.

We passed the joint and watched the moon as it descended, shining its white light on us like a gift. When it was close enough it covered us entirely, blotting out everything else but its yellow-white body.

'You see that?' I asked.

132

'Yeah,' Andray said. 'That's some fucked-up shit right there.'

I didn't know if we were talking about the same fucked-up shit. I felt my eyes close.

When I woke up, I was surprised to see Andray had changed his clothes. He was now in full Indian regalia: Vegas showgirl meets Buffalo Bill. He had on a big feathered headdress and an outrageous suit embroidered with beads and sequins, all bright green. He was smoking another brown cigarette and watching me calmly. When he crossed his legs his sequins rattled and shook. He exhaled an ocean of smoke.

From outside I heard drums and tambourines and brass. I looked out the window just in time to see the St Anne parade pass by – the Societé de Sainte Anne, as Constance used to call it.

My eyes focused in to see two women standing on the corner, watching the parade go by. Both women were in costume, the older one as Marie Antoinette and the younger one as generic French royalty.

I shivered in the cold.

'Stand still,' Constance snapped.

'I can hardly fucking breathe,' I complained. 'And I'm freezing.'

Constance shook her head. 'Hush,' she said.

'Is it always this cold on Mardi Gras?' I asked, kicking the ground. 'Because—'

Constance grabbed my arm and turned me around to face her.

'Do you know what the St Anne parade is really for?'

'For?' I said. 'I dunno. The parades aren't for anything, are they?'

Constance rolled her eyes. 'Most aren't,' she explained. 'But this one is. When the captain arrives you will see that he's holding a box. Almost no one else will see this, by the way, because almost no one else has your eyes, Claire. But he will have a box. And in that box are ashes. Someday I'll be there, in that box.'

I shivered again. Sometimes I would get this strange idea that Constance was going to kill me. I'd known her for two years by then, and she was extraordinarily good to me. But I couldn't believe it. Not until after she was gone was I really sure that she had nothing up her sleeve. I didn't know there were people like that: people who don't keep track of what they give, people who don't ask for payback.

'The procession goes to the Mississippi,' Constance told me. 'When they get there, he'll scatter the ashes into the river.'

'Who is it?' I asked. 'I mean, who was—'

'Society members,' Constance said. 'Friends, family. Me, someday, and I hope you too.'

She smiled at me but it was a funny kind of a smile, melancholy and secretive. Constance had always wanted me to take a more active part in New Orleans. She wanted me to love it like she did. And for a while, I did.

134

Finally the parade came, singing and dancing. One woman was a devil, another a baby doll, men dressed as women and women as men, cowboys and Indians and priests and nuns and cops and people with nothing on at all. I followed Constance's lead as she bowed deeply to the first man in the parade, and I noticed the wooden box he held in his hands.

We joined the parade in the second line, in between a group of kazoo players and an old brass band from Tremé. Someone handed me a mushroom. I figured it was probably the good kind and I ate it.

'What you don't understand,' Constance hissed at me, 'is not all spirits are *good*.'

Constance didn't have a problem with my using drugs. It was Constance who taught me how to use *Calea zacatechichi* for prophetic dreams and iboga to break bad habits. She'd taken ayauasca twice and was one of the first twelve people to smoke DMT.

But she said the best way was to forge your own path to the truth, not swallow someone else's.

The mushroom came on right about when the parade broke up. Constance went to a friend's house and I wandered around the Quarter looking for Mick, who I finally found sitting on a curb on Decatur.

I thought if I could design the most perfect place in the world it would be exactly this. I had never even let myself dream that someplace like this might exist. It felt like I had been given the key to the secret garden, been initiated into the biggest secret. I was in love with New Orleans.

'You look so beautiful,' Mick said when he saw me. 'Like an angel.'

'What the fuck did you take?' I asked him.

One year later, Constance would be dead, and her ashes would be in that box.

I wasn't there to see it. I left New Orleans less than a week after she died.

There are some things you can never forgive.

'Miss Claire,' I heard. 'Yo, Miss Claire.'

I opened my eyes. Andray was looking at me.

'I think you fell asleep,' Andray said.

'I think you're right,' I said. 'You'd be a hell of a private dick.'

Andray laughed. I was tired and hungry. All the adrenaline from our little shootout was gone, leaving me with low blood sugar and a headache. I asked Andray where I could drop him off.

'Anywhere's fine,' he said.

'Well, where?' I asked.

'Where you picked me up would be okay,' he said.

'Where you almost got *shot*?' I said. 'There?'

Andray looked at me as if we weren't speaking the same language. 'Miss Claire,' he said slowly, using the polite term a young person in New Orleans uses for an elder, 'they wasn't aiming at *me*.'

I drove him back to the hotel on Airline Highway, then drove myself home, picking up a po'boy on the way. I fell asleep with the po'boy on the dresser, watching me accusingly.

CHAPTER 19

That night I dreamed about Constance. We were in a rowboat with her old friend Jack Murray. They passed a bottle of brandy back and forth. I thought I was on the boat with them, but they ignored me and I wasn't sure if I was there or not. Constance wore her favorite Chanel suit, her white hair in a neat bun on her head. Jack wore an old suit and overcoat that weren't much more than rags. They laughed and whispered to each other; I couldn't hear what they said.

'Now listen,' Constance said sharply, turning to me suddenly. 'Jack has something important to tell you.'

A subway rattled overhead. I looked up; it was the double-R subway from New York. On the side of the train was a mural of a girl with a spray paint can in her hand, writing her name on the train. *Girldetective*, she wrote.

'You're not listening,' Constance said. 'He's telling you what you need to know.'

I looked at Jack. He opened his mouth to speak, but instead of sound birds came out of his mouth, hundreds of them; starlings, grackles, crows, pigeons.

'The clues are all around you,' Constance said sharply. 'All you have to do is open your eyes, Claire, and see.'

CHAPTER 20

After coffee the next morning I called Mick. I didn't tell him about my escapade with his little friend the night before. Mick probably thought he was at church, or maybe rehabbing houses in Lakeview.

'I need you to do something for me,' I said.

'Research?' Mick asked. 'Go through files?'

'Maybe,' I said. 'Maybe later.'

'Interview suspects?' he asked. 'Track down witnesses?'

'No,' I said. 'Probably. But not now. First, I need you to find Jack Murray.'

'Oh, Claire,' Mick said, his voice thick with disappointment. 'I don't know where he is. I wouldn't know where to begin.'

'You'd have a better chance than I would,' I said. 'I don't even live here.'

'Jesus,' Mick said. 'What am I, your fucking secretary?'

'You want to keep your little friend out of jail?' I asked.

Mick didn't say anything. We both knew the answer was yes.

'Then you're my fucking secretary,' I said. 'And while you're on it, yes, you can get started looking through Vic's work records – the cases he prosecuted, what he won, what he lost, all that. Got it?'

'I got it,' Mick grumbled. 'Jesus. Do you always have to make everything so fucking complicated?'

'Yes,' I said. 'Yes, I do.'

I hung up the phone.

'Simplicity,' Silette wrote. 'Is the refuge of fools.'

After breakfast, still slightly hungover, I walked back to Vic's house. I stood in his doorway and looked around as if I were starting my day.

This part of the quarter was almost too quiet. The loudest sounds on Vic's block were horse-drawn carriages and the calliope from the riverboat. No one was around. Across the street someone opened the door to a little cottage. A black cat came out and plopped down on the porch. The door shut behind him.

I closed my eyes. I knew the Quarter well enough to see a map of it in my mind's eye. The closest grocery was LaVanna's, on Royal. That was where Vic would go when he needed milk or toilet paper or cigarettes. I opened my eyes and walked over there. It was a bustling, busy little place, cram-packed full of junk food and beer and New Orleans tidbits like boudin at the meat counter and Hubig's pies in with the Twinkies.

141

At the counter was an old white woman in a blue housedress, thick glasses on her face, a heavy wood crucifix around her neck. I showed her Vic's picture and asked if she knew him.

'Vic?' she said. 'I knew him for years, poor kid. Why you wanna know? You a reporter?'

She had the fast-disappearing Yat accent, equal parts Brooklyn and Boston, and sharing the same origins. It used to be common in New Orleans; now it had moved out to Chalmette and up to the North Shore.

I explained who I was and why I was asking.

'Why 'poor kid'?' I asked.

'I thought he drowned,' she said. 'That's why I said that. What you told me about him disappearing, I didn't know that. I didn't know.'

'What was he like?'

'Vic? He was a hell of a guy.' She smiled. 'A sweetheart. Knew him all of his life. His momma, she came from down here, and she used to bring him down to see everyone. Always with a smile, something nice to say, something funny. Like a light, like a light in the room. Last time I see him he says "Miss Mary, Miss Mary," he says, "when are you gonna . . ."'

But she stopped talking and started to cry.

'Vic,' she said, counting on her fingers as she cried. 'Artie. Micky. Shawn, from over in the projects – Jesus, he was just a kid. Angie. Nate. Ferdie. Jesus Christ.' She shook her head. 'I'm sorry. Jesus.' She sniffed and stopped crying.

142

'Anyway, you wanna know about Vic, you come back and ask Shaniqua. She'll tell you.'

'Shaniqua?' I asked.

'Colored girl, works nights,' the woman said. 'Very nice, been working for me for years, never any trouble. I know her whole family, I know the kids since they were born. Good kids. Vic, he helped 'em out of a jam a, what, a year or two back.' She shook her head. 'How the police treat the coloreds around here, it's a crime. They got rights, you know. Not Vic, he didn't go for that. He helped Shaniqua and her kids, wouldn't take no money or nothing.'

'She's here every night?' I asked.

'Most,' the woman said. 'She'll be here tonight around six, you wanna come back. She'll tell you.'

'I'll be back,' I said. 'I'll be back around six.'

The woman shook her head.

'The coloreds,' she said sadly. 'They got the mayor, the DA, everybody. It's all black now. But still. They ain't never seem to catch a break.'

CHAPTER 21

'The first thing you need to know about being a detective,' Constance explained when she was interviewing me to be her assistant, 'is that no one will ever like you again. You will turn over their stones and solve their crimes and reveal their secrets and they will hate you for it. If you're stupid enough to marry, your husband will never trust you. Your friends will never relax around you. Your family will shut you out. The police, of course, will loathe you. Your clients will never forgive you for telling them the truth. Everyone pretends they want their mysteries solved but no one does.' She leaned toward me. I smelled her violet perfume, her expensive face powder. 'No one except us.'

I felt a thrill up my spine; her words, of course, were straight from Silette's *Détection*. Had she been there when he wrote them? Had she helped them take shape?

'That's okay,' I said. 'No one likes me anyway.'

She peered at me. 'Do you have family?'

'Yes,' I said. 'But I haven't seen them in years.'

'Do you have any friends?' she asked.

'I used to,' I said. 'They – one disappeared. The other hates me.'

Constance smiled.

'Good,' she said. 'That's perfect.'

I'd met Constance in Los Angeles in 1994. A detective named Sean Risling had set up an introduction, knowing I needed work and Constance needed help. She was in L.A. on the famous HappyBurger murder case. Of course I knew who she was: the famous detective, the student of Silette, the eccentric from New Orleans, admired by some, reviled by more. Silette and his followers have never been the most popular detectives. No matter how many cases we solved or how quickly we solved them, respect was always hard to come by. It was like an episode of *Quincy*, stretched out over fifty years. All the better, Constance explained later, when we were friends. High expectations from others can cripple you.

I didn't expect her to like me. I didn't let myself hope. I called her on the phone as per Sean's instructions. She picked the time to meet and the place, a small, dark restaurant in Little Tokyo.

'How will I know you?' I asked.

'I'll know *you*,' she said.

I thought she was nuts. That was the first thing I liked about her.

Since I'd left Brooklyn I'd been traveling around the country, taking it in a little bit at a time. A year in Chicago. Six months in Miami. Two years in Portland. I went from place to place, earning money when it was easy and acquiring it by other means when it wasn't. Sometimes I solved crimes, helping out other detectives when they needed it, going undercover where they couldn't. I was getting a reputation as a good detective but impossible to deal with. I had a temper. I had no patience.

I'd shot four people. I'd killed two. None were in self-defense.

I sat in the restaurant in Little Tokyo and read Bhukerjee's *Deadly and Medicinal Orchids of South America*. A side project I was working on for Sean. He'd been working on the world's definitive encyclopedia of flower poisons. And still was, as far as I knew.

Constance came in and sat at my table, barely glancing at the rest of the restaurant. She knew me, all right.

'Bhukerjee,' she said, looking at the book. 'Not bad.'

'Who do you like?' I asked.

'For orchids?' she said. 'Or poisons?'

'Both,' I answered.

She thought for a minute. 'Ivan Vesulka,' she said. 'He's a little sketchy on details. But I don't think you can beat him for theory.'

I reached into my purse and pulled out my own worn, creased copy of Vesulka's *Poison Orchids of Siberia: A Visionary Interpretation*.

146

We smiled at each other. I was hired.

I didn't try to impress her. I figured that wouldn't work. I just did my work and kept my mouth shut, watching her out of the corner of my eye when I could, taking in her fur, her spectator pumps, her Chanel suit, her big custom bag, the white hair in a knot on top of her head, the rocks on her fingers and around her neck.

Mostly in those first few days I ran errands for her. Bring this book to the Tibet Center, pick up dinner from the Korean barbecue joint, run to the herbalist for some new tea, find a Spiritual Church in Los Angeles and light a candle for Black Hawk. I tried to do a good job and keep my head down and my nose clean. After a few weeks she started giving me more substantial tasks: read this book on iridology and write up a report, go talk to this person about the history of poker chips. At the end of four weeks I sat in as she interviewed Vishnu Desai, the murderer – although, of course, we didn't know that at the time. Constance asked him a hundred questions or more in the room she'd taken to interview witnesses and suspects, two floors under her own room at the Chateau Marmont.

Desai didn't fold. He was good. At the end she turned to me.

'Anything you'd like to add, Claire?'

I figured she was cutting me a break. She'd missed the most important question of all. There was no way it had escaped her gaze, as sharp as an eagle's.

147

'Mr Desai,' I began gently. 'You say your wife, Sarafina, ran out at eleven o'clock for a bite from the HappyBurger down the block.'

'Yes,' Vishnu said politely, wearily. 'She was hungry. There was nothing in the house. HappyBurger was the only place around; she was going there to get a bite when—'

His voice broke, unable to form the words for what happened next.

'Mr Desai,' I said. 'Sarafina was a Sikh, am I right? She was a follower of Yogi Bhajan, wasn't she?'

Mr Desai nodded, confused.

'Yogi Bhajan's followers are vegans,' I said. 'They eat no animal products. What would Sarafina get from a HappyBurger?'

Mr Desai opened his mouth but nothing came out. His brown skin turned red.

'Even the french fries at HappyBurger have beef fat,' I said. 'Even the onion rings have lard. *Even the french fries*, Mr Desai. *Even the onion rings.*'

Mr Desai burst into tears.

'Oh, Sarafina,' he cried. 'Forgive me.'

He confessed. Constance broke the case. She'd thrown me a softball; all I had to do was catch it and not fumble.

One week later I committed to be her assistant. Three years later, she was gone.

CHAPTER 22

I got a sandwich at Central Grocery and then flipped through records at a store on Decatur Street for a while. I bought a vinyl import of the Wild Magnolias' *They Call Us Wild, a Best of Shirley & Lee* CD, and a CD reissue of T.Rex's *Electric Warrior*, somewhat overpriced but irresistible. Down the street I went to a bookstore, where I spent an hour looking at crime novels and picked up a copy of Jamal Verdigris's *Advanced Techniques in Locksmithing*, a steal at two hundred and fifty. After six I went back to the grocery store where Vic had shopped.

At the counter was a long-faced African American woman in jeans and a gray hooded sweatshirt, a bright red scarf around her hair. I would have guessed she was twenty-something if I didn't know she had children old enough to get into trouble. I introduced myself. She was Shaniqua. She said that the old woman, Florence, had told her about me.

'So no one knows what happened to Vic?' she said. The concern in her voice sounded real. 'That's terrible. He ought to be laid to rest. I just assumed, you know. I'm sorry he's gone, I tell you that. He was so nice to us. He was always nice – just friendly, fun, always tipping everybody. And then what happened was that my son, Lawrence, got in some trouble with the law. It wasn't his fault. He didn't really do anything – it was his friends.'

'Of course,' I said. 'Friends.'

'And Vic,' she went on. 'I mean, I just asked if I could ask him a few questions. Just to clear some things up. I was a wreck. You know, it's all so *confusing*. Like what kind of charges they could bring against him, what was real and what they were just scaring us with. I mean, you just don't know *what* to think. And Vic, he just fixed it all up for us. Just like that.' She snapped her fingers and looked amazed. 'Just talked to a few people and the whole thing just went away.'

'Wow,' I said. 'So if you don't mind my asking, what were the charges?'

'Oh, let's see,' Shaniqua said, counting off on her long fingers. 'Possession with intent to sell, possession of a handgun, driving with no license – what else? The big one, the scary one, was murder two. But Vic, he was like a magician. Just made it all go away.'

I asked if I could talk to her son, Lawrence. She gave me a long list of contact information that included two cell phones, a girlfriend's phone, a pager, and the number of a friend's house where he spent a lot of time.

'I mean, Mr Vic,' Shaniqua said. 'We are so grateful. He just made the whole thing go away. All that trouble. Just made it all disappear. Like, *poof.*'

'Poof,' I said.

'Poof,' Shaniqua confirmed. '*Poof.*'

CHAPTER 23

I met Mick for dinner later that night at a Middle Eastern joint on Magazine Street. That was the biggest change in New Orleans since I'd lived here: the dazzling array of Middle Eastern restaurants, at least a few in each of the busiest neighborhoods. That was a mystery itself, but one I could live without solving.

Mick had moved to the Irish Channel after losing his house in Mid-City. At first, he'd thought he would renovate or rebuild the house in Mid-City. But after a few months of dealing with contractors and insurance adjusters and copper thieves and one worker robbing him and another worker getting robbed and Mick's wife moving back to Detroit – after a few months, he decided to sell his house. It was bought by 'an evil vulture-type real estate yuppie who probably wants to put in a disgusting fucking McDonald's there,' as Mick described him. 'Or a Taco Bell.' But that was more or less how Mick described anyone who made more money than he did. Which, I was beginning to see, was almost everyone. Mick had done pretty well as a detective. As a teacher and a busy-as-a-bee volunteer, he wasn't exactly raking it in.

Now Mick was staying in a different apartment in the Irish Channel, the first one having had leaks and mice and neighbors who sold crack and carried guns. He'd gotten some insurance money, but not enough for a new house and new everything else. He'd lost *everything* in the flood; not just the things you think about, like a house and a car and maybe clothing and books and the good china. He'd also lost all of his socks and all of his utensils and his can opener and his kitchen spices and five packages of paper towels he'd bought on sale and some nice pens and his pillows and his sheets and his paper clips and some notebooks and a collection of tiki cups – all expenses he forgot to claim to the insurance company. Mick was lucky – not only was his house flooded, but most of the roof was blown off by the wind. That meant he got insurance coverage for some of his losses even though, like most New Orleaneans, he didn't have flood insurance.

'The thing is,' Mick said, eating his shawarma, 'if they put a fucking McDonald's in there? A McDonald's where my beautiful house from 1911 with three fireplaces stood? My house, which is gone because of the failure of the federal levees? If those fuckers put a McDonald's in there, I'll just blow it up. I can do that, no problem. I mean, I'm not even worried about it.'

I figured he was pretty worried about it.

'You know that's exactly what they wanted,' Mick went on, jabbing a finger in the air. 'That's been their fucking plan all along. Get out the poor, bring in the rich. Out with the black, in with the white.'

'I see that,' I said. 'A poor black man like you just can't make it in this day and age. What with McDonald's pulling the rug out from under you.'

Mick scowled.

'It isn't about *me*,' he said.

'People always say that,' I said. 'But it's always about them.'

'Please,' Mick said. 'They've been *dying* to get their hands on this city. Did you see the plans? The plans they made? You can get them on the Internet. They got plans for the whole city, all divied up. Fucking *Trump* is talking about a deal on Canal. Street. Fucking *Donald Trump*.'

'Right,' I said. 'I'm sure the powers that be are *very* concerned with this place. I'm sure Trump and Rockefeller are arguing over it as we speak. Dubai has *nothing* on New Orleans. That's why they let it—'

'It's like Iraq,' Mick said, ignoring me. 'They had this whole town bought and sold before it even began. Oil pipeline and everything.'

'Yeah,' I said. 'They're all fighting over a swamp. A swamp with the highest murder rate in the country. There's nothing anyone wants more.'

Mick rolled his eyes.

'Oh, that reminds me,' he said. 'I forgot. Guess what I found out?'

'The secret to life,' I guessed.

'No,' he said, looking a little hurt.

'The master key to riches,' I guessed again.

'No,' he said. Now he looked annoyed.

'I know,' I said. 'I can be really annoying.'

'Yeah,' Mick said. 'You really can be. I mean, this kind thing gets to you, you know?'

'I know,' I said. 'It's like a disease. I can't stop.'

'I mean, this is why I pretended I was busy,' Mick said, excited now. 'This is what the appointment thing was all about. I really need to prepare to see you. It's really difficult.'

'I know,' I said. 'I'm working on being as stupid as everyone else but I'm not there yet. I'm hoping more drugs will help. They say they kill brain cells.'

Mick shook his head sadly. 'The last thing you need is more drugs.'

'Okay,' I said. 'So what is it?'

'Well, the main thing is the *sarcasm*,' he said. 'It's like I can't say anything around—'

'No, I mean, what did you find out?' I asked. Now *I* was annoyed.

'Oh,' Mick said. 'Jack Murray. He's still alive.' Mick took a slip of paper from his pocket and handed it to me. 'Last known address.'

'Nice,' I said. 'Where'd you get that?' I hadn't expected him to actually accomplish anything in his state. Depression can make people stupid, as I well knew.

'I know people,' he said, shrugging. But under

155

the shrug he almost smiled. There was still a good detective in there somewhere.

Across the street from the restaurant, three big round people in shorts, showing white goose-fleshed legs in the gray cold, were taking pictures of a house covered with spray paint. It had the familiar X with cryptic numbers and letters in the hollows. Underneath was spray-painted in bright safety orange: OWNER HOME!! DO NOT TAKE CAT!! WE WILL SHOOT!! CAT RESCUERS GO FUCK YOURSELF!! GO HOME CAT PEOPLE!! GO HOME!!! CAT PEOPLE GO HOME!!

CHAPTER 24

Constance and Silette never stopped writing, and on his last trip to the United States, Silette, his wife, Marie, and their daughter, Belle, spent three days in New Orleans with Constance. I have a photo of them under a tree in Audubon Park. It's hard to believe the photo was taken in 1973. Constance looked like she was in the 1950s, Silette was dressed for about 1912 in his high-necked suit and tie, and Marie was in Pucci and Paraphernalia, holding the squirming Belle in her arms. They stood around a huge live oak. It was a photogenic tree and kind of a famous one; two of its giant limbs swooped down to the ground before shooting back up to the sky, and the strange Silette-Darling clan gathered in front of one of the low branches.

Six weeks later, Belle disappeared.

At home in California I had the picture on my wall next to one from 1985: me, Kelly, and Tracy in front of a graffiti-strewn bar on the corner of First Street and First Avenue in Manhattan. We held out our inner wrists to show off our new tattoos, each with the others' initials. If you blow

157

the picture up you can read the graffiti and handbills on the wall behind us. AIDS IS GENOCIDE, one of the posters reads, CREATED IN A LABORATORY TO KILL THE BLACK MAN. GOD MADE ADAM & EVE, NOT ADAM & STEVE. NO YUPPIE SCUM ON THE LOWER EAST SIDE. *ACT-UP*. MISSING FOUNDATION. 1933. PARTY'S OVER.

Two years later, Tracy disappeared.

'What will fill the void left by the missing person?' Silette wrote. 'Who will now breathe his air, eat his food, marry his wife? Who will fill the job that would have been his? Who will fill his seat at the university lecture, the football game, in the old armchair at home? Who will read his books? Wear his clothes? Watch his movies? And most important, who will attend to the mysteries that would have been his, and hold them until the missing person can return?'

CHAPTER 25

In my room that night I tried the numbers Shaniqua had given me for her son, Lawrence. This was the boy, corrupted by worthless friends, who Vic had saved from a legal jam.

One number was a fast food restaurant. Three were dead cell phones. One was a landline that rang and rang and rang and no one picked up and no answering machine came on and nothing happened.

I threw the I Ching again. Hexagram 62: Frightened rice.

> Hexagram 62: Frightened rice. Burned rice is scared of the woman who cooks it. Dry rice is scared of the farmer who grows it. Well-grown rice brings nourishment. Well-cooked rice brings joy. Spoiled rice brings bitterness to the king. Bitterness in the king spoils the country. Treat rice kindly and the king will be well fed.

CHAPTER 26

The next morning I called Leon to give him an update. He'd specifically requested an update every few days. I don't know why we PIs have to give constant updates. Scientists don't give updates. As far as I know no one asks a painter for an update, or a chef. But the private dick better give an update twice every week or people think she's slacking off.

'Good news, I hope?' Leon said.

'No,' I said. 'No news at all. Which in this case isn't good. Sometimes no news is good news. But not now. Now it's just no news.'

I gave Leon a rundown of what I'd done, exaggerating my confidence in Andray Fairview's innocence.

'I'm going to talk to someone now,' I said. 'I'm trying to track down a detective named Jack Murray. Last anyone heard he was in a rooming house in Central City. So that's today's plan.'

'And he might know something about Vic?' Leon said.

'Maybe,' I said. 'It's possible.'

'They knew each other?' Leon queried hopefully. 'They met?'

'No,' I said. 'I don't know. Maybe.'

'If you don't mind my asking,' he said. 'I mean, I'm not trying to tell you how to do your job or anything.'

Usually when people say that's exactly what they're doing.

'I'm just wondering,' Leon continued. 'You're always talking about seeing this person or trying to find that person. Couldn't you just call these people? Or e-mail them?'

'Well, Leon,' I began, 'Leon, when I ask people questions, I'm actually not just looking for their answer. I'm looking for a reaction. Like when I asked you about your sisters. Do you remember that, in our very first meeting? When I asked you about your sisters? You said they were great but you lied, Leon, didn't you? You don't really think they're so great, do you? In fact, I think you don't like them very much at all, and you haven't for a long time, not since they left. You people here in New Orleans don't like it when people leave. And you know, I don't think they like you very much either, and do you know how I found this out, Leon?'

I waited for him to answer.

'I don't know,' he finally murmured.

'You *don't know*,' I repeated. I suppose you could say I was a little annoyed. 'Well, I learned this from the *clues*, Leon. I learned this from your tics and tweaks. I learned this because you began shaking your right foot when you talked about your sisters. You do that when you aren't being honest with yourself. I learned that by being there, in person. This is what detectives do, Leon. If that's not what you wanted, maybe you should hire some rent-a-cop non-union hack from New Jersey with a mail-order badge and a magnifying glass from a Cracker Jack box and a—'

'Okay,' he said. 'Okay.'

'Now,' I said, 'why don't you come with me and see what I do? Because obviously you don't trust me. And I want you to trust me, Leon,' I lied. 'It's *important* to me that you trust me.'

I didn't care if Leon trusted me. But I did want him to keep paying me.

'Okay,' he finally said. 'I'll come with you. Not because I don't trust you' – now we were both lying – 'but just because I'm curious. But the thing is,' he said, 'my car is dead.'

'Dead?' I said.

'Well, no,' he said. 'Hopefully not dead. But it kind of, like, broke. And the place I usually go to is closed. It never reopened. And my friend told me about this other guy, but he's in Metairie and I can't get there. So I found this place on St Charles, but they're only open till one, and—'

I offered to pick him up. He accepted. Leon was on his porch waiting for me when I got there. I parked the car anyway. I got out and went to him.

'Can I use your bathroom?' I asked Leon.

He frowned. 'The house is already locked up,' he said apologetically. 'And it'll just take a minute to get back uptown. Literally.'

'Please?' I said. 'I really can't wait. Literally.'

From the outside Leon's house was an unremarkable shotgun on France Street. With a sigh he let me in and told me where the bathroom was. Inside the house I gasped and practically lost my balance.

Leon's house was *gorgeous*.

Leon collected Mardi Gras memorabilia from the golden age. Each room was lined with period glass cases that held lithographed invitations to balls, necklaces of glass beads, crowns of costume jewelry, aprons from skull & bones gangs, queen's sashes, and more of the same. Even without the Mardi Gras stuff the house was beautiful. The walls were painted a deep, rich red. The furniture was from the same era as the house, mid-1800s, but everything was pleasantly worn and just slightly out of place, just enough so you knew you didn't have to walk on eggshells.

Quickly, I took in what I could. In the second parlor I found a desk, and I rifled though credit card statements, electric bills, and other papers. Nothing told me anything. In a little bowl on the desk was a stack of cards – business cards, shopping cards, charge cards.

I looked at my watch. I'd been there three minutes. I figured I had seven, absolute maximum, before he noticed I was gone too long.

163

I jogged back to the last room, which Leon used as a bedroom.

My God.

Leon made his bed.

On his nightstand was a small pile of books: *Reading Indians and Writing Race*; *Mardi Gras in New Orleans*; *The Krewe of Comus*: *An Informal Oral History*; and *Cajun Mardi Gras Traditions*.

On the other nightstand was a pile of novels: Julie Smith, Poppy Z. Brite, James Lee Burke. There wasn't a novel anywhere else in the house: probably not Leon's. I looked in the drawer. One vibrator, one diaphragm, one packet of cough drops. Definitely not Leon's. So Leon had a girlfriend.

I looked at my watch. Eight minutes, all of them wasted. I'd learned a lot about Leon, but none of it would help me with Vic.

Leon was in the truck with the heat on full blast, frowning.

'Sorry,' I said. 'Female trouble. So. Mardi Gras.'

At the mention of Mardi Gras, Leon smiled. His whole face came to life. It was as if someone had flipped a switch and turned him on, a real man replacing the cardboard cutout that had been holding his place.

'Oh, yeah,' he said enthusiastically. 'I've been collecting Mardi Gras stuff since I was a kid. I been to pretty much every parade – well, pretty much every parade since I was born. Except 1989. I was in the hospital – man, that sucked. I missed the whole season that year. I'm in three krewes now; Krewe De Vieux, Zulu, and – oh, I'm not supposed to say I'm in that one, but one of the big ones.'

'You're a Zulu?' I asked.

Leon smiled again. He was like a different person now, a real person with things he liked and didn't like and even something similar to a personality. 'Oh, yeah,' he said. 'There's white guys in there. We do the makeup, the skirts, everything. No one cares. It's the best club I'm in. We got a clubhouse down on—'

He stopped. I knew why: the famous clubhouse was still closed, drowned in eight feet of water.

'Anyway,' Leon went on, skipping over the flood like a record skipping a groove. 'It's still the best krewe there is. Those guys *really* know how to party. There was this guy – John – he was an Indian too, and he was in about a hundred other clubs and masked Indian too. I mean he was just' – Leon took a deep breath, so great was John the Zulu – 'just *the best*. He got me into it. He used to say everyone had a mask on anyway, so, you know, who cares. Anyway, it *is* the best krewe. It was John who really helped me get into Mardi Gras. Saved me, really.'

'Saved you how?' I asked.

Leon wrinkled his brow. 'Well, not *saved*. It's not like I was – well, not *saved*, no. But I was, I don't know. Kind of just floating. Just not really doing anything and drinking too much and kind of, kind of drowning, if you know what I mean. Just kind of drowning in place.'

'I think I do,' I said.

'And then when I joined the Zulus it was like . . .' Leon looked down and frowned. 'Like John came and got me. You know? That feeling like someone really sees you? Really sees you for the first time?'

'I do,' I said. 'I really do.'

Leon looked at the floor and we drove the rest of the way uptown in silence.

CHAPTER 27

The last known address for Jack Murray was a rooming house on Jackson Avenue near St Charles. The house was a mansion, or had been. The porch was gone, its concrete pilings left to hold up nothing. A few traces of beauty still held on: a carved door, the crumbling haint blue porch roof. On the corner, a clot of thuggish boys hung out, trying to look murderous under the low gray sky. They gave Leon and me the long, slow fish-eye as we got out of the truck. I smiled at them.

'Hi,' I said, and waved.

They ignored me.

We climbed the makeshift wooden steps to the door. I tried the mammoth door, original to the house. It was unlocked.

Leon looked at me hesitatingly. I raised my eyebrows. He frowned. I shook my head. Finally he nodded and followed me inside. Leon was the type you have to bully once in a while if you want to get anywhere.

Inside the house told the same sad story, clinging to a few bits of past beauty like a woman showing off her 'best features.' I'd grown up in a house like this, a mansion my parents had inherited in a neighborhood where no one like my parents – rich and lazy – had lived in nearly a hundred years. Scraps of plaster trim hung on to the hallway walls under chipped paint. An original chandelier, covered in dust, hung precariously over the stairs. In a dusty sitting room a marble mantel proclaimed noble birth, a temporary dip in circumstances, a misunderstanding at the bank that would be settled any day now. It was a story I knew by heart, an old litany of excuses and apologies, born rich but somehow not quite staying there, poor but not poor enough to do something about it.

The manager came down the stairs under the swaying chandelier. To my surprise she was a white middle-aged woman with long white hair, barefoot, in jeans and a T-shirt.

'Sweetie!' she cried when she saw Leon.

'Marsha!' he said. They embraced.

This was fucking perfect.

'I'm so glad to see you!' the woman cried. 'I been thinking of you.'

'Me too,' said Leon. 'I heard about you from—'

'Me too,' Marsha said. 'But it's still good to see you. How'd you make out?'

'Eh,' Leon said. 'How about you?'

'Eh,' she said. They smiled sadly at each other.

'Hi,' I said.

'Oh,' Leon said. 'This is Claire. I don't know if you heard about my uncle?'

'Your uncle?' she said. Leon told her the whole story and why we were there.

'Ah,' Marsha said. 'Well, come on in, for Christ's sake. Have some tea.'

We sat on thrift-shop chairs in the dusty parlor and drank green tea. I explained to Marsha what we wanted.

'I'm sorry you came all this way,' she said when I was done. 'I could have told you over the phone. Jack Murray doesn't live here anymore. After the storm he started drinking again and, you know. It wasn't that he got behind on his rent, although he *was*. But a lot of the guys here are in recovery and, God, I couldn't risk it. It could be like dominoes.' She laughed and flipped her hands over in time, like dominoes falling. 'I was going to ask him to leave, but I didn't have to. He just up and left. That was it. I heard from one of the guys that he's staying in Congo Square now,' she said. 'I hope he isn't. But that's what I heard.'

'Did he leave anything behind?' I asked.

'Yeah,' she said suspiciously. 'How'd you know that?'

'People always leave something behind,' I said. 'You think I could see?'

Marsha looked at Leon. He shrugged.

'It wasn't much,' she said, wavering. 'But it was everything he had.'

'He left it behind,' I said. 'He hasn't come back for it. Legally, that makes it garbage.'

169

'I guess,' she said. The idea seemed to make her sad. 'Come on.'

Leon and I followed Marsha to a closet under the main staircase. It was full of sloppily stacked mismatched boxes. She struggled to pull a box out from the middle. Leon and I both jumped in to help. Somehow they ended up talking and I ended up unstacking and restacking the boxes.

'I don't know why I keep it all,' Marsha said. 'Some of this shit is twenty years old. But, you know. There's no one else.'

While they were talking and I was stacking, a man, another tenant, came over to us. He was Creole, probably handsome once, probably happy once, probably healthy and strong. Now he was old and none of those things.

He looked down at the floor, about to speak.

'It's okay,' Marsha said before he had a chance. 'Next week.'

He nodded. He looked like he was going to cry.

'Thank you,' he said.

Marsha nodded and smiled, as if it wasn't worth thanking anyone over. The man turned and walked away.

'You talk to Mark Dylan?' Marsha said to Leon. 'I haven't—'

'Oh, yeah,' Leon said. 'He's in Dallas. He's doing okay. Dyin' to come home, though.'

They both laughed. 'Talk to Jesse?' Leon said.

'Not for a while,' Marsha said. 'I got an e-mail from her. A group thing. She's staying in

New York, I guess. Her kids are there, she's got grandkids.'

'Why not?' Leon said. 'She's got nothing left down here.'

'She sure doesn't,' Marsha said. 'Less than nothing. You know, she never even came to see the house. Where the house used to be. Said she'd rather remember it as it was.'

'I don't blame her,' Leon said. They were silent for a minute. Then Leon said, 'I heard about Brad.'

Marsha didn't say anything.

'I'm so sorry,' Leon said.

'I miss him every day,' Marsha said. 'I think about him all the time. All the time. Every day.'

No one said anything.

It was the first time I'd heard anyone talk about the storm since I'd first met with Leon. People talked a lot about the response to the storm and the effects of the storm and the future the storm would bring. But they didn't talk much about the incident itself.

Finally I had Jack Murray's box out and open. But there was almost nothing in it. A few items of filthy clothing. A copy of *Aunt Sally's Policy Players Book*, a book that decoded dream images into lottery numbers. A chip from the casino downtown for two dollars. Mardi Gras beads.

And a postcard. It was from the Spot of Mystery in California. On the front was a picture of the house itself, a benign-looking cabin in the redwoods.

'Shit,' I said.

'What?' Leon said.

'Fuck,' I said. 'I said that out loud?'

Marsha and Leon nodded and looked concerned.

'What is it?' Marsha asked. 'Is it a clue?'

'Yes, it is,' I said. 'A very valuable clue. *Very valuable indeed.* Lucky we came here *in person.* I wouldn't have wanted to miss this *important clue.*'

'Ooh,' Marsha said. 'That's kind of exciting.'

'It always is,' I said smugly.

Leon smiled politely and looked rigid and unhappy.

I turned over the postcard. It was addressed to Jack, at this address. The postmark was January 1, a few days before I'd come to New Orleans. Next to the address someone had written a message in black ballpoint ink:

The Case of the Green Parrot.

CHAPTER 28

My family had not been popular in our Brooklyn neighborhood. We were poor, white, and strange, with no good excuse for it. We lived in a neighborhood of African Americans and Puerto Ricans and Dominicans and Haitians and Jamaicans, some of whom strived to be working class, most of whom had given up. The fact that Mother and Father openly loathed people of color didn't help.

The house had been in my father's family for generations. There had been a few people in line before my father for the ancestral mansion, but he could whine and wheedle his way into anything. Besides, no one much wanted it; it had been vacant for years, and the garage had become a bathroom, the garden shed a shooting gallery. The houses on either side had long ago been turned into rooming houses. The east and north had been taken over by row after row of ugly brick projects. From what I understood, Mother and Dad lusted after the house for years before they finally managed to get their hands on it. I always suspected it was the house that kept them together. Neither would let the other have it.

My parents were both beautiful, both intelligent, and as far as I could tell both entirely incompetent. My father chased the squatters off with a shotgun but did little else to improve the property. The hot water was sporadic and even the cold water wasn't entirely reliable. In the bedrooms the heat was just enough to keep a red-blooded mammal alive, and there was none on whole floors and wings. The back staircase was so rotted, it couldn't be used. The front stairs were made precarious by the original runners, slick with age, which no one bothered to replace.

Settled in their little patch of hell, my parents surrounded themselves with dethroned royalty and snake-oil peddlers, mail-order Ph.D.s and ouija board readers – in other words, their people.

'Shut up and listen, *darling*,' Mother would snap if I wasn't attentive enough to one of her houseguests. 'This is your *education*.' In her Austrian accent *education* came out as a long slur, something obscene.

There was the raw-vinegar-and-oil proponent; the psychic who promised that *any day now* their fortune would arrive; the astrologer who convinced Mother she was Isis reincarnate; the third cousin who was a count, a fitting counterpart for my mother the marquise.

Oh, yes, we were royalty, or so my mother insisted – although she also insisted raw vinegar

174

was a wholesome food for children. Even if she wasn't technically quite as close to the queen of Hapsburg as she imagined, she was another kind of royalty: beautiful and almost famous. My parents knew Andy Warhol and the owners of Studio 54; they knew counts and duchesses and movie stars. My mother drove a sports car around town and tossed the tickets in the boot; my father collected rare books that he got on credit based on his family name. Before they got the house they lived at the Chelsea Hotel and ran up a legendary bill at El Quixote, which they never paid.

Regardless of their literal bloodline, my parents were both from old, rich families, my mother's from Austria and my father's from right here in the United States. Mother despised that Father's money came from actual work – his grandfather had done something with steel – and never let him forget it.

'I never should have married an American!' she would scream when they fought. 'Look, you can see the dirt on his hands. He has calluses!' Except with her accent it came out as calOOSES.

'He has calOOSES! He has calOOSES!'

'Look at the *princess*!' Father would reply. 'Look at the *princess*! *Madam* isn't happy with the help today, is she?'

'She is not! She is not!'

But Mother's insults were entirely unfounded – my father never worked a day in his life. The family fortunes in both cases were many times divided now, and while their combined income from their relative shares of the family pie would have been more than enough for us to live comfortably, it was never enough for them. They had no interest in getting by or getting jobs. They wanted to be rich again, and they were sure they could find the back door in. A dividend payment that could have fed us for a year turned into one bag of groceries, a payment to Dr Bradley, 'Chakraologist,' a rabbit fur stole for Mother, and an investment in a scheme to import essential oils from Bavaria that, shockingly, never seemed to get off the ground. As far as I could tell, money and glamour were the only things that mattered to them. And what they didn't have in the first they made up for with the second. Neither would leave the house without at least an hour of primping. They refused to miss a good party and didn't pretend to care about the PTA or the bills or any of the dull matter of everyday life.

When we moved in, the house was full of the detritus and debris of DeWitts past, but most valuables had long ago been removed and sold: art, silver, china, all of the better fixtures. A whole panel of stained glass had been sold from the front parlor, replaced with plywood. Chandeliers, doorknobs, mantels – all sacrificed to DeWitts' greed. What was left were the common-edition books, the scrapbooks, the trunks of old clothes, boxes and boxes of chipped dishes. Like a crackhead who picks up pieces of white lint and tries to smoke them, my mother would comb through the attic and closets when she needed cash. Sometimes she surprised us, turning up a silver fork or a set of pearl buttons.

Big houses are full of mysteries, lives lived on top of each other year after year, leaving only their clues behind. As a child I pored over every inch of the crumbling mansion. Who was Great-Aunt Eve, and why was her copy of *Das Kapital* missing the first three pages? Why was there a switch on the first floor that turned on a light on the third? Who thought to build a hallway connecting the master bedroom with the maid's room, and who sealed it off years later? Why was Mother crying? Why was Father screaming? Why was enough never enough?

And the biggest mystery of all: Why was everyone so unhappy?

I investigated these mysteries alone until I met Kelly and Tracy. After that, we were a team, and we investigated together.

On the first day of fourth grade I sat next to Tracy in school. I'd vaguely noticed her before, along with the other white girl, Kelly, she hung out with. Neither made much of an impact. I sat next to her because there was an empty seat there and I was fairly certain she wouldn't hit me. I was never seriously injured, but slaps and hair-pullings were common currency in my neighborhood, more annoying than actually frightening or painful.

Then I spotted Tracy's Official Cynthia Silverton Girl Detective Decoder Ring. She wore it on the ring finger of her left hand, as if she were married.

'You got it,' I whispered.

I'd seen the ring advertised in the back of the latest *Cynthia Silverton Mystery Digest*. Teen detective and junior college student Cynthia Silverton knew her Aunt Agnes hadn't stolen the Bangkok Emerald. But then who had?

Without the ring, I would never know.

Tracy looked up at me and smiled. The room seemed to go quiet as she held out the hand with the ring, showing it off like a new bride.

'I got it,' she whispered. We looked at the ring in awe. Now, I was sure, we would understand everything. All secrets would be split open and laid bare; all mysteries would be solved.

'So who did it?' I asked. 'Who stole the emerald?'

Tracy looked at me and bit her lip, thinking. She looked around; unable to guarantee our privacy, she instead wrote the guilty party's name on a carefully guarded scrap of paper. She handed it to me when the teacher wasn't looking.

Duane Edwards, she had written. *The butlar did it*.

I sucked in my breath, unable to quite believe it.

The butler? *Really?*

I stared out the window and let my mind wander. Life could not be predicted, I was already starting to see. No one could be trusted.

★   ★   ★

178

Five years later, Kelly and Tracy and I weren't friends anymore. We were sisters. Or so we thought. It was about then, when we were fourteen, that we gave each other the tattoos with a needle dipped in ink from a Bic pen and had our picture taken in front of the bar on First Avenue. I had a *T* and a *K*, Trace had a *C* and a *K*, and Kel had a *T* and a *C*. We would be friends forever, we swore. Sisters till the end.

But forever never lasts as long as you think it will. Two years later Tracy disappeared. Soon after that, Kelly stopped speaking to me, and I'd spoken to her a dozen or less times since.

Life could not be predicted, I saw. And no one could be trusted.

CHAPTER 29

I spent the rest of the day in the coffee shop, reading what I could find about Vic Willing online. It wasn't much. A little bit here and there about cases he tried, the usual litany of murders, assaults, and drug sales. Just thinking about trying to track down the cases and their actors gave me a headache – record keeping had long been a lost art in New Orleans, and since the storm most records were, literally, lost. Occasionally Vic popped up in the society columns. *Mr Willing accompanies Mrs Branford Stepman to a fundraiser for our troops. Prosecutor Vic Willing enjoys a laugh with Ms Stephanie Ludwig at the book release party for* That Was New Orleans.

My phone rang. It was Mick.

'You busy?' he said.

'Very,' I said. 'But what's up?'

'I'm over by Coops,' he said. He sounded cold. Cold and alone. 'You want to maybe get something to eat? Maybe some dinner?'

I said I would. I walked to Coops. Mick was already there, eating something fried, with a side dish of something else fried.

180

'How are you not a thousand pounds?' I asked.

'How are *you?*' he asked. 'You've been inhaling food since you got here.'

'It's illegal where I live,' I explained. 'If you get fat in San Francisco, they kick you out.'

I got rabbit jambalaya. Just when I was about to bite into it, Mick's phone rang. He checked the number.

He answered it. It was the drop-in center where he volunteered. I heard a thin, high, worried voice on the other end, but I couldn't make out the words.

'No,' Mick said vehemently. 'Don't call an ambulance, don't call the cops. Don't call anyone . . . No . . . I'll be there in, like, a minute.'

He stood up and put on his jacket.

'I'm almost there. Just wait.'

He hung up.

'Do you mind?' he said. 'They've got a little situation there – if this girl gets locked up it's gonna be bad news.'

'I don't mind,' I said. I left two twenties on the table and put on my coat. 'What happened?'

'This girl,' Mick said. 'Her name's Diamond. Sweet kid. Her mom got sent upstate today. They weren't living together, but still. She was all she had. So sometimes she, Diamond, stays in this abandoned house in the Upper Ninth. A bunch of girls stay there. They all turn tricks. A while back some trick followed them home, so now they've got a gun. Which would be fine, except

181

I'm worried Diamond – the girl – might use it on herself. Apparently she's totally freaking out. No one knows what to do with her.'

The drop-in center was a big depressing room on Canal Street near Claiborne. It used to be a grocery store, and the linoleum floor still bore marks where the refrigerators and coolers had been. A puddle of dirty water sat in one corner where a pipe leaked. Cheap plastic institutional chairs and tables were scattered around, handed down too many times. A buffet table offered coffee, colored sugar water, and doughnuts. A bin in the corner held old clothes and shoes. Two girls sifted through it, laughing and inspecting the clothes as if they were shopping in a mall.

The kids in the center had divided themselves into affiliation groups: white punks, black thugs, white thugs, trannies and queer boys, a group of girls of different races who were obviously streetwalkers. Some of the kids in the center had children with them themselves, toddlers or babies. When Mick and I walked in, about half the kids waved at him and a few came running over.

One young girl, one of the streetwalkers, was holding back tears. When Mick reached out a hand to her, she burst out crying. Everyone looked at her.

'Oh, Mr Mick,' she said. 'Mr Mick.'

Mick put his hand on the girl's shoulder and pulled her in to his chest. She collapsed against him and sobbed. The other kids stepped away to give them space. I guessed that was Diamond.

Mick led the girl to an empty table. I wandered over to the buffet and got a cup of coffee. The kids in the center sounded just like kids everywhere – loud, laughing, nearly hysterical. But they weren't like kids everywhere. They were kids like Mick had been once, kids for whom no adult on earth could muster up enough love or money or responsibility to care for. Abandoned children had long been a problem in New Orleans. Since the storm it was an epidemic. Thousands of parents stayed where they landed, sending their kids back to New Orleans with a promise of *We'll send for you when we can.*

Mick had already been on his own for years when he met Constance in his early twenties. She'd found him holding up a convenience store where she was buying an Evian. Mick had tried to rob Constance. But she saw something else in him, and after a long conversation he bought her her Evian and Constance turned him into a private eye. Or, according to Silette, revealed him as such.

I took my coffee and sat near a group of boys who looked like Andray – young, black, poor, so full of life that it took everything they had to suppress it and look cool. I tried to eavesdrop, but their accents were so thick that I could make out only every third or fourth word, and it was always *nigga.* After a while one boy and then another noticed me listening. It was obvious that I made them uncomfortable – there was no explanation for my presence there or my interest in them.

But I knew I was there for a reason. There are no coincidences. Just opportunities you've been too dumb to take, doors you've been too blind to step through.

'Excuse me,' I said to the boy sitting closest to me. He was small and not much more than thirteen or fourteen. His face was round and adorable. 'Can I ask you a question?'

He looked at me and nodded, unsure. His friends stopped talking and looked at me.

'Do you know a young man, about your age, named Lawrence? His mother's Shaniqua, works at LaVanna downtown?'

Lawrence was the boy who Vic Willing had supposedly helped out of legal trouble, from the goodness of his heart. I'd tried calling the numbers his mother had given me, but they were all disconnected or clearly fake.

'Yeah,' one of the other boys said cautiously. He was taller and older and looked serious. 'I know him.'

'You know where I can find him?' I asked.

The boys shut up and started to turn away from me.

'I'm not a cop,' I explained quickly. 'I'm a private eye. Like on TV. Look.' From my wallet I took out my California PI license and showed it to the boys. 'I'm investigating a case. Lawrence might be an important witness.'

The boys all laughed in astonishment.

'Like *Magnum*, P.I.,' one said.

'Just like that,' I said. 'But without the boss.'

'Get outta here,' the boy I'd first spoken to, the cute one, said. 'You ain't no PI.'

'Am too,' I said. 'I'll prove it to you.'

'Go on,' he said. The boys laughed again.

'Okay,' I said to the boy. 'Tell me one thing about yourself.'

'Like what?' he said.

'Anything,' I said. 'One thing.'

'Okay,' he said. His voice was husky and a little raw, as if he'd been shouting. 'All right. Lemme think . . . Okay. When I was a little kid, my sister called me NeeNee. That was her nickname for me.'

The boys laughed and kept talking. I looked at the boy; his height, his weight, his tattoos, the slightly overdeveloped muscle in his right forearm. I listened to his layers of accents as he talked to his friends. His shoes were worn, his pants big and denim but not very clean. I watched the way he carried himself, saw the curves of his emotions in his back, the set of his shoulders and his jaw, the slight overbite, the lines in his face, the tension in his belly. He blinked twenty percent more than he should have. Once I had all the information, I closed my eyes and let it all fall together into a whole.

In two minutes I had it.

'You were born in Atlanta, Georgia,' I began,

opening my eyes. Slowly, the boys stopped talking and laughing and turned toward me. 'You were born in 1992. You moved here when you were four, maybe five, with your mother. Your name is Nicholas, Nicholas something. You worked scooping ice cream last summer in the French Quarter before the storm came. Your mother left when you were eight. You lived with your aunt and uncle but you came back from Houston without them three—maybe four – months ago.'

Now all the boys were listening. 'Your father is in Angola,' I said. 'You miss your sister. You've been looking for her. You had a girlfriend but – well, I won't talk about that. You do better in school than you should. And you like airplanes. Someday,' I said, 'you'll fly in one.'

The boys looked at Nicholas – the cute boy— for confirmation. Eyes wide, he nodded his head.

'The ice cream place,' he said, slowly. 'It was Uptown. On Carrolton.'

'Holy shit,' one of the boys said.

'Fuck,' another said.

'How you do that?' another said. 'I mean – what the fuck?'

'Told you,' I said. 'I'm a private eye.'

'Now,' I said, 'you guys can help me with something. Something for a *very important case*.'

From my purse I got my picture of Vic Willing.

'Any of you know this guy?'

I handed the picture to Nicholas. He said he didn't know him. I watched his face as he looked

186

at the picture. He was telling the truth. So was the next boy, and the next.

The tall boy with the serious face took the picture and, like the rest of them, shook his head.

'Uh-uh,' he said, his eyes darting a little to the left. 'Never seen him.'

He was lying. He knew Vic Willing.

When we finished with the pictures the boys went back to their conversation. Nicholas, the cute boy, came and sat next to me.

'That was fucked up,' he said, pretending to laugh.

'Thank you,' I said.

'So,' he said, looking at the floor. 'My sister. You know where she's at?'

I looked at him. He didn't look like a boy anymore. He looked like a little old man, with the burdens of an unfair life on his back.

'You been looking for her?' I asked.

He nodded. He looked bone-weary tired.

'Few years now,' he said.

'You didn't lose her in the storm?' I asked.

He shook his head.

'Foster care?' I guessed.

He nodded. 'I ain't seen her in five years,' he said.

'I don't know where she is,' I said. 'But I can tell you how to find her. But the thing is – people change. You know that, right?'

He nodded.

'She might not be the person you're thinking of. She might not even be someone you want to know. You understand that?'

He nodded again, his old-man face serious.

'Okay. You know that guy over there, Mr Mick?' I asked, pointing at Mick.

'Yeah.'

'Well, you give him everything you know about her – her full name, her date of birth, her Social if you have it – and he'll find her for you. Shouldn't take him more than one, two days. But he probably can't get to it until he's done with this thing he's helping me with, 'cause I'm keeping him pretty busy. You tell him I promised, okay? Tell him I promised.'

The boy nodded and thanked me. I didn't know if he would do it or not. I would've offered to help him myself, but Mick would do it faster – he knew the ins and outs of the system in Louisiana. Besides, why steal his chance to be a do-gooder?

The boy wandered off and I pretended to read a magazine for a while, all the while keeping my eyes on the tall boy who'd lied about not knowing Vic. After a while he got up to use the bathroom. I was waiting for him when he came out.

'Hi,' I said.

The boy jumped.

'What the fuck?' he said. 'You waiting for me?'

'So you knew Vic,' I said.

His whole body tensed. You didn't have to be a

detective to know something was wrong. He frowned.

'You seem like a nice lady,' he said. 'But everyone around here know. You talk to the crazy lady about the DA, you dead.'

'Really,' I said. 'Where'd you hear that from?'

The tall boy laughed and shook his head.

'Sorry,' he said. 'I ain't fucking around with that.'

'Thanks anyway,' I said. He nodded.

I turned to walk away. Then I heard the boy inhale and I turned back. He had something else to say.

We looked at each other. His long, serious face looked tired. Tired of fighting, tired of keeping secrets, tired, probably, of living in a world where if you say the wrong thing to the wrong person, you die.

'If you wanna find Lawrence,' he said. 'He hangs out at this park up in the Irish Channel. Third and Annunciation, around there. Little guy, big dreads. If he ain't there, you just go on back another day.' He looked at me. 'He there. You find him. You find him easy.'

He hoped that whatever he wouldn't tell me about Vic, Lawrence would.

CHAPTER 30

Congo Square was a small cobblestone-paved plaza on the edge of Louis Armstrong Park, preserved as the spot where African and Haitian and Indian slaves in the eighteenth century, allowed slightly more freedom in New Orleans than elsewhere in the South, came to play music, dance, and worship. The square was widely regarded as the birthplace of American music, the spot that held the key to understanding what would later become jazz and then become rhythm and blues, rock-and-roll, and everything that followed.

It was preserved, but not protected. A regular crew of alcoholics and addicts had claimed it and held it tight. Anyone else who stepped in that corner of the park did so at their own risk. The police never came around. Neither did the Salvation Army or the National Guard.

There were a few benches scattered around the perimeter. Three were empty and two had men sleeping on them. Toward Rampart Street there was a picnic table, anchored in place. Five men sat at the table. Each was over fifty and poor, probably homeless, wearing clothes that hadn't been washed this year. They were the same type of man you could see in any city in America, in a little park or square just off downtown, halfway to skid row. I think they started making them after the Civil War; fighters who'd lost their wars and lost their fight. Even when their side won, they lost.

One of them was Jack Murray. Under layers of dirt and spilled liquor and despair, the men were barely distinguishable from one another, but I recognized him from the day on Constance's porch. I was sure he wouldn't remember me.

Jack Murray, PI, began life as a good upper-middle-class boy from Uptown. Like Vic Willing, he'd graduated from Tulane and started off full of ambition. Jack Murray wanted to be the best PI alive, and he was on his way there. He solved the murder in the Blue Room in less than ten minutes when he was just twenty-six. At thirty, he solved the murder in the wax museum, open since 1957. At thirty-five Jack Murray got James 'Slim' McNeil exonerated for the Abita Springs slayings and sent the real guilty party – McNeil's own brother! – straight to the pen. Murray was the detective to beat back in 1979. Made the cover of *Detective's Quarterly* no less than five times. He was ready to take over the world – or at least his little corner of it.

But at forty, Jack Murray discovered Jacques Silette. And everything changed.

I'd read interviews with him from that time. He

seemed genuinely shaken by what he'd learned. From *International Detection*, 1988:

Interviewer: So how has your discovery of Silette changed your approach to solving crimes?

Murray: (Long pause.) I think that now I'm more interested in seeing how my mysteries solve me.

Soon Jack was turning down all the best cases that came his way. He passed up the Case of the Baghdad Bandit and its fifty-thou commission. He didn't even try to find out who shot the police chief's mistress. And he totally ignored the Murder on Rue Royal, despite a personal plea from the editor of the *Times Picayune* to get involved in the case.

Instead, it seemed like he was accepting the worst offers he could get, all of them pro bono. He devoted months to solving the murder of a homeless man by the railroad tracks in Metairie. He found a serial killer who'd been preying on the working girls of New Orleans for years. But no one cared about homeless men or working girls – no one except the victims themselves. Murray wasn't making any money, and after a year or so of this he got kicked out of his house. He started drinking more. Everyone tried to help him; friends, other detectives, family. But he said he wasn't the one who needed help.

After he'd been on the street for a few years, a determined writer tracked him down to interview him for the *Journal of Silettian Studies*. The journal lasted for exactly two issues due to complete lack of interest from the world at large.

Interviewer: What does it mean to you to be a Silettian detective?

Murray: (Pause.) It means I was blind, and now I can see.

Interviewer: And the drinking?

Murray: Well. Some people need glasses to see, you know.

After that, Murray wouldn't answer any more questions.

I'd heard of him when I worked for Constance, although not from her. The older guys never mentioned his name; it was us young Pls, full of gossip, who were fascinated by him. The brilliant detective reduced to a bum and a drunk. I'd thought he was more legend than reality. I didn't know how complicated life could be until one day he showed up on Constance's doorstep and rang the bell.

I saw him at the door, held up one finger in a *wait* gesture, and went to find Constance in her office.

'Constance,' I began. 'I think you—'

But she was already up and coming toward the door. When she opened it the big man smiled broadly, as gray and soiled as his old coat and hat, and they fell into each other's arms. They both laughed as the man waltzed her around the porch.

I stood and watched until a ringing phone pulled me away. There was always something going on at the big house on Prytania Street. The day before it had been Constance's meditation teacher, Dorje, in his saffron robes, making mushroom tea in the kitchen. The day before that we'd interviewed a German shepherd. Life was never dull with Constance.

I went back to work and didn't see Constance for a few days. When I saw her again I asked about the man at the door.

'Jack Murray,' she said. 'If you see him again, Claire, please let him in, or give him money if he needs it, will you?'

'Of course,' I said. I was burning with questions, but I didn't know if I should ask them.

'Jack's path is a strange one,' Constance said, seeing the questions on my face. 'But he is where he's supposed to be. We needn't worry about him. And if he needs help, he knows he can always come here.'

She looked at my face and saw that I was still confused.

'Sometimes you have to accept things that you can't understand, Claire,' she said.

I frowned. So did Constance.

'Well, I suppose you don't have to *accept*

them,' Constance clarified. 'But they exist all the same.'

Jack disappeared back into the twilight world of shelters and hotels, park benches and bus stops, liquor stores and rooming houses. I never saw Jack after that. I doubt Constance did either.

Six months later, she was dead.

There was a seat at the next picnic table over, and I went and sat near the men. They smelled strong even in the fresh cold air. This was a mean crowd, I saw that. But I had never let anyone get the better of me yet, and I didn't plan on letting that happen now.

They ignored me, passing around a forty-ounce bottle of malt liquor.

'A girl could die of thirst around here,' I said with a little smile.

They ignored me. They kept ignoring me.

They ignored me until I left.

That afternoon I drove by the park on Annunciation and Third. A group of boys hung around, trying to look important and busy. But I didn't see any little guys with big dreads, no one who met Lawrence's description. I went to a sandwich shop on Magazine and First and got a shrimp po'boy and a root beer and then went back. Still no Lawrence.

On Jackson, between Magazine and Constance, I saw the cherry picker again, illegally parked by a fire hydrant. No one was in it.

Clean me, someone had written in the dust on the rear window.

Kill me, someone else had written underneath.

I'd been on the case for two weeks. I had clues, I had leads, I had questions. What I didn't have were answers.

'Only a fool looks for answers,' Silette wrote. 'The wise detective seeks only questions.'

Silette didn't have a client paying him by the day and watching the clock. He had book royalties and a trust fund from his father, who'd made a fortune in textiles.

CHAPTER 31

That night I went to dinner at a restaurant on the corner of Frenchman and Chartres that served Creole food and had just reopened a few weeks ago. Like a lot of restaurants, they didn't quite have it together yet. The food came out in Wonderland-type portions: an iced tea was served in a little juice glass and a pile of fried okra was bigger than my head.

I'd just paid the bill and stepped outside into the cool, wet air when I felt it.

First the pressure dropped. Then it was like someone flipped a switch and the world turned to slow motion, its energies made almost visible. I felt fear rise up from my root and into my belly, where acid rushed to meet it.

Someone was going to die.

I looked around. I saw someone else hear it before I heard it. I glanced at the face of a woman across the street, and I saw in slow motion as her mouth opened and she started to let out a scream. Then – it seemed like an hour later but it had been less than a second – I heard the rat-a-tat-tat of gunshot from an automatic weapon. I looked

197

around and saw the panic spread across the street, saw as one person and then another opened their mouths and then dropped down or ran or stood and screamed.

I heard the shots. But I didn't see the shooter.

I jumped down behind a newspaper box and stayed down, covering my head and my heart in a ball. I heard screaming, saw feet running in every direction. The plate glass behind me shattered as one shot and then another hit the window. That was the last shot.

I opened my eyes and unwound myself. All was quiet. I stood up. Everyone was gone or hugging the pavement. Everyone except me. I ran to the corner just in time to see a black Hummer with no plates drive away, a long brown arm pulling an AK-47 in through the window.

There was a tattoo, in fancy script, across the back of his hand. I didn't have time to read it.

I looked around. Next to the service entrance to the restaurant on Chartres a boy slumped against a wall, half lying, half sitting. His eyes were rolled open and his mouth was frozen in an O of terror. I thought he'd been shot.

Then his eyes rolled down. He smiled.

We looked at each other. In the wall behind him was a spray of bullet holes.

His face glowed. We started to laugh.

'Fuck,' he said.

'Man,' I said. 'Wow. You all right?'

He nodded and laughed.

'I guess,' he said. 'I ain't dead yet.'

He stood up and we both looked him over for bullet holes. There were none. People came out of hiding one at a time, coming over to look at the holes in the wall behind him.

I didn't know if the bullets were meant for me. Maybe. Maybe not. I'd been asking questions, and it wasn't impossible.

The boy who hadn't been shot grinned and did a little dance.

In New Orleans, it's hard to tell where your murder case ends and everyone else's begins.

CHAPTER 32

Most people assume Constance was killed working on an important, dangerous case. She wasn't. Constance was having dinner with a friend at a restaurant in the French Quarter when she was killed. Two boys came in with AK-47s and killed everyone in the place. Eight patrons, three staff members, and one off-duty cop who was supposed to be guarding the place. He did his best. His gun was in his hand when they found him – a .22-caliber revolver. It was a toy compared to what the two boys had. I've never seen anyone say no to an automatic weapon. The boys who shot her didn't have to kill her to get her money. They killed her anyway.

Constance was worth millions. I'd seen her give a thousand dollars to a beggar. She bought her maid a house. She sent her cook's kids to Harvard. She would have given those boys anything they'd asked for, even without a gun. But they didn't ask. They just shot her.

A lot of people thought there was more to it. Conspiracies. Webs. Plans. Connections. Constance had never stopped working on the disappearance of Belle, Silette's daughter. Some detectives thought she must have found something: clues, stories, suspects. Silette had other followers too, and not all of them agreed with the way Constance kept the torch. Not everyone thought she was the rightful heir to the throne.

Those people didn't know what life is like in the city of the dead. They didn't know how easy it is to die.

Mick spent years studying Constance's murder. He studied each detail, followed every clue. Other detectives helped. Kevin McShane came out of retirement to work the case with Mick. The Red Detective came down from the hills of Oakland to whisper theories in my ear. The Oracle of Broad Street volunteered her services for free. Every detective in the world wanted to crack the case.

But in the end, there was no case. No mystery. Just a plain fucking murder. There was nothing more to it than two poor kids who wanted money and didn't know or care who they were killing to get it.

The big conspiracy that killed Constance wasn't the Federal Reserve or the Octopus or the Anti-Silettians. It was the biggest, oldest conspiracy in the world – the conspiracy that produced kids like the two who shot her for pocket change. It was the conspiracy that began when the first man looked at his neighbor and said, 'Hey, I think I'd like *that* cave.'

Constance was always trying to get me to see

201

something better in people, something that would lead us up a little higher. I didn't see it.

'This world was supposed to be paradise,' she told me once, biting into an apple at her big kitchen table. 'If people would wake up, it still could be.'

'I don't know what it was supposed to be,' I said, 'but it's pretty fucking close to hell. Listen to that.'

A siren wailed past the house, the fifth one that night. There was some kind of battle on the streets Uptown: four murders in three days.

Constance smiled. 'When you get to hell, Claire, believe me, you'll know it. It's *much* hotter than this, for example. And dark – they don't have light bulbs there yet, or so I'm told.'

Constance was shot through the head, right at her third eye. And with her gone, I became the best detective in the world.

CHAPTER 33

Disguise is one of the arts of detection, and like most of our arts, it has fallen on hard times. Your average hack detective today thinks putting on a suit from the Goodwill and getting a haircut qualifies as a disguise. It does not. Neither does slapping on a little makeup or a wig, although, certainly, costuming is a good skill to have, and one you'll need. But disguise is far more than a new outfit and a change of facial hair. For a worthwhile disguise the detective must not only *appear* to be someone else, she must *believe* herself to be someone else. She must let her ego dissolve into the ether and must reach out into the collective unconscious and pull up a new person, fully formed, to borrow for as long as she needs her. She must let herself be possessed, if you will, by this new person, regardless of how unpleasant she may find her new persona to be. But this isn't the biggest challenge. The challenge for the detective who needs a disguise isn't taking on the new personality – it is letting her old personality go. To let go of the self is the highest calling of the self, something that few achieve. And something that every self, whether she knows it or not, aspires to.

In the afternoon I went back to Congo Square. This time I went as Elmyra Catalone, African-Italian American recovering crack addict from Memphis, Tennessee, raised Baptist, now occasionally Pentecostal, occasional sex worker, victim of sexual abuse at the hands of a cousin, mother of four children, one dead, one in foster care, one in Angola, one living in the town of Celebration, Florida, with a wife and two children. Elmyra is off the crack cocaine but she likes her liquor and has a schnapps now and then to be sociable.

Elmyra came to the park shyly at first, looking for a friend from Tallahassee she'd heard might be around here. She didn't see the friend but it looked like a place she could have a drink without causing too much trouble. If there was one thing Elmyra had had enough of in her life, it was trouble. From her plastic bag she took out a little bottle of peppermint schnapps and had a swig and found a bench to sit on. Trying to stay warm, Elmyra drank her schnapps and waited for her friend.

The men at the picnic table were not kind to Elmyra.

'Lookie here, there that same white bitch in dirty clothes.'

'She put some kinda shit on her face thinking we won't see.'

'Bitch.'

'White bitch.'

Jack Murray was silent.

I had a slug of schnapps and threw my wig in the trash and left. On my way to the truck on North Rampart I saw Leon coming out of a record store. I thought I could avoid him but he spotted me when I opened the door to the massive truck with its ear-blasting remote.

'Claire?' he said. 'Is that you?'

We made small talk. He asked how the case was going. I lied and said it was going swell.

'Are you okay?' he asked. 'Is everything okay?'

'Of course,' I said. 'Thanks for asking.'

Leon acted strange and confused. When I got back to my hotel I remembered that I was still in Elmyra's clothes – some of which I had bought at a thrift shop and some of which I found in the garbage – and that I had splashed myself with some schnapps before going to the park, for effect. And that I was actually kind of drunk when I saw him. And that I smelled like crack from the pipe they'd been passing around in Congo Square.

This day wasn't working out as I'd hoped.

CHAPTER 34

The hardest thing about buying a gun in Louisiana was that there were so many options I hardly knew where to begin. I heard shots at least once a day. Half the men in the city wore clothes so big, they could carry an arsenal under them. Out of the sliver by the river, spent casings and shells crunched underfoot on the sidewalk like crack vials or fall leaves. The suburbs west of the city were lined with pawnshops that advertised $99 SPECIAL ON 9 MILLIMETER and HANDGUN SALE and SPECIAL ON UZIS.

But I decided a pawnshop was too risky. It wouldn't be as helpful to have a *registered* gun; besides, I wasn't sure if I would pass the criminal background check. I'd only brought paperwork for two other names with me, and I didn't want to waste them.

Instead I drove around Central City. As always, there was a small group of young men on every third or fourth corner. It was like looking at a long strip of fast food restaurants and convenience stores at a highway exit. They all looked equally good, or bad. It wouldn't be a complicated transaction, but a lot could go wrong – I could get robbed, the police could show up, or the kids could refuse to deal with me.

From a pocket in my purse I pulled out two dice. One was lapis, one was jade. They had been Constance's. I held the dice in my hand for a minute and let them warm up. Then I tossed them on the passenger seat.

I got seven. I made a left on the next block and a right on Seventh Street. After two blocks I saw a group of kids, slightly larger than the other groups, maybe eight or ten young men on the steps of a cottage, laughing. They were laughing at something the kid on the top step had said. The kid on top stood above them, not smiling even though he'd just made the others laugh.

As I got closer I saw that the kid on the top step was Andray Fairview.

I pulled up beside them. Two kids who stayed down on the street put their hands on their waistbands and looked at me. I rolled down my window and leaned over.

'Hey, Andray,' I said. 'Remember me?'

As the other boys looked on, amused, he came toward the truck and leaned toward the window.

'What's up, Miss Claire?' he said. His face wasn't that different than it had been in OPP: vacant and depressed, devoid of qi. Again, it was clear that he'd shut his doors tight and had no inclination to let me in. It was like the night we'd gotten high together had never happened. I didn't blame him.

'Come on,' I said. 'Get in the car. You can do me a favor and get on my good side.'

Without arguing he got in the passenger side of the truck and shut the door behind him.

'What's up?' he said again, looking straight ahead.

I thought about giving him some kind of I'm-not-the-enemy-here speech, but that wasn't exactly true. I liked Andray, but I kind of *was* the enemy. I wasn't at all sure he didn't kill Vic Willing.

'So, listen,' I said. 'I need a gun.'

Andray turned and looked at me, his face a big question.

'Yeah,' I said. 'Shocking, isn't it? A nice lady like me.'

He laughed. 'I don't carry no more,' he said. 'If you gonna buy one anyway, I can hook you up.'

'Thanks,' I said. 'Seriously. I need some protection.'

'I hear that,' Andray said. He lifted up his shirt to reveal a narrow washboard waist and a nine-millimeter pistol tattooed on his belly, tucked neatly into his fancy boxer shorts. 'Turning the other cheek and all – that shit's hard.'

'Tell me about it,' I said. 'You ever think about moving? You know, people shoot each other much less in other places.'

We laughed. I don't know why. Yesterday more Americans had been killed in New Orleans than in Iraq. I figured when you counted up the kids shot in every city in America you probably had the Iraqis beat too.

'Shit,' Andray said, still smiling. 'I ain't never leavin'. I love this city. I love New Orleans.'

'How do you know?' I asked. 'You've never been anywhere else.'

Andray shook his head, smiling. 'I couldn't love no place else more,' he said.

'Andray,' I asked. 'How many times you been shot?'

'Three,' he said. 'How about you?'

'Four,' I said. 'Well, four and a half. But that's not the point. I'm a private detective. You're a kid. No offense. But you're supposed to be in school, not dodging bullets.'

Andray laughed again. 'This one, right here?' he pointed at his chest, at the scar I'd seen under his shirt in jail. 'I *got* this in school.'

I shook my head. I felt like Grandma lecturing the kids about rock-and-roll. We middle-aged white ladies shot our wad a hundred years ago, with our lectures and nagging and Temperance Union. I didn't know how you explained to a young man that this time it *really was* different.

'That doesn't happen in other places,' I said.

Andray shook his head. 'Last time I got shot,' he said, trying to explain his love of New Orleans to me, 'you know how many people came to see me in the hospital? My uncle, aunt, all my friends, cousins. Shit, my room was full every day. I got people here – I wouldn't have that nowhere else.'

'I thought you grew up in foster care,' I said. 'Who are all these aunts and uncles?'

'Oh, that wasn't my real aunt and uncle,' Andray explained. 'That was this guy, Mr John.'

'Was he the Indian?' I asked.

'Yeah,' Andray said, smiling a little. 'I told you 'bout him, I forgot. Mr John, he wasn't related or nothing. He was just this guy. Had a house over on Chippewa Street. Sometimes, at night, he'd go out to houses where kids stayed. He brought blankets, sandwiches, shit like that. Sometimes I'd go stay with him. He had a room with all these beds in it, lined up like an orphanage or some shit.' He laughed a little. 'Sometimes, he took me out to Indian practice. Introduce me to his friends, like—'

Andray stopped talking. He stopped smiling. Earlier, he'd told me Mr John was shot coming home from work one night. Andray shook his head and made himself laugh, pretending he was fine. 'I got real family too. My mom's around. She's just, you know, busy. I got cousins, aunts, uncles.' He laughed again. 'Shit. You a trip, Miss Claire, you know that?'

'I'm often told,' I said. 'So, Andray. Why don't you tell me about Vic Willing?'

Andray smiled a forced, tight-lipped smile. 'I told you, Miss Claire. I cleaned his pool a few times, he invited me in, we got to talking about birds and shit and—' A quick frown flashed across his face. 'And that's it.'

210

There was something he wasn't telling me – maybe a lot he wasn't telling me. But I had no idea how to get it out of him.

'So,' Andray said. 'You want a nine? An Uzi? Or what? Chief over there, he can get you an M-sixteen, and he got a flame-thrower at home. That shit *works*, too.'

I stopped and stared at him for a while. Then I told him that a simple handgun would do.

Andray leaned out the window. 'Terrell,' he called.

Terrell came out from inside the house. The windows were boarded up with plywood. Terrell held his pants up around his slim waist with his right hand. The boys who hung out on street corners in New Orleans were so achingly thin, I wondered if it was a fashion trend or they were trying not to exist, even less than they already did in the eyes of the world. Terrell wore a black sweatshirt with a skeletal white spine on the back, as if he were already dead.

Terrell smiled. 'What up?' he asked me. It was so rare that someone was happy to see me that I wondered what his angle was. Then I remembered I'd saved his life. Still, though.

'What happened to the hotel?' I asked.

Terrell laughed. 'I got things to do! I can't be hiding out out there.'

I wanted to argue but I didn't. *Eat your breakfast. Don't listen to jazz, it's the devil's music. Don't hang out on the same corner where someone tried to shoot you.*

'You still got that thirty-eight?' Andray asked Terrell.

Terrell looked at Andray like he was crazy. Andray nodded. Terrell made an it's-your-life face and nodded.

'I can get it,' he said.

'All right,' Andray said, opening the door. 'Come on. We gonna hook Miss Claire up.'

Andray moved over and Terrell got in, shutting the door behind him. Terrell started to thank me again for the other night. I stopped him. Andray and Terrell broke out into a giggly conversation. When they spoke to each other their accents were so thick and their dialect so heavy that the only words I could make out were *mothafucka* and *nigga*.

'How about you?' I asked Terrell. 'You know a guy named Vic Willing?'

Terrell busied himself getting a pack of cigarettes from his voluminous pants and lighting one up.

'Shit,' Andray said, laughing. 'Terrell with me all weekend. I with him from Friday night till we get to Texas. Don't even fuck with that, lady. He ain't even know no lawyers. Boy never hardly met a cop.'

Both boys laughed. But nothing was that funny.

'Where were you that weekend?' I asked Terrell. 'During the storm?'

Terrell kept the smile on his face, but it was forced. Cigarette in hand, he reached up and

212

pushed his hair back, holding his dreads up in the air for a minute before dropping them back down his back.

'Went to the Superdome first,' he recited. 'Then the Convention Center. Then we met up with some other people – Peanut, Lali, and them.'

Terrell looked at Andray, as if to check that he was getting the story right. Andray looked straight ahead and ignored him. Andray was right. Terrell was no criminal mastermind. He was a bright, funny kid who, if he had lived anywhere else, probably would have listed underage-beer-buying as his worst crime. I couldn't imagine any circumstance other than being born in New Orleans that would have led Terrell to pick up a gun.

'And then we drove to Houston,' Terrell went on. 'Went to the Astrodome, but they ain't let us in.'

'So what'd you do after that?' I asked. 'What'd you do after you got turned away from the Astrodome?'

Terrell froze, doubtless trying to remember the story Andray had fed him to back up his alibi. Then he burst out laughing.

'Shit, lady,' he said. 'I like to help you. But I try to forget all that. I don't want to think about it no more.'

I gave up. Trying to get these boys to talk was like trying to lasso cats. Terrell directed me to an abandoned, half-collapsed house a few blocks away. Stuck in the lawn, half buried in the rubble

213

and garbage, was a construction sign. I guessed the house was halfway renovated before the storm brought it back to the beginning:

Another FINE job from
Ninth Ward Construction.
Call Frank!! I can Help!!

The sign was ringed in yellowish-brown water-mark lines.

I parked in front and Terrell sprinted inside while Andray and I waited in the truck. A few minutes later Terrell came back and we drove to another deserted block and parked again. He took the gun out of his pants and laid it on the dashboard.

'May I?' I asked. Both boys nodded. I picked it up and looked at it and fiddled around with it for a few minutes. It was loaded. It looked good.

'What do you want for it?' I said.

Terrell looked at Andray and then me and then back at the gun. 'Nothin',' he said. 'You saved my life. I don't need to make no money from you.'

'I can give you what you paid for it, at least,' I said. Usually I didn't buy contraband from children, but I figured if I was going to, I might as well not profit off it.

We haggled over the price and settled on one hundred. I took the gun and gave him five twenties. Terrell reached into the endless pockets of his huge pants and pulled out a small plastic bag of dark brown hand-rolled cigarettes before he pulled out a fat roll of money. He added the money I'd given him to his roll and started to put the money and bag away, but Andray stopped him.

'Hook a friend up,' he said to Terrell.

Terrell looked at me.

'Go ahead,' I said. Terrell took out one of the long, thin, crinkly cigarettes and lit it. We passed it around. When it came to me I inhaled deeply and held the poisoned air in as long as I could.

Drugs take you places – some fun, some terrible. But the important thing about those places isn't whether or not they're fun. The important thing is that, sometimes, in some places, you can find clues.

Soon I was sleepy and pretty sure the truck was listing to one side, but I was more or less awake. The two boys started talking. I could hardly understand a word of it. I watched them as they talked: They were different boys together than they were alone. Together they were alive and hopeful and maybe even happy. They had their own language, forged from years of exchanging secrets and truths.

As I watched them I noticed something I hadn't before: Terrell and Andray had matching tattoos, a combination of two Ts and an A in a circular, almost Celtic sort of design on the inside of their right forearm, just past the crease of their elbow.

'Who's the other T?' I asked, interrupting their conversation.

They stopped talking and looked at me.

215

'Your tattoos,' I said. 'Who's the other T?'

Neither of them said anything, but I felt the mood in the truck change instantly. All laughter was gone, flown far away.

'You guys know each other a long time?' I asked, looking for another way in.

'All our lives,' Terrell said. 'Andray my brother.' The boys did some kind of special handshake and smiled. But something was missing. You could smell the sadness in the truck.

'Who was the other T?' I asked.

No one said anything. We passed the cigarette around again. Now I was sure we were parked on a steep angle of some sort and the truck was leaning far to the left. I was surprised I didn't tumble out of my seat. I thought maybe it had been a mistake to disconnect the airbags.

After a long while, Andray said, 'It was Trey. He the other T.'

'Where is he?' I asked.

For another long while we smoked and no one said anything.

'I shot him,' Andray finally said.

'You shot him?' I repeated. He handed me the brown cigarette but he didn't look at me. I took it and took another big inhale.

Andray nodded. 'Yep. I shot him.' He was so reserved – or so high – that it was impossible to tell what he was thinking. He leaned back and closed his eyes. Terrell did too.

'What happened?' I asked.

'See, when we got back,' Terrell began, 'we—'

'No, no,' Andray said. 'Lemme start at the beginning. See, the three of us, we grew up together. We were friends all our lives.'

'*Real* friends,' Terrell said. 'Not like people around here, always sayin' they your friend when they don't give a shit if you live or die. No. Us, we was like brothers.'

'I don't even remember when we met,' Andray said. 'I don't even remember not knowing them two. We didn't even live together. Terrell was always in one foster home and Trey in another and me in mine. But somehow it was like – like we always found each other. We were always running into each other. And then we started working together. Eleven, twelve, we started working for the same people together. And that – that was good.' He smiled. 'I mean, now it wouldn't seem like nothin'. Just a little bit of money. But shit, we bought CDs, sneakers. Trey, his mom was doing good, she was slinging too' – I thought that meant selling drugs, but I wasn't sure – 'and she bought us a car. A beat-up piece-a-shit ole Mercury. But man, we thought it was the shit. We went all over in that car, playing music, taking out girls. Just doing stupid shit. Just having fun. We was like brothers. Always together. We knew everything going on with each other. Everything. We collected money for each other, we made deals for each other. Trust, you know? We got these together, eighth grade.' He looked at his tattoo.

'Trey a goofy mothafucka,' Terrell said, laughing. 'Like a fucking clown. Always, always, always with a joke. I remember once—'

'Once,' Andray picked up, now laughing himself, 'he got in a thing with this kid Deuce—'

'And Deuce comes up on him with a fucking nine in his back—'

'A fucking nine—'

'And Trey, he says, 'Deuce, man, you happy to see me or what?"

We laughed. It was an old Mae West line but still a good one.

'Cold,' Andray said, clearly meaning it as a compliment.

'Stone cold,' Terrell agreed.

'But then,' Andray went on, 'it all changed. See, three, four years ago, we all started moving up. Making money. Meeting people. And soon we weren't working together no more. We was competition. At first it didn't matter. There was plenty for everyone. But, you know – it was little things. We each had kids working for us then, and sometimes the kids would fight. Then we had to settle it. But you know, we always did. Settle it.'

Terrell nodded glumly. 'Until the storm,' he said.

'Yeah, the storm,' Andray said, nodding. 'It all changed. See, Trey and Terrell, they went to Houston. And me, I went from Houston to Dallas. We each stayed away like three months, and when we came back, it was all different. See, business-wise, everything changed. We all hooked up with new people in Texas. So we weren't even with the same people anymore. Now we was *really*, like, rivals. And there was hardly no one else back yet. Not just customers, but sellers. Most were stuck, you know, California, Wisconsin, shit like that. Wherever the storm took them, they was stuck. So it was pretty much just me and Terrell and Trey and a few other guys.'

'But mostly,' Terrell said, 'just us.'

Andray nodded. 'Just us. And a chance to make *a lot* of money, fast, before the rest of the mothafuckas came back in town. I – well, I think I was a little fucked up in the head anyway. 'Cause of the storm and shit. You know, some of the shit I saw – I was angry *all the time*. It was like—'

'Like a sickness,' Terrell said. 'Like a sickness, being angry all the time.'

Andray nodded. 'So, Trey, he just one more thing to get angry about. He's taking half my fucking customers away. Every day, I'm getting angrier and angrier. Meanwhile Trey's making all my fucking money. But it wasn't just that. It was like – like something else. Shit, I can't explain it.'

We passed the long brown cigarette around. 'Were you scared?' I asked.

'No,' Andray said indignantly, almost laughing. Then he thought about it for a minute. 'Yeah, maybe,' he conceded. 'Not of Trey. Not of anything, really. I just *was*. Like, I was always thinking someone was coming up behind me and shit.'

'It's called post-traumatic stress disorder,' I said. 'It's like when something fucked up happens to you and you feel like it's happening again and again. You're scared even when there's nothing to be scared of.'

The boys nodded and looked at each other. They didn't need me to explain it to them.

Andray frowned. 'Yeah. That was pretty much it. Scared all the time, but not scared of anything. Angry for no reason. Anyway,' he went on, 'finally, one day I say, Okay. Enough. Any other motha-fucka stepping on my profits like this, I would have taken care of him long ago. Now it's time for Trey to go. So I tell him, Meet me over by the Calliope at midnight. This was in January – last January, about a year ago. Just like normal, Meet me over at the Calliope.' He pronounced the name of the housing project, named for the muse of music, KALI-ope. 'So about eleven something, me and some of my boys, we get to Calliope. Trey, he already there. Alone. He didn't even look like he had a weapon. Nothing. He was just Trey. It was like he knew.

'So there we was. Me and my boys down at one end of the block. Trey at the other. The projects was closed. No one else was around. Just us.

'Trey, he ain't say a word when he saw me. Just stood there. Looked at me. And then he put his arms up, like he was gonna hug me from all the way away. Wide open. The easiest fucking target in the world.

'And then Terrell comes up. Running up on the street between us like a fucking crazy person.' Andray shook his head. Terrell didn't say anything. 'But I had my mind made up. My stupid fucking mind. I got Terrell outta the way and got a bead on Trey.

'I shot Trey.

'I shot him.

'I ain't see just where I'd hit him, but I knew I hit him somewhere. And Trey, he was still for a second. Less than a second, just a tiny little moment – he stood still and he just looked at me. He looked at me, like, *Andray*.

'And right then, that look on his face, that tiny little second – I saw what I done. I killed my best friend. See, he wasn't dead yet, but he was dying. I saw that. I killed him – the only person who ever was good to me. The only one who ever loved me, for real. My brother. Just him and Terrell. I killed him. I didn't even know why anymore. Just anger. Just being fucking crazy. Just, you know, like you said. 'Cause I was thinking he was gonna do me first. I don't even know why. But I thought that mothafucka was gonna kill me.

'So then Trey falls back, you know, like normal. Blood coming out of him all over the place – his chest, his mouth, his ears, his eyes. I just ran to him. I didn't give a shit who saw. I didn't care about nothing no more. Not nothing. Looking like a fag-got – shit, that didn't mean nothing no more. I knew I'd just made the biggest fucking mistake of my life.

'I told him I loved him. I told him I was so sorry. I started to cry – fuck, I ain't cried like that since I was a little kid. Just really let go. I felt all the blood pumping right out of him. His heart was beating and it was like it didn't know the blood was all just going out to the ground. I held him and his blood was all over me, in my face, in my eyes. And I said, I love you. I fucked up, and I know it, but I love you. I love you so much.'

Andray stopped and laughed a little to cover up that he was crying.

'And then it was like – like time slowed down for a minute. Like time kind of stopped. And I felt this – like a – well, shit, I can't explain it. Something happened. Like a breeze, like it was hot and cold at the same time.

'And then Trey, he sits right up and says, "Why you cryin', Andray?"'

Andray laughed again, but it worked less well now to cover up his crying. He leaned over Terrell and leaned out the window and spit.

'I nearly jumped out my fucking skin,' he went on. 'Nearly passed right out. But he was fine. He just stood right up and he was fine. We was both covered in blood, but he was all healed up. Not a mark on his body. Not one scratch.'

I looked at Terrell. He looked at me and nodded solemnly. 'God's truth,' he said. 'I seen the whole fucking thing myself. That mothafucka, he up and walking, just the same goofy fuck he always was.'

Both boys laughed nervously.

'I started cryin' all over again.' Andray said, shaking his head. 'Trey, he told me to stop cryin'. He says to me, 'It's all over now. You ain't going nowhere. So stop crying and shut the fuck up.'

'See, he knew. I decided – see, I couldn't live with that. If he died, I was gonna die too. Right next to him. He hugged me and we both just, like – we was so happy.'

'And then it start to rain,' Terrell said, smiling.

'Just like *that*,' Andray said, snapping his fingers. 'Just quick like that, a big storm, and all the blood was washed away. We was both just soaked, clean, like after a shower. And it wasn't no dirty water, like usual. It was real clean, like from a bottle. And then it stopped, just like it came.' He snapped his fingers again.

'But when it was over,' Andray concluded, 'it was over. Trey, he never would say a word about it. Never tell me how he did it. I seen a lot of fucked-up shit, but that, that's the real thing.'

'But Trey,' Terrell said solemnly. 'He ain't never the same.'

'Well, he'd been shot,' I said.

'No,' Terrell said, shaking his head. 'It ain't like that. In his body, he just the same. No scars, no nothing. But in his head – he changed.'

'Stopped hanging out with us,' Andray said. 'Saw him less and less.'

223

'He started ridin' trains,' Terrell said. 'Like some hobo shit.'

'With white kids,' Andray said. 'Those dirty kids, white kids with dreadlocks and shit like that. Punks. Went longer and longer each time.'

'Started making friends all over the place,' Terrell said. 'He went to the library, e-mailing some girl he met in Portland.'

'Oregon,' Andray clarified, assuming I found Portland as mysterious as he did.

'Portland, Los Angeles – shit, he went all over,' Terrell said. 'Ridin' trains. Then one time he just didn't come back.'

'That about six months ago now,' Andray said.

'About seven,' Terrell said. 'Seven months.'

'That's a long time,' Andray said.

We sat and I smoked the rest of the cigarette. Andray looked at me.

'Why you breathing like that?'

'That's just how I breathe,' I said.

I felt myself falling and I wondered if the truck had finally tipped over – it was, after all, at an impossible angle. I had as strong a grip on physics as anyone else.

'Hey, lady,' I heard from far away.

As I fell I saw Trey making the girls laugh in Portland, marveling at the clean streets and whole houses. Trey in Los Angeles, taking meetings at the Brown Derby. Trey in Boston, exploring Harvard Yard. Trey in Miami, wrestling alligators. Trey in Alaska, teaching Yukon Jack to shoot nines

224

and sling rock. Trey, laughing his way around the country, seeing everything, living in the sun.

'Her name Miss Claire. Yo, Miss Claire.'

'Fuck. Hey, lady, *wake up.*'

'Hey, CLAIRE. Claire DeWhatever-the-fuck-your-name-is. WAKE UP.'

Suddenly someone's hands were on my shoulders. Trey?

'Oh lady oh lady oh lady please wake up oh fuck oh fuck PLEASE wake up.'

Thump-*thump*. Thump-*thump*.

I felt my heart pound in my chest. My eyes popped open. I was high and very much alive. Terrell was leaning over me, eyes and mouth open. Andray was gone.

'Oh, man,' he said. 'I thought you was gone, lady.'

He laughed, not because anything was funny, but because he was glad I wasn't dead.

I realized I was slouched down low in the seat, my head near the bottom. I sat up.

'Hey,' I said. My throat was burnt and dry. 'Can I have some more?'

Terrell shook his head and ignored my request. He was used to idiots on drugs. 'You really looked dead, lady. You was all white and your eyes was all up in your head like a movie.'

'That's just what I look like,' I croaked.

Terrell looked at me. Then he instructed me to drive to the all-night gas station on Magazine and Washington. He dashed in and came out with a corn-syrup-and-food-coloring orange drink in a little plastic tub.

'Juice,' he said, handing it to me. 'You drink this. Good for you.'

I drank the sugar water and I did feel a little better. I understood why he and Andray were friends. He was a kind boy. We drove back toward his corner. About a block away I stopped to let Terrell out.

'You sure you gonna be okay?' he asked. 'You need help or something?'

'I'll be okay,' I said. 'Thanks for the juice.'

He nodded, shook my hand, and got out of the car.

His skin was leathery and tough, as if he'd been working hard.

CHAPTER 35

I t was night. The bar was dark and smelled
like beer and felt familiar. Maybe I'd been
there before. Little Christmas lights lit up the
bar. Tom Waits played on the jukebox. I was on
lower Decatur in the Quarter, a strip of antique
stores during the day and dive bars at night. I
didn't remember when I'd gotten there. But there
I was.

Tracy and Andray sat at the bar, drinking
together. Andray was drinking a martini in a big
oversize glass and smoking a cigar. Tracy was
drinking a glass of beer and smoking a cigarette.
Andray must have come straight here from the
truck where I last saw him.

So that's where Tracy's been all these years, I
thought. Here I was thinking she was dead. But
she's been in New Orleans. It made a strange kind
of sense. Tracy would love New Orleans – the
murder, the music, the people. She was my age –
her age – and she looked hard and bleached and
a little bit scary. Just like I always knew she would.
She wore a black fur coat that was falling apart
at the seams and big cocktail rings on her fingers.

227

Under her coat I could see the tattoos on her wrists: C, K. Around them were new tattoos: snakes, roses, names of boys she loved, however briefly.

I wanted to talk to them but they couldn't hear me, even though I could hear them.

'The thing is,' Andray was saying, 'people come down here thinking it's some kinda Damon Runyon story. Thinking they gonna see some parades—'

'See some voodoo shit,' Tracy said, in full agreement. 'See some little black kids tap dancing in a puddle. Maybe see an old black guy playin' guitar down in the Quarter.'

Andray laughed. It made so much sense that they would like each other. Of course they would be friends.

'But once they here,' Andray said, 'they gonna find out. This ain't no Damon Runyon shit.'

Tracy laughed.

'More like Jim Thompson,' she said.

'Or Donald Goines,' Andray said.

'Maybe even like Chandler,' Tracy said. 'Like how things never make any sense.'

'Yeah,' Andray said. 'You got it. if anybody looking for *that* kind of story, the kind where every little thing gets tied up in the end, they best stay on the train and go right through to Texas.'

'Don't even get off,' Tracy said. 'Stay right on the train. I heard they got some good stories up in Oxford, Miss.'

Andray laughed.

'Got some in Miami, what I hear,' Andray said.

'Got plenty in California,' Tracy said. They laughed again.

'The thing about this city,' Andray said. 'It knows how to tell a beautiful story. It truly does. But if you're looking for a happy ending, you better be lookin' somewhere else.'

Tracy cackled.

'You got it, pal,' she said, lighting a cigarette. 'There's a lot to love about this place. But it ain't for the weak of heart. And it ain't no place for happy endings.'

CHAPTER 36

I woke up and got my phone and called Kelly. I hadn't spoken to her in five years. I got her answering machine. Her voice was clipped and mean, just like the last time I heard it.

'You've reached the McCallen detective agency. Leave a message.'

'It's me,' I said. 'I had a dream.'

I hung up.

We started our careers as detectives by solving the mysteries in our own homes. Where was Kelly's mother going at quarter after one every afternoon? To the liquor store, as we found out. What did Tracy's dad keep in the mysterious box under his bed? Bondage porn, photographs I wished I'd never seen. And who was my mother making such mysterious calls to after my father fell asleep at night? We found out it was my father's brother.

It wasn't long before we had proven Silette's first rule of solving mysteries: most people don't want their mysteries solved. Including us. But it was too late for us to stop.

Next, we started solving mysteries in the

neighborhood. There was no shortage of crimes, but the solutions weren't very challenging. Everyone knew who'd shot Dwayne. Everyone knew about La Tisha's dad. The problem wasn't solving the crime. The problem was that no one cared.

As we got older we spent hours on the subway. From the Cloisters to Coney Island, New York was ours. It cost seventy-five cents for a subway token, and a can of Krylon was two bucks. And turnstiles were easy to jump, and spray paint was easy to steal. We rode the trains and left our mark where we could. Some kids lived or died for graffiti. We just wanted to leave some evidence we'd been alive.

New York was our own private mystery. Like children alone in the woods, we followed our trail of crumbs wherever it led us. No one looked for us. Nobody missed us. Our only encounter with adult authority was the cops, and all they ever said was *Pour it out, Put it in a paper bag,* or *Put it out.*

Together we wrote graffiti, together we bought records, together we combed thrift shops for clothes and books, together we bought nickel bags of weed and pints of vodka on Myrtle Avenue, together we faked the age on our bus passes to sneak into shows, together we rode the subway to the end of the line, together we met other kids like us – a whole city of kids like us, from neighborhoods and houses they wanted to be away from as much as possible.

But there was one difference between us and the other kids we met. We had read *Détection*. They hadn't.

By 1985 we'd started reading the papers and watching the news and trying to solve the crimes we read about. That year more than a thousand people were murdered in New York City. There were one or two shootings a week in our neighborhood alone.

But the city at large, we found, wasn't so different from our neighborhood. Sometimes the problem wasn't cracking the case. It was finding someone to care after you cracked it.

'The clue that can be named is not the eternal clue,' Silette wrote.
'The mystery that can be named is not the eternal mystery.'

CHAPTER 37

The next day I drove to the park on Annunciation and Third again. In front of me was the big white truck with a cherry picker I'd seen around the city. I still didn't know what it did. I looked at the license plate; it was covered with mud. I tried to catch sight of the people inside but I couldn't make much out, just two people in white jumpsuits. At Josephine it made a right turn and I didn't follow.

The park on Annunciation was supposed to be a playground. No one was playing in it. But the same boys were hanging out, trying to sell the same drugs. One of them was small and had great big dreadlocks. I knew it was Lawrence.

I parked and went over to Lawrence and introduced myself. Lawrence had flawless dark skin and a good-looking-enough face, but his best feature was his hair, which cascaded out and around him in well-tended locks like those of Shiva, the Hindu god. He wore tremendously large pants with an equally disproportionate gun in the waistband and a huge T-shirt that had a picture of a dead boy on it. HUSTLER 4 LIFE, the T-shirt said under the picture of the boy. In the cold I saw goose bumps on Lawrence's perfect brown arm.

I shivered as we stood and looked at each other. Nearby, his friends, concealing enough weaponry to subdue Fallujah, watched us. I was glad for the .38 tucked into my jeans.

Lawrence sneered at me. Only a mother could think Lawrence was innocent of anything. As far as I was concerned everyone was guilty of everything. Especially Lawrence.

'Can I buy you lunch?' I asked. 'It's kind of cold out.'

Lawrence shook his head and didn't say anything. He was playing it tough.

I was tougher.

'It's about Vic Willing,' I said softly. 'The lawyer.'

Lawrence pulled his lips together. He still didn't say anything.

'Yeah, I know,' I said. 'Don't talk to the crazy lady about the lawyer.'

He didn't say anything. But his eyes were dying to talk. The story was strong. But Lawrence was stronger.

'So I'm gonna guess,' I said. 'I'm gonna guess what happened between you and Vic Willing.'

Lawrence looked sideways, ignoring me, setting his jaw. But he didn't leave.

I watched Lawrence. He stood tall and erect, but his back was stiff and rigid; it was bravado, not pride that held him upright. His shoulders pulled forward in a self-protective gesture. He stuck his hands in his pockets so I wouldn't see how hard it was for him to keep them still. I measured his rate of breath and the depth of his inhalations: fast and shallow. I looked into his eyes and read the marks on his irirses. I studied his tattoos. In addition to the usual gang and neighborhood markers, a zipper was inked across his neck; it screamed *suicidal ideation.*

It wasn't a hard tale to read. Just an old, sad one. One I knew better than I wanted to.

'Vic heard about you from your mother, Shaniqua,' I began. 'She asked him some questions and told him all about you. And he offered to help. And he *did* help, didn't he? Got the charges dropped, got your record cleared. And he was so *nice*. He was about the nicest, coolest guy in the world. Right?'

Lawrence said nothing.

'Just like everyone said he was,' I went on. 'And after the case was over, he didn't leave. Not like – well, like just about everyone else except your mom, right? Vic didn't leave. He stuck around. And he was probably a good friend at first. Interested in you, listened to you, gave you good advice.'

Lawrence kept his eyes fixed on a spot on the other side of the playground and clenched his jaw. His chest puffed out like he was ready to fight.

'But then one day,' I said, shivering, 'he wasn't so nice anymore, was he? He wanted more. He told you it was okay, that everyone did it. He wanted – well, he wanted sex. And when you said no, at first that was okay. He said it was fine. You didn't have to do anything you didn't want to do. And you could still be friends, right?'

Lawrence didn't move a muscle. But shiny little pools formed in the corners of his eyes.

'But he wouldn't stop trying. He wouldn't let it go. He took you to nice places. Bought you things. But he wouldn't stop trying. He said you could still be friends. And you wanted to still be friends. But he wouldn't stop. He just *wouldn't stop.*

'And then one day he laid down the law. He wasn't asking anymore. He *told* you. You get with the program, or he would get the charges reinstated. Murder two – that's a big one. No one in the world wants to go to Angola for that kind of time.' Of course, it was unlikely Vic could bring the charges back once they'd been dropped. But there was no point in telling Lawrence that now. 'So you did it,' I went on. 'You—'

Lawrence shook his head.

'Uh-uh,' he said, his voice full of emotion. 'No. We did *not* – no.'

He made a strange motion with his head and sighed, turning his head toward the park, avoiding my eyes.

I didn't say anything.

'I just watched,' Lawrence mumbled. 'He liked to have someone watching. Some other boy did the . . . you know.'

236

'How old were you?' I asked.

'Fourteen,' he muttered. 'Thirteen and then fourteen.'

His eyes were glued on something twenty feet in the distance. It started to rain, almost as if he had made it happen by staring hard enough. I didn't think Lawrence just watched.

We stood in the rain and tried living with what I'd just said.

Neither of us liked it very much.

If there was a cure for self-loathing, I'd give it to Lawrence, after taking a sip for myself. But there is no magic potion. Everyone has to find his own way out. Everyone has to carve his own road through the wilderness.

But sometimes, maybe, you can leave a clue.

'When it happened to me,' I said, 'I wanted to die.'

Lawrence kept his eyes fixed in the distance.

'I mean,' I went on, 'I really, really just wanted to die, you know? To be honest, the only reason I didn't do it was because I was scared. Scared of what would happen after, scared of dying. And then, of course, I hated myself for being scared, too, so there was that. Then I found this book. And this guy, in this book, he said something I thought was really smart. It kind of changed things for me. It kind of like changed everything, like changed my whole life.'

I looked at Lawrence. He was still looking away. In the inner corner of his left eye, a well of tears shook and then broke and streamed down his face. He froze, trying to pretend they weren't there. Fast food wrappers and empty soda bottles rattled on the ground around our ankles, driven by the wind.

'In this book,' I went on, as if we both weren't crying, 'this guy, he says, 'Be grateful for every scar life inflicts on you.' He says, 'Where we're *un*hurt is where we are false. Where we're wounded and healed is where our real self gets to show itself.' That's where you get to show who you are.'

Lawrence turned and looked at me. He didn't say anything. But he looked at me like he was drowning and I was holding out a rope.

'From here,' I said carefully, 'you can go anywhere you want. Anywhere in the whole world. You don't ever have to be the same person you were yesterday. The same things will have happened to you, but you don't have to be the same person.'

Lawrence laughed and pretended he didn't understand what I meant.

'This story,' I said, '*your* story – it doesn't have to be the story where the victim dies alone and broke in a hotel room on Canal Street. It doesn't have to end at Angola. This can be a story where no day is ever this boring again. I mean, you've already lived through the worst possible outcome of any risk. You've really got nothing to lose.'

We looked at each other for a long minute.

'I think you crazy,' Lawrence finally said, laughing, choking back tears.

'I am,' I said. 'Officially. Come on. Let me buy you lunch. I'll tell you about it.'

'Yeah,' Lawrence said. 'Okay.'

We walked up to Parasol's and got roast beef sandwiches and root beer and laughed some more until neither of us was crying. We didn't talk about Vic or the case. I just told Lawrence stories. I told him about the time the state of Utah had me declared officially insane. I told him a few stories about Brooklyn and then I told him a few about the rest of the world: Paris, Buenos Aires, Mexico City, San Francisco. I told him about solving mysteries and going crazy and getting kicked out of a tattoo convention in L.A. and being banned from the Sands in Vegas for life.

There are no coincidences. Just opportunities you're too dumb to see, doors you've been too blind to step through.

And for every one you miss there's some poor fucking soul who's been left behind, waiting for someone to come along and show him the way out.

CHAPTER 38

Once, when I worked for Constance, a friend of hers showed up at the house with a dozen or more little children. He was an Indian, the witch doctor from the White Hawks. He wasn't in costume, but I recognized him from Saint Joseph's Day, when we'd seen him performing in the park. He'd worn white that day, with a headpiece three feet high, and long synthetic braids coming down each side of his face. The man was fifty-ish and had a mean face – if he hadn't been in the company of a group of kids who adored him, he might have scared me. But the children clearly worshiped him; they ran around and climbed on top of him and crawled over him. They all called him Uncle, although I was fairly certain that none of them were related. The kids were unruly and not terribly clean and I figured they were system kids – fosters, group home children, or street kids.

I had no idea what they were doing there. They all went out to the garden, where Constance grew her herbs, the most dangerous kept behind a locked gate. The children gathered around the

240

man and he took out a tambourine and began teaching them chants. I'd been in New Orleans long enough by then to recognize the Indian songs, even though I didn't know what they meant. But I was surprised that Constance knew all the chants without missing a beat, and taught along with him.

I watched them for a while and then went back to work, sifting through files. We were working on the Case of the Missing Miners and I was researching the genealogy of the mine owner, Alfred Stern – which turned out to be a waste of time because the miners, in the end, were never really missing at all. Just misplaced. When I needed a break I went in the kitchen to get a drink. Constance was sitting at the table with one of the little boys, reading his tea leaves. The boy beamed; her attention was like a life vest to a drowning child.

'When the time comes,' I heard her say to the boy, 'you'll know it. Okay?'

The boy nodded, smiling. Constance reached over and rubbed his head.

'Remember,' she said. 'Remember this.'

I went back to work. The man and the kids stayed until dark. After they left, Constance and I cleaned up together, picking up half-full glasses of lemonade and plates of cookie crumbs from around the house. Constance answered my question before I asked it.

'You can't change anyone's life,' she said. 'You can't erase anyone else's karma.'

241

'But—' I began.

Constance stopped me, shaking her head. 'All you can do is leave clues,' she said. 'And hope that they understand, and choose to follow.'

CHAPTER 39

Back in my room that afternoon, I called Leon.

'Was your uncle abused as a child?' I asked.

'Huh,' Leon said. 'Abused? No. I mean, him and his dad weren't close, but I don't think it was abusive. And his mom was kind of cold, but—'

'No,' I said. 'Sexually. Sexually abused.'

'Oh, God,' Leon said. 'No. I mean, not that I know of. God, no.'

We hung up. I called Mick and told him what I'd found out. As we talked I threw the I Ching.

'Jesus,' Mick said. 'Jesus. Out of everything I would have guessed.'

I added up the coins and checked the book. Hexagram 55: Lonely smoke.

'I know,' I said. 'That's the thing about the truth. It's just like your car keys – always in the last place you look. Did Vic ever prosecute Andray?' I asked. 'Or try to?'

'No,' Mick said. 'I looked into that right away. Never.'

Smoke without a fire misses his sister. The wise man

243

follows the smoke to its spark. A lonely king cannot rule his people. Love spoils the rice and sours the clouds.

'Are you there?' Mick said.

'I'm here,' I said.

'So what do we do now?' he asked. 'I mean, do you think this is why he was killed? I've been going through all his financials, and I think—'

'Forget about his financials,' I said. 'This is it.'

'What do you mean? You mean Lawrence—'

'Not Lawrence,' I said. 'But this is it – this is the mystery. It has to be.'

'How can you be sure?' Mick asked, always suspicious.

'I'm never sure of anything,' I said. 'But I'm fairly fucking certain this, uh, *proclivity* of his has something to do with why Vic was killed.'

'Well, I still think I should keep going through his records,' Mick said. 'You never know—'

'You do whatever you want,' I said. 'I'm gonna go try to get an alcoholic in Congo Square to be my friend.'

I was on my way out the door when Leon called back.

'Hi, Claire,' he said.

'Hi, Leon.'

'So, I was thinking – my mother never left me alone with Vic.'

'Never?' I said. 'Never ever?'

'Never ever,' Leon said, sounding a little queasy.

'I mean, that doesn't mean – it doesn't – I remember once she made a comment like, oh, Uncle Vic doesn't know anything about kids. Something, you know, totally innocent.'

'Not even once?' I said. 'Not even if she ran out for cigarettes?'

'No,' Leon said. 'If she had to go somewhere she took me with her. Always. Not even once.'

Most people who've been abused as children never hurt a fly. But of all the people who hurt flies, almost all of them have had their wings broken themselves.

She knew. Leon's mother knew.

CHAPTER 40

That evening I went to Congo Square for the last time. I didn't try to be friendly or work any disguises. I didn't try anything at all. Instead I just sat in the square and watched the men ignore me. Jack Murray was at his usual place at the picnic table. I took three packs of cigarettes with me. I was robbed of the first one in ten minutes.

'Got a cigarette?' the man had said to me. He was at least fifty, wearing clothes that hadn't been washed in a year.

'Sure,' I said.

When I took the pack out of my purse to give him one, he snatched the whole thing out of my hands and walked away. I suppose I could have killed him, but it hardly seemed worth it. Cigarettes are cheap in Louisiana.

I heard someone laugh. I turned around and saw a woman sitting in the grass behind me. She was as regal as a president, holding a forty-ounce bottle of malt liquor, a bright green wrap on her head, sitting under a tree with all her possessions in a shopping cart next to her, laughing at me.

I turned back around.

My next visitor was another old man, forgotten long ago, in the shabby trench coat all hard-living men acquire somewhere in between jail and the Goodwill, the liquor store and the halfway house.

'You got a dollar?' he asked.

'No,' I said. 'Sorry.' I should have thought to bring small bills and change with me, but I hadn't.

The old man lunged for my purse. I pulled back and put a hand on his chest. The men at the picnic table, including Jack Murray, watched, bored.

The black alligator purse had been Constance's. Supposedly it had been custom made for Constance in Paris by Mademoiselle herself. It was bigger on the inside than on the outside and could get almost anything through an x-ray machine or a Geiger counter. It had pockets inside pockets, secrets inside secrets. The solution to approximately seventeen mysteries could be found in this purse at any given moment. In a jam it could unfold into a tent and I could live in it until circumstances improved.

'No,' I said to the man.

He swatted at my hand and kept fighting.

'Stop,' I said. 'Really. Stop.'

He pushed my hand away and went for my purse again.

'Seriously,' I said. 'Come on. I don't want to hurt you.'

The woman behind me laughed again, more of a cackle. The man and I squirmed around for a few minutes, not exactly fighting but wrestling our way toward my purse.

'Come on,' I said. 'Just go.'

'Gimme that purse,' he panted, getting winded.

'No!' I said, annoyed now. 'Go away!'

But he didn't go away. Instead we squirmed around for another minute, and then I lost patience. I stood still and pushed hard to get a little space and then kicked him in the hip with my left leg, and as he contracted toward the pain as I knew he would, being just a man made old before his time and not much of a fighter, I smacked him in the face with my right hand and then with my left.

I didn't hurt him too bad. Not physically. But he seemed wounded in some other way. He stood and looked at me with his mouth open, looking crestfallen.

'Fuck YOU,' he said, looking hurt, as if I'd started it. Everyone was watching us now.

'Fuck YOU,' he said again.

'Okay,' I said softly.

He stood and looked at me for another minute. Maybe he was expecting some kind of resolution. I didn't give him any. Finally he shambled off.

I went back to doing nothing for a while. I figured I'd come here every day for the rest of my life if that's what it took. I was glad I wasn't pretty anymore. It was so much easier to do things like this without being pretty. I'd come here every day and beat people up until Jack Murray talked to me. True, I'd go through a lot of cigarettes, but at least I'd keep in shape. I'd studied martial arts for years – Constance had insisted on it – but I hadn't been to the studio in ages and my chops were way down. Constantly being mugged, I'd get my high kicks back. I was absorbed in a daydream of actually doing this, living in the park for the rest of my life, when a bike stopped in front of me. On the bike was a boy. He was white, with dirty-blond dreadlocks, and tattoos on his face. His kind seemed to have made a mass migration to New Orleans lately, apparently under the impression that New Orleans didn't have *enough* jobless, antisocial ne'er-do-wells of their own fighting for scraps.

'Got a cigarette?' he said.

I heard another cackle behind me. I turned around to see the regal woman's face, ruler of all she surveyed.

'Boy, you fucking crazy,' she said. She had a slight Gullah accent, probably from the Georgia Sea Islands. 'You go on and get out of here.'

The boy on the bike laughed. 'I ain't scared,' he said.

'Then you one stupid fuck,' the lady said. She cackled loudly, and this time I cackled along with her. The boy left and we kept cackling.

'You want me to tell you something?' the woman said.

'Okay,' I said.

'Good,' she said. 'You go get me a little bottle and I'll tell you something.'

I jogged across the street to a grocery store and got her a forty. When I came back she was sitting on my bench. I sat next to her and gave her the bottle.

'Now tell me something,' I said.

She took a long sip of the malt liquor. 'You a crazy bitch,' she said.

We both cackled again.

'I already knew that,' I said. She took a sip from the bottle and then handed it to me. I had a drink and gave it back. After a while I took a joint out of my purse, lit it up, and handed it to her.

'Bless your heart,' she said with a smile, and handed the bottle back to me.

We started cackling all over again. I couldn't have said what exactly was so funny, but something was.

'You a crazy bitch,' she said affectionately.

'I told you, I know that,' I said again. We cackled.

We passed the liquor and we passed the joint and cackled until the sun went down and the moon came up. When the first forty was dead I ran to a store on North Rampart and got us another, and when that was gone I ran and got us another.

'Bless your heart,' the woman, whose name was Sandra, said over and over again. 'Bless your heart.'

We drank and smoked and talked about childhood

and about men and about liquor and drugs and work and birds. Jack Murray ignored me until, when the sun was coming up, I looked over and saw he was gone.

CHAPTER 41

Vic was sitting in his chair. His chair where he watched the birds. He looked out the window with a soft, dreamy look on his face. In between his chair and the window was the foot of the bed. Lying the wrong way on the bed, with his head at the foot, was a boy, or young man. He had long dreadlocks and dark skin. I couldn't see his face.

I wasn't sure if he was alive. Maybe sleeping.

I looked back to Vic. Tears were running down his face. He looked through the bedroom to the terrace. It was empty. No birds today.

I heard a howl. Vic was sobbing. He let out a scream.

The sky turned black outside. It started to pour, great lashes of rain sweeping into the bedroom, lightning shooting into the living room.

Vic cried and wailed. His pain was tangible. It knocked me down like a wave, crushing me. The storm whipped the house, tearing it to pieces.

I woke up screaming.

CHAPTER 42

I'd just finished my coffee the next morning when my phone rang.

It was Kelly. I picked up. She didn't say hello or hey or how are you.

'Tell me about the dream,' she said.

I told her about the dream about Tracy at the bar with Andray. I wasn't sure what it meant. Dreams are slippery things. There's no easy translation from that world to this one.

'What was she wearing?' Kelly asked.

I told her.

'Huh. How old was she?'

'Our age. The age she would be if . . .'

'Huh.' That was all she said about it. 'While I've got you on the phone,' she said, 'do you remember the name of the boy, the boy hanging out by the keg at the, at a, at a Broadway-Houston party on – let me see, hmm, wait, I dropped it. Shit.' I heard some papers rustling. Then I heard the phone fall to the ground and a crackle as she picked it back up.

'December 30, 1984,' she said. 'He wore jeans and a black T-shirt and black creepers. About five-seven-and-a-half, dark hair. Oh, and he had a little star tattoo on his elbow. Near his elbow, sort of on the side of his arm. I think the last time you saw him was at Julian's on June 11, 1986. The pool hall,' she clarified, in case I'd forgotten. I hadn't. A Broadway-Houston party was a kind of party kids had in the eighties, and maybe before: they would rent one of the dance studios near the corner of Broadway and Houston in Manhattan, buy a few kegs, and charge other kids four or five dollars to get in. Julian's was a pool hall on Fourteenth Street. One of the soda machines dispensed beer at night.

Now the corner of Broadway and Houston was some of the most expensive real estate in the world. Julian's had been torn down long ago to build brick-façade housing for NYU.

I heard a gunshot in the distance.

'Julian's,' I said. 'I'm thinking.' Tattoos were relatively uncommon in New York City back then, especially on young people. When we did our first tattoos on our wrists – a K for Kelly, T for Tracy, C for Claire – some people didn't know what they were. They thought they would wash off.

'I think I do remember him. I think his name was Oscar. No, no. Oliver, maybe? I don't know his last name. I'm pretty sure he lived in Manhattan. Maybe Queens. Definitely not Brooklyn. He had a lot of friends from Stuyvesant but I don't know if he actually went there. For some reason I'm thinking Bronx Science. I don't know why.'

'Known associates?' she asked.

'Huh. Hannah. You remember that girl Hannah? Livie. Todd. Nakita. Rain. Rain from Stuyvesant, not Rain from Midwood.'

'Known to frequent?'

'Julian's pool hall. Maude's. Cherry Tavern. Blanche's. Sheep's Meadow – I remember seeing him there at least once.'

'Anything else?' she asked.

I thought for a minute. Another gun responded to the first, a semiautomatic, pop-pop-popping in rapid succession.

'He was cute,' I said. 'He dated this girl, a mod girl. She had red hair, long hair, bangs.'

'Like Manic Panic red?'

'No, like a dark strawberry blond. Not natural but almost a natural-type color. Almost. Sometimes she wore a black and white checked miniskirt, a checkerboard check. She wore that with black tights and creepers, the tall ones.'

'Two and a quarter inch?'

'Maybe even three inch,' I said. 'And she had this white leather jacket. This great vintage white leather coat with black fake fur collar. The kind of fake fur that's like a stuffed animal. It was a man's coat from, hmm, '73, '74, something like that. It was very sharp.'

'Wait,' she said. I heard papers rustle as she looked through her files. 'I knew it,' she said. 'The white jacket. I think we're talking about Nicole Abramowitz. I'm almost sure. Do you know she went to Packer? So, hmm, under her known acquaintances we have an Oscar Goldstein. Do—'

'No,' I said. 'I remember Oscar Goldstein. He wasn't the boy with the tattoo.'

'Hmm,' she said again. 'Okay. Well, I've got nothing on him, then.'

'What's up?' I asked. 'Did you find something?'

But I knew what the answer was.

'No,' she said.

Kelly hung up.

In the distance I heard sirens from police cars. My head pounded and my mouth was dry.

I sat up in bed and looked out the window. The coroner's truck drove by.

Today wasn't a good day for happy endings.

CHAPTER 43

Early in the morning on January 11, 1987, Kelly and Tracy and me stood on the subway platform underground at the Brooklyn Bridge station in Lower Manhattan. Kids would start to gather there in a few hours to see the graffiti that had been done the night before. At night graffiti artists snuck into the train yards to do entire cars, and other kids waited on the platform to see them as they came in, before they went off to be cleaned. We'd been out all night, first to a Broadway-Houston party and then writing on trains and then breakfast at the Square Diner in TriBeCa with some boys we knew. We had been drunk and high but now we were just tired, or at least Kelly and I were. Tracy wanted to see the trains come in. A boy she liked had gone to the train yards the night before and she wanted to see what he'd done, if anything.

'You bitches do what you want,' I said. 'I'm going home.'

'Me too,' Kel said. 'You coming?' she said to Tracy.

'Cunts,' Tracy said. 'I wanna see Marcus's train. I'm staying.'

We lit cigarettes. There was no one to tell us not to. Rules and laws were for other people in other places; we did as we pleased. New York was our oyster; smoking on the subway platform was the best pearl we could wrench from it.

We heard the clang of metal on metal and felt the rush of wind. A train was coming. We would take the 4 up to Union Square and get the L back into Brooklyn; at Lorimer we would switch to the G and take that the rest of the way home.

I hugged Trace as the train curled around the tunnel toward us. 'G'night, bitch,' I said. 'Call me tomorrow.'

She smelled like the subway and cigarettes and her thrift-store leather jacket, with *die yuppie scum* written over her heart in silver paint pen. She wore her blond hair with short bangs; a thriftshop sixties dress in green lamé; black tights; and real Doc Martens, a Christmas present from her father, who saved for months to buy them for her. Her voice was young but also a bit gravelly. She already smoked about a pack a day. She is always in that moment and always will be; she's stuck, dead, frozen, on the northbound 4/5/6 platform in 1987; this is where she will spend eternity.

'Night, slut,' she said. 'Love you. Talk to you tomorrow.'

Kelly and Tracy hugged and whispered similar words. An Uptown 4 pulled in to the station and Kelly and I got on. We waved goodbye to Tracy through the glass. As we took off she blew us a kiss off the palm of her right hand.

No one ever saw Tracy again. No one ever found a clue, no one ever found a suspect, no one ever found a lead.

Not even me. Especially not me.

Tracy had been missing for almost a full day before her father called me. Her mother had died in an accident when Tracy was two. Her father was a poor, broken-down Irish-Italian drunk who'd lived in the projects all his life. But Tracy loved him, and all he wanted was to get his kid the hell out of Brooklyn. Less than a year later he died from alcohol poisoning and heartbreak.

I'd thought it was strange that Tracy hadn't called me after coffee that morning, but it wasn't a big deal. When her father called, it still wasn't a big deal. I called Kel and her phone was busy; sure enough, she'd been talking to Tracy's father too. None of us had heard from Trace. Kel and I figured she'd hooked up with the boy whose graffiti she'd been waiting to see.

We spent a sleepy, hungover day at the coffee shop on Myrtle Avenue. By four o'clock it was already dark. We took the G to Williamsburg and walked to Domsey's to shop for vintage clothes at two dollars a pound. I got a purple minidress, Kel got a bowling shirt. LYDIA, the shirt said across the breast. POLICE ATHLETIC LEAGUE BOWLING TEAM, it said across the back. We had dinner in a little Polish diner on Broadway and took the subway home. We watched TV at my place for a while, watching a Movie of the Week on my little black-and-white TV I'd thrifted from a Goodwill on Fifth Avenue. Valerie Bertinelli was held hostage by her obsessive ex-husband. Would she escape? Or would she be trapped there, forever, in the place she used to call home?

'I wonder what happened to Trace?' I said as I kissed Kel good night on the cheek. 'I wonder where she is?'

Kelly shrugged.

I did too. She would turn up.

The next morning, when we still hadn't heard from her, we started to worry. Her father called again. We told him we were sure everything was fine. But we weren't sure. She should have called us. We didn't begrudge her whatever adventure she'd run into. But she should have called us.

That afternoon Kel came to my house and we drank coffee and smoked cigarettes and made calls. We called friends, acquaintances, boys. No one had seen her. At eight we took a break and went out for cheeseburgers and disco fries. After cheeseburgers, we started looking for Tracy. We found Marcus, the boy whose piece she'd been waiting for, drinking at Mona's on Avenue A. Mona's was one of a string of East Village bars that would serve a toddler with a fake ID. Marcus hadn't seen her at all. He didn't even know she liked him. We went to all the bars where teenagers went in the East Village: Lizmar Lounge, Alcatraz, Downtown Beirut, Mars Bar, Blue & Gold, Cherry Tavern, Holiday, International.

No one had seen Tracy.

Another day went by. Her father called the police. He called other parents. He called Kel and me every day. We told him we were sure everything was fine. But now we were sure it wasn't.

We expanded our circle of phone calls. We searched Tracy's room, her locker, her pockets. We looked through every scrap of everything Tracy had owned or touched or been near. A phone number on a scrap of paper, a notation in a V. C. Andrews book, a stain on a T-shirt, a lone high-heeled shoe, a crooked poster on the wall – nothing went unexamined.

But none of it helped. Weeks passed, and we still had no sign of Tracy. The police got involved but lost interest quickly. The papers and the local news had a burst of interest in the first few weeks, but as they learned more about her family and her past, short as it was, they lost interest. Despite blond hair and blue eyes, Tracy was not a marketable victim.

We got clever. We tracked down the MTA employees who'd been on duty that night. We found kids we'd seen but whose names we didn't know. We learned how to get people to talk to us who didn't want to tell us anything at all. We showed up at one boy's house as very believable counselors from Stuyvesant High; we showed up at a another girl's house as less believable, but still convincing, STD social workers.

We stopped going to school. We stopped going to parties, stopped writing graffiti. Tracy's disappearance, the lack of her, became our world. Our lives revolved around the hole where Tracy had been. We applied Silette's principles of *Détection* to every facet of it. We threw ourselves into the case full-time. We fingerprinted her room, her clothes, her books. We broke into the school office and got her records. We tried to talk to her teachers, and when they didn't want to, we found ways of making them. We followed up on every matchbook we found in her school bag, every note on a scrap of paper, every bird that flew overhead, every flower that bloomed. Omens were all around. Clues were everywhere.

But somehow, we still couldn't see.

'Mysteries exist independently of us,' Silette wrote. 'A mystery lives in the ether; it floats into our world on the wind like an umbrella and lands where gravity pulls it. And all the elements around it are now rearranged into the elements of a mystery: a tightly woven lace of clues and detectives, villains and victims. Yesterday's peaceful cottage is now a murder scene. The previously unremarkable butter knife on the counter is now an ominous weapon. The bland, unnoticed doorman is now a suspect.

'Those who step into this pattern, often through

262

no fault of their own, have no choice but to follow the mystery through to its end. That, or live their lives stuck in its web. It isn't a matter of deserving or undeserving, good or bad. It is only what the facts tell us.'

But in an *Interview* interview in 1979, Silette amended his words: 'Perhaps, though, it isn't mysteries that create these webs,' he said. 'Perhaps the mystery is only what allows us to see them. Maybe that doorman really was capable of great evil all along. Maybe the butter knife was always been a complicated, portentous thing. But it was only their proximity to a mystery that allowed us to see it.'

Months passed. Tracy's father had her declared legally dead. Less than a year later, he died himself. Alcohol. We had learned absolutely nothing about what had happened to Tracy. We were no closer to the truth than we had been the day after she vanished.

We'd had nothing to do for weeks. I had a list of possibilities, all of them equally likely. In my heart, I was almost sure of one of them: she'd gone out writing graffiti, slipped in front of a train, and been crushed. As for why no one had found her body, I figured we just hadn't looked in the right place yet. New York City had hundreds of miles of subway tunnels, some of them abandoned by the MTA and used only by graffiti writers and the homeless. We'd been in plenty of them. But no one had been in all of them. It would take years to cover them all. As far as I was concerned, the mystery was solved by default. There was no other possibility.

I missed her every day. If I found her body, I wouldn't miss her any less.

Maybe I didn't really want to know. Maybe, like everyone who hires a detective, I didn't want to solve my own mystery. Maybe I wanted to keep Tracy as she was, blond hair and bangs, vintage dress and Doc Martens, smelling like subway and cigarettes. Maybe even detectives don't want to solve their own crimes. Because once a crime is solved, you have to close the case and move on.

But Kelly didn't give up. Kelly never gave up. She kept talking to people, kept riding the trains, kept looking for clues. When Tracy's father died she broke in to the projects and walled off Tracy's room, preserving the evidence forever. She plastered the wall over and facsimile-aged the plaster to match. The housing authority thought it was a paperwork issue that had changed a two-bedroom apartment in the projects into a one-bedroom. You could hardly blame them for not guessing the truth.

'Maybe,' I said to Kelly one day over coffee, 'it's time to take a break.' We drank gallons of coffee; we lived in coffee shops.

'What?' Kelly said sharply. 'Take a break from what?'

'You know,' I said nervously. 'The case. Tracy. I think maybe we've gone as far as we—'

'When we find her,' Kelly said. 'That's when we will have gone far enough.'

I didn't say anything. I picked at my bagel. I'd turned seventeen a few months before. I hadn't been to school in nearly a year. I hated Brooklyn – hated its filthy streets, its dying trees, its rows of colorless brownstones, its attached houses that suffocated you, and most of all hated the rich yuppies who were taking it over neighborhood by neighborhood, murdering what little was good. It used to be a miserable, poor place where people talked to each other. Now it was a miserable, expensive place where people ignored anyone outside their clan. At least the kids who had pulled my hair and slapped my face had acknowledged my existence. The rich put on their Walkmans and looked right through you. They walked expensive dogs and rolled expensive babies in designer carriages and glared if you tried to pet either. I wanted to go.

I didn't leave home. Home left me, block by block.

Kelly had wanted to go too, once. That was the plan, the three of us. When we turned sixteen we were going to leave together. It didn't matter where. We weren't going *to*. We were going *away from*.

'I thought we were going to leave,' I said finally. Kelly was going through her file of interviews, double-checking the testimony of a transit officer who may have maybe seen someone who kind of maybe looked like Tracy ten minutes after we left her. 'I don't want to stay here forever.'

Kelly looked at me as if she couldn't believe what I'd said.

'Yes,' she said, astonished. 'We were going to leave. Together. *The three of us.*'

'Even if we find her,' I said, 'she's not coming with us.'

We spent the rest of the day in silence. After that day, I saw that I had to make a choice. I started giving things away, lightening my baggage. Kelly talked to me less and less. A crack had developed between us; soon it would grow into a valley. I started stealing more money from my parents to save; they were drinking more and didn't notice. I also started stealing more from stores, things I could sell: mostly books, which were easy to take and easy to sell to the Strand.

I didn't tell Kelly. She knew.

When I had a decent bankroll together, I packed what little I had and told my parents I was going to summer camp. They barely noticed.

I went to Kelly's apartment to say goodbye.

She opened the door. When she saw me standing there with my suitcase, she turned her back on me and closed it again.

I went to Port Authority and got a ticket for the next bus that was going far away. It was going to San Francisco. I got kicked off in Cleveland.

I knew if I stayed in Brooklyn, I'd be locked in that room forever, like Tracy and Kelly, walled off, slowly running out of air to breathe. I would drown in the Case of the Girl Gone Missing if I didn't let it go.

But Kelly never left. She never stopped. And slowly, a little bit at a time, she did drown. She opened a detective agency, but it was just a side project to fund her search. Nothing else mattered to her. She'd left an air-shaft window open to Tracy's room, and she was arrested a few times for breaking in to the projects, even though no one found the room. Twenty years of working on the same case had made her a great detective. And it had broken her. Everything that could have been hadn't and everything that should have been wasn't. It should have been the three of us traveling the world, the three of us solving mysteries, the three of us growing rich. But it was only me. There wasn't a moment I lived that I wasn't living for three of us. It's not the way to do it. But it was the only way I knew how. It wasn't enough to take one bite for myself. I had to take a bite for Trace and a bite for Kel too. I couldn't go back there, but I also couldn't let go, not really. It would be like losing them all over again.

Kelly and I talked once every few years, when we had dreams about her or other clues to share. Now, twenty years later, sometimes I still expected Trace to call me up on the phone. *What's up, bitch, meet me at Mars Bar at ten tonight.* I still expected

Kel to be waiting for me at the G train to go write graffiti. *What's up, bitch, you're late.*

It isn't the dead we should feel sorry for. It's the living.

I didn't know how to solve the Case of the Girl Gone Missing. And I didn't know how to solve the Case of the Broken Levees. I didn't know how to save a city from drowning and I didn't think anyone else did, either. I could barely keep my own head above the water. The water line was already up to my eyes, and it wasn't getting any lower. I would have liked to rewrite both stories and give them a happier ending. But I couldn't do that. All I could do was solve mysteries, and go on.

'There are moments in life that are quicksand,' Silette wrote. 'A gun goes off. A levee breaks. A girl goes missing. These moments of time are different from the others. Quicksand is a dangerous place to be. We will drown there if we can't get out. But it tricks us. It tricks us into confusing it with safety. At first, it may seem like a solid place to stay. But slowly we're sinking. You will never move forward. Never move back. In quicksand you will slowly sink until you drown. The deeper you let yourself sink, the harder it is to claw yourself out.

'These spots of quicksand are unsolved mysteries. Only the detective can descend into the quicksand and come out alive. Only the detective can pull things and people out of quicksand and get them back on solid ground.'

But how the detective pulls herself back up – well, Silette never wrote about that. And I still don't know.

CHAPTER 44

When I got off the phone with Kelly my head was pounding too loudly for me to go back to sleep. There were plenty of other symptoms too, but I could sleep through those. After a thousand cups of coffee and one of the Vicodin I'd stolen from Vic Willing's house, I felt well enough to check my voice messages. Leon had called while I was sleeping.

I had a shower and more coffee and called Leon back. I gave him a vague report on what I'd learned. He sounded unhappy. Clients are often unhappy. Especially when you tell them their uncles might be pedophiles and you still don't know who killed them. They're funny about that.

'Are you sure?' Leon kept saying. '*Really?*' He asked if I could come over to his house a little later. I was pretty sure what was coming, but there was nothing to do but let it come.

I got to Leon's house at about three. We sat down in the living room. He fixed me a drink right away. I knew *that* was too good to be true.

He sat on the chair opposite me. 'We need to talk,' he said.

I rolled my eyes. Clients.

'I don't think things are working out,' Leon said gently, as if we were breaking up. 'This isn't going the way I hoped it would. I really hoped we would have made more progress by now.'

I sighed and began my standard lecture for impatient clients. 'Leon,' I began. 'In these busy, fast-paced times, people often have unrealistic expectations of how private investigation works. This isn't *Matlock*, Leon. This isn't *Magnum, P.I.*—'

Leon frowned and interrupted me: 'I don't watch *Matlock*. I didn't think this was *Matlock*.'

'Okay,' I continued. 'You don't watch *Matlock*. No one's accusing you of anything, Leon. I was explaining that detection isn't a sprint. It's a marathon. Anyone can jump to conclusions. You don't need a private dick for that. You want the truth. As do I. We're united in—'

'Thanks,' Leon said, frowning again. 'Thanks, but no. I don't think it's going to work out.'

'Leon,' I said. 'At some point in the development of the detective/client relationship, it's natural for the client to want to fire the PI. It's a part of the process, and that's okay. But we need to move past that, to a better place – a place of healing, if you will.'

I didn't think any of that was true, about clients wanting to fire their private dicks. They usually wanted to fire me. That was true enought.

Almost always they wanted to fire me. Actually, every time. Every time except one, the time in Dallas when the guy killed his own mother and then hired me to find the killer because he didn't know the murderer was one of his other personalities. *He* never fired me.

'No,' Leon said. 'I don't think so. I think this is over. I'll pay you for what you've already—'

'Leon,' I said. 'You can't fire me. I'm going to keep working on the case. Then, when I solve it, you're going to see how truly wonderful and clever I am. Then you're going to pay me for the whole time, and you are going to do it *happily*. You are going to do it *with bells on*. So let's just—'

Leon let out a little breath of frustration.

'No,' he said again. 'No. I – I really don't – I mean, I just can't imagine that. No. This is over. This is completely over. I haven't been happy with your, uh, performance. To begin with, you don't check in enough. And as far as I can tell you haven't, you know, accomplished anything. And the' – he looked at the bottle and made a little tipping-back gesture with his hand – 'the drinking and the, the everything else, whatever it is you're doing, smoking morning glory seeds or whatever—'

'Ololiuqui,' I said. 'It's not exactly a morning glory. It's a flowering shrub—'

'And the voodoo or whatever—'

'Oh, come on!' I cried. 'No one was even possessed!'

'No,' he said again, cutting me off with a frown. 'No. I don't want to give you the wrong idea. Here.' He handed me a check for the work I'd done so far and a piece of typed paper. It was an official notice of termination. On the bottom was a seal; I saw that it had been notarized by a notary public. He wasn't taking any chances.

'I think that makes it official,' he said, standing up. 'I think we're all done.'

I stood up. 'You'll see,' I said.

'Sure,' Leon said. 'Okay. I think you should leave now.'

I stood up and left.

'I'm right,' I said at the door. 'I'm always right.'

'Yep, okay,' Leon said as he closed the door in my face. 'That's fine.'

'You'll see,' I said. 'You *will* see.'

He shut the door and didn't say anything, and I knew I was right.

And I knew something else too: when a client fires you, it means you're getting close to the truth.

'The client exists not as a part of the whole but as an external source of power,' Silette wrote. 'If the mystery is Shiva, the client is Shakti. The client initiates the descent into the mystery, but after that she is no longer needed; the detective proceeds of his own accord. The detective will more often than not solve the mystery despite the client, not because of her.

'The client is the errant goat that leads

Persephone to the weak spot of earth where Pluto can let her in.

'No one remembers the name of the goat. Everybody remembers the name of the first detective, Persephone.'

CHAPTER 45

I drove away from Leon's house and parked a few blocks away even though I had nowhere to go. I didn't want to seem stalker-y. I didn't know what to do. I wasn't hungry. I was tired of liquor and drugs. I wasn't interested in going to any museums or malls or tourist attractions, most of which were closed, anyway. There was no one in New Orleans I wanted to see.

I wanted to know who killed Vic Willing. That was all I wanted.

I drove to the Quarter and parked the truck across the street from Vic's apartment. Jackson, the homeless man who'd known Vic, was sitting on the steps of a house nearby. We were only a few blocks from his regular spot in Jackson Square.

I got out of the truck.

'Hey, Jackson,' I said.

He nodded sagely. 'Hello, ma'am.'

'How you doing?' I asked.

'Blessed,' he answered. 'And you?'

'Not so blessed,' I said. 'They keep trying to bless me. But I don't think it's sticking.'

He laughed. 'They got the truck there,' he said.

He looked toward Vic's. I followed his eyes. In front of Vic's building was the same white cherry picker truck I'd seen all over the city.

'What is that thing?' I asked.

Jackson shook his head. 'Don't know,' he said. 'I do not know. I thought you was a detective, anyway.'

'That's true,' I said. 'I am.'

I checked my gun, making sure it was loaded and within easy reach in my waistband. Jackson raised his eyebrows but didn't say anything. Dealing with municipal authorities in New Orleans might require heavy artillery.

I crossed the street; as I did a man in a white jumpsuit got out of the truck and walked over to the oak tree by Vic's window. Vic's tree, where he fed his birds.

The man held an aluminum clipboard and looked up at the terrace, where the bird feeder hung.

'Hi,' I said.

The man jumped and turned around.

'You scared me,' he said, looking annoyed. 'Is that your apartment?'

'No,' I said. 'It's my friend's. What do you want with it?'

He reached into his jumpsuit and pulled out a badge holder and flashed me a badge and an ID. He was an ugly man, short, with an unpleasant face and a lumpy body. He had black hair and brown skin with acne marks and a frown.

'Wildlife and Game,' he said, snapping the wallet back closed. 'We're—'

'Easy, pal,' I said. 'Let's see that again.'

He shrugged and tossed it to me. I caught it and looked at his ID. It was good. I gave it back to him.

'So what are you doing here?' I asked.

'We had reports of an invasive species being fed here,' he said. 'The Quaker parakeet. They're illegal, you know.'

'How can a bird be illegal?' I asked. 'Was he dealing? Soliciting?'

The man shrugged. 'Ask my boss. My job is just to eliminate them.'

'Eliminate them?' I repeated.

He nodded. We looked at each other.

'You from here?' I asked.

'From here?' He looked confused and shook his head. 'No. I'm from D.C. I'm just here for the elimination project.'

'Well, you're in New Orleans now, pal,' I said. 'And no one's getting eliminated.'

He scowled. 'As a representative of the federal government, I have the right to—'

'You have the right to get your ass out of here without me shooting you,' I said. I reached to my waist and put my hand on my gun. 'But only if you leave right now.'

The man didn't look shocked or surprised. Just resigned. I guessed he was used to this kind of reaction. He gathered up his work case and his clipboard and got ready to leave.

'You were taking down their nests,' I said, suddenly getting it. 'They like the warmth so they build on transformers. You were taking down their houses.'

'They're a hazard,' the man said. 'They could start a fire.'

'Right,' I said. 'People *never* do that.'

'They eat crops,' the man said.

'Right,' I said. 'The wheat fields of New Orleans will recover. I promise you.'

The ugly man looked at me. Maybe he wasn't so ugly. Maybe I just didn't like him.

'What's your problem?' he said. 'Why do you care?'

'I don't,' I said. 'Now go fuck yourself.'

I looked up. In the tree were two fat, ungainly little parrots. Mates. Many birds, maybe most, mate for life, or at least closer to life than most humans get.

The man got in his truck, made some notes in his clipboard, and left. I looked up. The two parrots looked down at me. One squawked.

'Yeah, you're welcome,' I said.

I looked down at the base of the tree; sprinkled around it was some kind of blue powder, like the poison they use on rats in New York City.

Jackson and I spent the rest of the morning spraying off the tree with the hose from Vic's building, washing off the blue poison and hoping no one would catch us before we finished the job.

CHAPTER 46

That night I drove around, still hoping something would happen. Nothing did. Not to me. Things happened to other people; people laughed, guns went off, people drank, prayers went unheard, lives were conceived, people fell in love. A house fell down on Josephine Street. I was on Magazine Street when I heard a big boom, like a cannon. A cannon didn't seem impossible, but when I drove closer to the scene I saw a big dome of sawdust and ash, like a mushroom cloud. I'd noticed the house before. It was an old, pretty shotgun, or had been. The storm had knocked the roof off. Then a fire had gutted it, leaving a black ashy mess. But it had still stood up, until tonight. A crowd gathered around the collapsed house, astonished, laughing and shaking their heads.

On my way back downtown to my hotel, I stopped in the all-night gas station on the corner of Magazine and Washington for a few bottles of water. Theoretically the water in New Orleans was as clean as before the storm. Even if that was true, it wasn't exactly an endorsement.

The store at the gas station was the only one open at night for a few miles, and the lot was full. I parked the truck on Washington, in front of something called the New Orleans Firefighters Museum. Inside, the gas station/store was a cross section of New Orleans, each nominated representative of each subculture eyeing the other suspiciously: punk giving the fish-eye to frat boy, thug warily watching punk, Egyptian store worker following crackhead lady, crackhead lady eyeing Egyptian store worker for signs of disrespect.

On my way out of the store I ran into Terrell, Andray's friend. He was loitering with another boy near an Oldsmobile high up on oversize wheels. He had his phone out and was about to make a call.

'Hey, Miss Claire,' he said, uneasily. Terrell looked tense, different from his usual happy self. I figured he was hanging out with the cool kids and trying to look tough. I waved a hello. He waved back and went back to his phone.

I walked back up the block to my truck. I was almost there when I heard someone come up behind me. I turned around.

It was Andray. He wasn't alone. Behind him were three other young men, men I didn't know. Each wore the uniform of huge pants and big hooded sweatshirt, along with the accompanying almost-sneer.

I didn't see Terrell. They'd been looking for me, I now saw, and Terrell had been the advance team.

If I had seen that five minutes ago, it would have been much more helpful than it was now.

'What's up, Miss Claire?' Andray said. If he had any recollection that we had almost been sort-of kind-of friends, he kept it a secret.

I reached into my waistband for my gun – the gun Terrell had sold me. That was a dumb move. The youngest of the boys behind Andray, a kid about sixteen with skin nearly as dark as his black hair, had a nine-millimeter out and pointed at me nearly as soon as I got the idea.

'Fuck,' I said. 'Fucking Quick Draw McGraw.'

The boys all laughed. But the young one didn't put down his gun.

'Shit,' Andray said. 'You always funny, Miss Claire. But listen, we gotta talk to you. So you gonna come with us for a little drive, okay?'

I looked at Andray. I looked for a crack in a window, an easily picked lock on a door to his psyche.

Nothing. He was sealed up tight.

'You're the boss,' I said.

Andray's friends hung back as we walked together up toward Prytania. We didn't talk. Andray's sneakers were quiet in the night air, his breath soft and white in front of him. Around the corner I saw what I'd been dreading.

A black Hummer. Just like the one driven by whoever shot at the kid in front of the restaurant the other day.

Or shot at *me*.

281

We stopped in front of the car.

'You gonna kill me, Andray?' I asked. I heard my heart beating in my chest.

Andray shook his head as if I'd said something stupid and didn't answer.

That was when I got scared.

The other boys caught up with us and the youngest one tossed his gun to one of the others, two medium-size, unremarkable-looking young men. One of the unremarkable boys caught the gun by the handle in the air. He was like a circus performer. Then the young one used a key to open the Hummer and then popped the rest of the locks and we all got in – me in the front between Andray and the driver, the two unremarkable boys in the back.

'You don't have a remote?' I asked.

'I lost that shit!' the driver exclaimed. 'Like the first mothafucking day I had it, I lost that shit! And you know what they want for another one at the dealer's?'

'I can imagine,' I said. 'Look on eBay.'

'Yeah,' he said, looking over his shoulder to pull out. 'I gotta get with that shit.'

The driver put on the radio. To my surprise he didn't put on one of the ten million hip-hop stations in New Orleans. Instead he put on WWOZ, where the Oak Street Brass Band was doing an in-studio show.

The two unremarkable boys fell into a series

of hoots and hollers as the band started 'Eliza Jane.'

'We got friends in that band,' one of the boys explained to me.

'You play?' I asked, turning around.

'Oh, yeah,' the unremarkable boy on the driver's side said, smiling. 'Tuba. I play with them fuckers sometimes. I played with 'em at Maple Leaf few months back. We opened for Bo Dollis,' he said proudly.

'No shit,' I said, turning around. 'I seen Bo Dollis play, gee, five times, at least. How about you?' I said to the other boy. 'What do you play?'

'Fuck, I ain't play nothing,' the boy said, laughing. He had light skin and freckles and a funny, friendly face. 'I play a little drums. I ain't no good. I play tambourine when I go out with the Red Eagles.'

'You're in the Red Eagles?' I asked, incredulous. The Red Eagles were one of the most spectacular Indian gangs in New Orleans. 'Shit, I saw you guys parade – Jesus, more than ten years ago – 1995.'

The boy let out a hoot. ''Ninety-five?' he said. 'I was there. I was four years old. That my first parade.'

I remembered that day. Constance had taken me to the park to see the Indian practice. The men in their elaborate beaded outfits and headdresses huddled together to chant and drink, surrounded by uncostumed men playing percussion:

tambourine, block, cowbell. With them had been a tiny boy, not much higher than my knee, in full costume. He played a little half-tambourine and danced and let out a wild pseudo-Indian yelp every once in a while. The mother of the little boy was a friend of Constance's, and she'd made the boy come over and say hello. She picked him up so Constance could kiss him, a little ball of baby fat dressed in fifty pounds of sequins and feathers.

Everyone knew Constance. Nearby, the Big Chief, sweating in his costume, chanted. His eyes rolled back in his head as he went into a kind of trance.

New Orleans was the first place I'd been where magic was real.

'Holy shit,' I said to the boy in the back seat. 'I remember you. I saw you. I met your mother.'

'Shit,' the kid said.

'Yeah,' I said. 'Your mother – she knew my friend. This lady I used to work for.'

The boys in the back seat looked at each other. No one laughed anymore.

We kept driving.

In Central City we pulled over in an empty lot on Washington just before Dryades.

No one said anything. The band was doing a version of 'Iko Iko.' When they finished the driver turned off the radio.

I breathed slowly, and prayed. Constance had sent me to study with a lama in Santa Cruz for two months, and the prayers he taught me came

284

back, just like he'd promised they would when I needed them.

Om dum durgeya namaah.

The driver popped the locks. Everyone except me grabbed for a door handle.

Om gum gunaputayi swaha, I silently repeated.

'Wait up,' Andray said, loudly. 'Wait up, niggas.'

Everyone waited.

Aham prema. Thy will be done.

'We ain't need four guys for this shit. I can take care of her.'

In the rearview mirror I caught the eye of the kid I'd seen parade. He looked away.

Om shanti shanti shanti. Thy kingdom come, thy will be done.

The driver looked at Andray. 'You got it?' he said.

Andray nodded.

St Jude, hear my prayer.

'Yo, Quan,' the driver said to the boy with the gun. 'Give it to Andray.'

Quan took the gun out of his pants and gave it to Andray.

'Shit,' Andray said. 'This be *warm.*'

Everyone laughed again.

Saint Joseph, protect me.

'You got it?' the driver said to Andray again. 'You gonna take of this?'

Lord, forgive my sins, of which there are too fucking many to count.

Andray nodded.

285

'Awright,' the driver said. Andray opened his door and hopped out of the Hummer. I followed.

'Yo, shut the door,' the driver said, annoyed with my poor manners.

I shut the door. The Hummer drove away.

I turned and looked at Andray. We stood in the cold air and looked at each other. Andray shook his head, as if I'd let him down.

'I kind of like you, Miss Claire,' he said.

'Thanks, Andray,' I said. 'I kind of like you too.'

Some people got meaner when they got a gun. The rush of power could be intense. But not Andray. He looked like he'd been given a job he didn't want.

I hoped to God I was right.

'I like those tattoos you got,' he said, looking at my wrists.

'What those letters mean?'

'My friends,' I said. 'It was for them. I was young when I got them. Younger than you.'

'They still your friends?' Andray asked.

'No,' I said. 'One's dead. The other hates me.'

Andray frowned, as if he'd expected a better story. On one side of the lot was a brick warehouse, long abandoned. An old mural was barely left on the wall: NEW ORLEANS COMES TO LIFE WITH COMMUNITY COFFEE!

'You got more?' he said. 'More tattoos?'

'About ten,' I said. 'Maybe twenty. *Live free or die*. You haven't seen that one. It's on my back. I got like ten more.'

'What's that on your arm?' he asked, pointing with the gun.

I looked to where he was pointing. I pushed up my sleeve so he could see. It was a magnifying glass. Above that was a fingerprint.

Om shanti shanti shanti.

Andray nodded.

'I like that. *Live free or die.* Take no shit from no one. But first,' he said, 'I gotta take care of this.' He stomped his feet against the cold and looked around.

'Now, Miss Claire,' he said, turning toward me and looking me in the eye. 'You gonna forget all about what you seen since you been in New Orleans, right?'

'I've already forgotten,' I said. 'So now we can—'

'I mean, you *really* gonna forget, okay?' Andray said.

'Okay,' I said. I had no idea what he was referring to. It could have been Vic. Or it could have been the shooting in front of the restaurant the other day. I had the thought that maybe he wanted me to forget everything – the ruin, the despair, the blood. Maybe he was part of a committee to help people remember New Orleans before and forget New Orleans now.

'And these guys,' Andray went on, 'they want to make sure you remember to forget. And just to know you really forgot, they want you to get the hell out of New Orleans, all right?'

'I've forgotten,' I said. 'I'm on the next flight.'

'You got to leave,' Andray said, firmly. 'You got to get out of town. Just like the old movies. You hear me?'

'I hear you,' I said. 'I'm already out. I'm not even looking back.'

'The thing is,' Andray went on, 'I gotta make sure you forget. I'm sorry. You a nice lady. I almost like you. But that's how it's gotta be.'

'That's okay,' I said. 'I understand. But if you—'

I didn't finish my sentence, which was going to be something like *But if you kill me I'll never forgive you*. Andray pulled back the hand with the gun up above his head, and my heart stopped.

Then he swung it down to crack me on the forehead.

I saw a thousand little Lite-Brite lights in the sky. I fell back and felt the cold earth hit my bones.

As I fell, I saw that the Hummer was parked across Dryades. We were being watched.

'You gon' be okay,' I heard Andray say from far away. 'This time, you livin' free. And you ain't dead yet. As long as you get your ass out of New Orleans, you gonna be just fine, Miss Claire DeWitt.'

When I came to, it was still night. Andray and I were sitting on the levee, looking over the Mississippi, watching it roll by like slow, sticky molasses.

'Shit,' Andray said. 'He been talking about you, you know.'

He passed me a fat brown spliff. I took it and took an elephant-size hit. When I exhaled the smoke spread out on the Mississippi, settling over it like fog.

'He told me to tell you not to worry,' Andray said.

'He always says that,' I said.

'He said he knows it's hard,' Andray said, nodding. 'He say he knows that. But you gotta be patient, Miss Claire. He ain't working on your time. You oughta know that.'

'It's just that—' I said. 'You know, he's been saying that a long time now, and it's like—'

'He said he got a spot all saved for you,' Andray said. 'A seat right next to him. He say all the detectives, they gonna go home when the flood comes. The *real* flood. And you gonna get, what you call it, recompense for all the burdens you bear. For carrying his burdens and shit. We all gonna get our recompense, but people like us, people who take on burdens, we gonna get to sit by his side. He promised me that.'

Andray took the joint and closed his eyes and took a huge hit, filling the city with smoke when he exhaled, like a dragon.

'All the saints gonna be waiting for us,' Andray said, smiling.

'All the birds, they gonna sing for us when we come home. The dogs is gonna cry and the cats is gonna laugh. They all waiting for us, up at the castle. And every one gonna say thank you. That's gonna be nice, huh? *Thank you.*

'See, they know all about people like us, Miss Claire. They ain't forget us. We workin' for them down here. They know that. He ask us to do our turn and we did it for him. We forgot. But him, he ain't forgot nothing. He know why we're here. He remember for us. He asked us to come down here and do his work, and where you think you're gonna do that? Shit, happy people, they ain't need us. They got what they need. They ain't our people, Miss Claire. People like you and me, we born sad. That way we always recognize our own.'

My eyelids felt heavy and I felt myself drifting away.

'You my sister, girl,' Andray said, smiling. 'We on the same team. And I'm-a see you again for sure.'

We were standing next to each other on the street in Central City. No one else was around, and I heard the water curl through the streets. It rose up around us, wrapping us tight but leaving us dry. Birds flew overhead: parrots, pigeons, doves, starlings, blue jays, all singing together, flying in a whirlwind above us. Andray leaned toward me and whispered in my ear, his breath hot on my skin.

'Your girl, she up there waiting for you. She want me to tell you. She ain't never forget you. She know she in your heart, every minute. Like a little bird in there, beating her wings. She waiting for you up there. She saving you a seat right by her side. She say you getting closer. She say the time is almost here. She say soon, girl. Soon.

'And your girl, she say the whole world stranger than you ever gonna believe. And she say she laugh so hard, sometimes, at the things she see you do, she almost fall off her throne and fall back down to earth.'

I gasped and opened my eyes. I was lying in a filthy lot in Central City. Hovering above me was a man of indeterminate age and features, kicking me lightly. Andray was gone. I didn't know when he'd left.

I sat up. The old man shuffled back a little and mumbled something, his breath forming clouds in front of his mouth.

'Better luck next time, pal,' I croaked, my throat dry and painful. 'Not dead yet.'

The man left. I lay still for maybe a minute or two, or maybe I fell back asleep for a while. Eventually I got up and checked for damage. I didn't think I had a concussion, and if I did, the last place I wanted to be was a New Orleans emergency room. I checked my purse and pockets, and everything important and lethal seemed to be in place. I looked at my phone. It was three in the morning. I'd been out for hours.

From my purse I took out a compact mirror and looked at the bump on my head. It was a little mountain, all right, but the skin was barely broken. I wiped up the small smear of blood that was there and stood up.

I saw more Lite-Brite lights. I sat back down.

I did this a few times before I was stable enough to keep standing. Then I walked. I made it as far as the steps of a church on Dryades. I sat on the steps and tried to stay awake. I was feeling a little punch drunk. The cold air helped a little.

'Hey, miss,' I heard behind me. 'Miss.' I turned around. A man was behind me. Not one man, I saw after a moment. Men. A bunch of them were huddled up in sleeping bags and newspapers and rags by the door of the church, about five feet from where I was sitting, trying to sleep and stay warm.

'Hey, miss, 'scuse me.' One of the men scootched forward and sat near me. He was skinny and short and old.

'Yeah?' I said.

'You got a smoke?' he said. 'I don't mean to bother you. But you got a smoke? All I want is a cigarette.'

I shook my head. 'Uh-uh,' I said. 'Sorry. I don't have one.'

He looked at me like he didn't believe me.

'Really,' I said.

He mumbled something under his breath.

'You want a dollar?' I said. I was worried about a rebellion of men on the church steps. ''Cause I really don't have a cigarette.'

He smiled. 'Yeah,' he said. 'That'd be nice. Thanks.'

I reached into my pocket and found a five-dollar bill and gave it to him.

'Thanks,' he said again. 'Bless you.'

'You too,' I said.

I stood up and my head spun. I sat back down.

'Hey,' the man said. 'How about you? You want a cigarette?'

'Sure,' I said. 'I'd like that.'

He reached into his pocket and pulled out a half-smoked 100. I took it and he lit it for me with a matchbook.

When he lit the match, he saw the bump on my head.

'That don't look good,' he said, frowning.

'It don't feel good,' I said.

The cigarette tasted good. I sat and smoked it. The man pulled a pint bottle out from his overcoat and opened it up and handed it to me.

'Thank you,' I said. I took a long, burning sip and handed it back to him.

'You welcome,' he said. The man smiled. As I looked at him his coat kind of shook and then rattled. I thought I was seeing things, but then something crawled out from the coat and onto the man's shoulders.

It was a rat. A pretty, clean brown and white rat.

'Oh!' I said.

'That's Boo,' the man said. He reached a hand up to pet the rat.

'Hey, Boo,' I said. I reached out to pet him, but Boo shrank away.

'Sorry,' I said.

'That's okay,' the man said. 'He just shy.'

We passed the bottle for a while, not a good idea if you might have a concussion, but a good idea if you're depressed and lonely and it's four o'clock in the morning in the most godforsaken place in the USA and you are very, very thirsty.

We drank for a while and then we smoked more half-cigarettes. Then he pulled out one of the long brown joints and we smoked that.

We talked about the storm. The man told me he'd hidden in a spot he knew, a spot he would not reveal, but from which he could watch all the madness of the city without being seen by any authority.

'You leave people to their own, woulda been fine,' the man said. 'Once the cops and the Guard come in, start telling everyone what to do, that's when it gets all fucked up.'

'I have great faith,' I said, 'in people's ability to fuck things up without the cops.'

The man laughed.

Me and Boo had been eyeing each other the whole time. Now, finally, he leaned in closer to me. I reached out my hand and let him sniff it. His sharp little nose took in everything. He made a face like something smelled foul. That means something coming from a rat.

'I know,' I said. 'It's been a hard night.'

The rat looked at me and leaned toward me, moving his whiskers up and down as he weighed what I'd said. I held my hand still. Finally he sat back down on the man's shoulder. The man smiled.

'That means he like you,' the man said. 'He don't like everyone. That means you can pet him.'

With one finger I petted his soft, clean little head. 'Hey, Boo,' I said. 'You're a good boy.'

'He is that,' the man said proudly. 'He a real good boy.'

I scratched the top of his head. He seemed to like it.

Boo's owner turned to the men behind him. 'Hey, Jack,' he said. 'Look at this. Check it out.'

A big lumbering shadow came toward us. Between the play of lights and my head injury and my general intoxication, it looked like a shadow cast by a backlit giant. The shadow came into focus as a man in a big overcoat.

'Boo don't like just anyone,' the shadow said. I thought the voice was familiar, but I couldn't . . .

'He sure don't,' Boo's owner said.

The shadow got closer and I felt its eyes on me.

My head spun. I looked back at the shadow, but now it wasn't a shadow anymore.

It was Jack Murray.

'Come on, DeWitt,' the shadow said. 'You and me, we going for a walk.'

I followed Jack, walking silently behind him. He wore the same tired overcoat from Congo Square, over an old suit that might have started off as any color but was gray now. He took us to the Moon

Walk, the pathway by the river. We took up a few benches, and his strong unwashed smell was enough to guarantee our privacy. I was far from sober but I managed to get out a few questions, and I was just sober enough to remember his answers the next day. I remembered his face wobbling in the dark, spinning – or so it seemed to me – lit only by our cigarettes, or maybe they were joints, or maybe freebase, or maybe wet, the same long brown cigarettes soaked in poison I'd been smoking. Or maybe I should just say we each held something small and burning but I don't know what. I forgot my questions, but I remembered Jack's answers.

'I knew Vic from way back,' Jack Murray said. 'We went to nursery school together, me and him. All the way up through Tulane. Two good little boys from Uptown, me and Vic.' He laughed. 'Yes. I do know what happened to him. But you got to find out for yourself, DeWitt.

'You got all the clues you need. You just got to put them together. You trying to think with your head. But you got to remember what the man said. There ain't no coincidences. Believe nothing. Questions everything. Follow the clues. Especially the first one.'

And later, after we'd smoked too much of whatever we were smoking and had drunk twice as much as was wise:

'Now, me, I'm happy with my lot,' Jack said. His face was calm above the light of his cigarette, his eyes clear and intent. 'I solved my mysteries,' Jack continued. 'I found my answers, and that's between me and God. Me and God and no one else. I know it looks like I got nothing, but I got everything. I got my peace and that's all I ever wanted. You, DeWitt, I don't envy you. You still got a long way to go. I feel for you, 'cause you're gonna go to hell and back before you solve your mysteries. You already halfway there, but that ain't nothing.'

I was just sober enough to remember I'd never told him my name.

'Being a good detective, see, people think that makes it easy for us,' he explained. 'But it makes it harder. Maybe some things come easy to you, but that just means you gotta do more. It means more's expected from you. It means you got a place, and that place needs you. It means there's a job for you. A job that only you can do. It means there's a book out there that only you can read. Constance knew that,' he said. 'She knew the truth isn't always in a book. It isn't always in a file, or on a piece of paper somewhere. It can be buried like a treasure. It can be in the sky. It can be in the water. It can be in here.' He looked at his PCP-laced cigarette. 'It can be inside you, in your own heart. You can leave little bits of it everywhere, once you know how. That way it's only for the people who have eyes to see. Ears to hear. You make it easy for people, you ain't doing 'em no favors. See, she understood. You can't do someone's job for them. You can't solve their mystery for them. Even after they gone, you can't solve it. It just go unsolved until they come around again. All you can do is hold it for 'em till they get back.

'She ain't teach you everything, not by a long shot. There's a lot you still got to learn, DeWitt. She still teaching you. But you gone and closed your eyes. You shut your ears. The whole world teaching you. The whole world your school. But you stopped listening, just 'cause you lost your favorite teacher.'

And later, he said:

'Now us detectives, our reward's in heaven. We ain't get much here on earth, but when we go upstairs, we gonna get ours. I been promised that, and I believe it. But a man like Vic, he don't know about that. He think he got to take his reward right here. So what was his reward?'

'I don't understand,' I said. 'How do I find that out?'

'I already told you too much,' Jack said, scowling above the red light of whatever he was smoking. 'And that's all I'm gonna tell you. That's all I *can* tell you. You got to find the rest out on your own. You got to find your own buried treasure, girl. Solve your own mysteries. I solved mine. I fucking been to hell and back, but I solved mine.'

I had a hard time staying awake. But I wasn't so drunk that I didn't see the tattoo above his heart when he reached into his chest pocket, looking for a cigarette butt.

Constance.

'I tell you one more thing,' Jack said, before he left me alone and disappeared. 'If you hoping for a happy ending, DeWitt, you lookin' in the wrong city.'

CHAPTER 47

I woke up on a park bench in Congo Square. I was panting. I heard a shrill squawk in my ear.

It was my phone. I picked it up and checked the display. It was Mick. It was one in the afternoon. I ignored it.

I stood up, dusted myself off, and found a taxi to take me back uptown to get my truck.

I'd lied to Andray. There was no way I was leaving New Orleans.

'Not one detective in a thousand will hear my words,' Silette wrote, 'and of those, one in one hundred will understand. It is for them who I write.'

Detectives are superstitious, and over the years people started to read more into *Détection*. It was code for a secret plan. If you said it all at once, without stopping, you could crack any case. If you put every seventh or ninth or forty-fourth or one hundred and eighth word together you would get something that meant something else. It hadn't been written by one person, but by a secret cabal of detectives. It was a channeled message, and Silette didn't understand it any better than the rest of us.

People thought that because they didn't understand. They weren't the one in one hundred in one thousand.

Silette hadn't written for them. He had written for me.

CHAPTER 48

I went back to my room and went back to sleep.
When I woke up again it was dark. I went to
a restaurant on Frenchman Street and
ordered sunny-side-up eggs. But when they came,
they didn't look like eggs at all. They looked like
something terrible and inedible. They looked
like punishment.

It's a great thing to be at rock bottom, I
reminded myself. There's nowhere to go but up.

After breakfast – or maybe it was dinner – I
called Mick. I didn't plan on telling him what had
happened with Andray. On a different day it
might have been fun to break his heart. Not today.
I told him I'd fallen asleep early the night before
and hadn't learned anything new.

Then I told him my truck had died. I asked if
I could borrow his car, a dark gray sporty little
Nissan from 1990-ish.

'Died?' he said.

'Well, hopefully not died,' I said. 'That would
be sad. But it's not running.'

'Won't the rental place give you a new one?'

I exhaled a loud, annoyed sigh.

'Then *you* call them,' I said. 'Maybe they can give *you* a car before noon tomorrow, which probably means four or five. Maybe for *you* they'll have a spare car of any kind at any price, because for me they certainly—'

'Okay,' Mick said. 'Okay. Take a cab on up and meet me here. Give it back to me tomorrow morning.'

I went back to my hotel room and got my gun from where I'd hidden it in the box of tissues in the funny little slot hotels always have, as if there were something untoward about a bare tissue box. I gave it a quick check for functionality, and when everything looked good I went back out and got a cab on Decatur to take me uptown. Mick met me out in front of his place. He gave me the keys to his car with some instructions: *Sometimes the lights stick and you have to jiggle the thing a little. Sometimes it stalls at red lights. The driver's window only goes down halfway and then you have to push it down, but don't because it's a bitch to get back up.*

I'd forgotten what it's like to be poor.

'So where are you going?' Mick asked. 'Did you get some leads, or—'

'Nope,' I lied. 'No leads. No plan, really. Just figured I'd drive around and see what happens.'

Mick nodded and pretended he thought that was a good idea. I knew he didn't.

He would have liked the truth worse.

It was less than five minutes from Mick's house to Central City. Andray and Terrell were in the same place on their regular corner. Some other boys were with them, but I didn't recognize any of them.

Terrell saw me first. He nudged Andray and pointed me out. They thought, of course, that I was Mick. I drove past them and parked at the end of the block. Andray walked down the street to see what I—Mick—wanted.

He came to the car and leaned down toward the window.

I rolled it down and pointed my gun at him.

'Surprise,' I said.

Andray ran. He ran back into a house nearby, probably to go through a back door and come out on the other side of the block. I drove around the block until I saw him running out of the front yard of another house. I left the car running, jumped out, and caught him on the corner, just as he was about to step off the crumbling curb and into the street. I grabbed Andray by the shoulder with one hand and pointed the gun at him with the other. Both of us were panting, our breath visible in the cold air.

Andray rolled his eyes and tried to look blasé and tough. But for a second he had the same look he had had on his face when I first saw him. As if he were drowning. As if he hoped I would just shoot him already and get it over with.

It passed as quickly as it had come.

'Fuck,' he said.

I pointed the gun at him and held it there while

I searched him. I pulled out a nine-millimeter pistol and a hunting knife, both of which I stuck in my purse.

'We're going to the car now,' I said.

Andray shook his head.

'I'm not going to hurt you,' I said. 'We're just going to talk.'

He shook his head again, fighting to keep his face calm. 'If you gonna shoot me,' he said, 'you can shoot me right here. I can die right here.'

I realized he was terrified. He thought I was going to kill him. Like a lot of people who thought about suicide, Andray didn't actually want to die. Dying was the hard part. He just wanted to be dead already.

By then some of the other boys had come around the corner to see. They kept an eye on us, but none of them rushed to help Andray. I saw what he and Terrell had meant about false friends. The other boys seemed more amused than anything else.

'I am not going to hurt you,' I said again, softly and slowly. 'But—'

'I ain't getting with you in that car, lady,' he said again. 'No fucking way.'

I looked around. I could have put my gun down. But I wasn't sure about the boys around us.

I'd done some dumb things before, but I was realizing that this was one of the dumber.

'Okay,' I said to Andray. 'You're going to tell your friends that everything's cool. When you do that, I will lower my gun. We won't get in the car. Forget about the car. Okay?'

He nodded and swallowed.

'Tell your friends everything's cool.'

'Yo, G,' he called out to one of the boys. I lowered my gun. 'It's cool. She my friend, man. She just pissed off, it's okay.'

The boy, G, looked at us.

'It cool,' Andray said again. 'Just back off, G. We need some space, that's all. She need to calm down.'

G looked at us long and hard. Then he turned to the other boys and led them toward the corner. I inhaled and put my gun away.

Andray shifted his weight from one foot to the other, eyes wide. He reminded me of everyone I knew in New Orleans – scared of everything he shouldn't have been and accepting what should have terrified him.

'Where can we talk?' I said.

He shrugged. He tried to swallow but couldn't and instead he spat.

'Listen,' I said. 'I don't want to hurt you. I don't want to shoot you. And I *really* don't want to kill you. But if you hurt me again, if you *try* to hurt me again, I will do any and all of those things. Okay?'

He nodded.

'And if you don't, I won't,' I said. 'I like you, Andray. I'd rather be friends. Or at least not kill each other. Okay?'

He nodded again.

'Will you get in the car now?' I said.

'No fuckin' way,' he said, shaking his head.

'Okay,' I said. 'We'll walk.'

The daiquiri was the national drink of New Orleans. Different chains of daiquiri shops sold them like slushies, in sixteen- or thirty-two- or sixty-four-ounce plastic cups from big machines. There were even daiquiri drive-thrus, although not in this neighborhood. The nearest daiquiri shop to Andray's corner was on St Charles and Josephine. We walked there silently.

Inside the daiquiri joint everything was painted black. We got a table in the corner and I got us each a daiquiri, strawberry for Andray and coconut for me. Old soul music came from the speakers, which suited the clientele, mostly my age and up. A few drunk couples danced, but mostly people sat at tables, talking loud and laughing or talking quietly and looking very serious.

I'd put Andray through a confusing and stressful hour, and when I looked at him now I saw what every foster parent and drug dealer had seen in him before – an ache that would never be relieved but that he would do anything to dull for a while. He looked at me with big, pretty eyes. *You did it*, the eyes said. *Now fix it*.

'Andray,' I said. 'I know you didn't kill Vic Willing. I'm pretty sure I know what happened to him. But I still need to know why you took me that night, and I need to know what you know about Vic. Because I know you've been lying, and I have to find out the truth. That's what I do. No matter what it is, l promise, no going to the cops, okay?'

He nodded. I didn't know what he was thinking.

'Don't believe me because I'm an authority figure,' I said. 'Believe me because I'm friends with Mick, and he's never been anything but good to you. Believe me because you know me, at least a little bit, and *I've* been pretty good to you.'

Andray looked away, then looked at me and nodded. He took a deep breath and relaxed a little. So did I. We'd made a deal.

'What the fuck?' I said. 'What was that all about?'

'Shit,' he said. 'I'm sorry, Miss Claire.'

'Well, yeah,' I said. 'But what the fuck? Why'd you do that?'

Andray sighed deeply. 'Shit,' he said again. 'Those boys I was with – they was looking for you. They heard you saw that kid Deuce almost get shot on Frenchman Street the other day. They wanted to, you know. When I hear them talking about crazy white lady there, see the whole thing, I figure it was you. I told 'em I handle it.'

'You mean they were going to kill me,' I said. 'They thought I was a witness and they were going to kill me.'

Andray nodded.

'You stopped them,' I said.

He didn't say anything.

'That is so fucking noble,' I said. 'My heart is bursting, Andray. *Bursting.* As we speak. Why—' I paused. 'You hear that? It's the pieces of my heart, falling to the floor.'

He laughed. He looked at me, and for the first time he looked to me like an ordinary boy, with an ordinary smile on his face. In a quick vision I saw what Andray might have been if he had been born anywhere else but here. An endless arc of possibilities flashed before my eyes. None of them involved guns or foster parents or jail.

'Andray,' I said. 'I need to know the truth. What happened between you and Vic Willing?'

He sighed and looked around the room.

'Look,' I said. 'I could have had you arrested twice already – once for Vic and once for the other night. I didn't do it either time. Use your head. Can you trust me, or not?'

He sighed again. I could almost see his mind waver: yes, no, yes, back to no again.

'Stop sighing,' I said. 'It's annoying. Think. Can you trust me?'

Yes, no, yes, no.

He sighed again.

Yes.

'Okay,' Andray finally said, decisively. He looked me straight in the eye. 'I was there. I knew that fucker have beer and water and shit like that. So I went to get some. I – I been there before.'

I gave him time but he didn't say anything.

'When?' I said gently. 'When had you been there before?'

'Mr Vic,' he said, looking at the table. 'He paid – shit. If he got you in a case he would. You know. You could work that off. And sometimes, he also paid guys to come to his place with him and, you know.' I nodded. I knew. 'So I went there a few times – I mean, I didn't do nothing. I mean, *nothing*. But he liked people to watch, so I watched. It was easy money. But I only did it a few times. I ain't like that shit at all. Not just 'cause it's two guys. I – I don't know. It was just sad. Just sad all around. Like, one person needing one thing so bad – money – and the other person just needing something else so bad. I – I don't know. Just sad.'

I nodded. I doubted he was telling the truth about just watching, but I didn't care. That was his own business.

'Why'd you tell people not to talk to me?' I asked.

''Cause I knew you ain't believe me,' Andray said. 'You had your mind already made up. I told everyone they help you, they dead. Besides, most people, they know that without me saying anything. They know you don't talk to cops.'

I mulled it over. It made sense.

'How did you meet Vic?' I asked.

'First working on his pool,' he said. 'That was the truth. And then, like I said, he took me in. We had a nice lunch, told me about the birds and stuff. At first I thought – I thought he was just being nice. He said I reminded him of an old friend. We hung out a few times. I thought he was cool. But then, you know, he said if I needed money we could. So I didn't hang out with him no more after that. But then, once, I really did need the money. I was hungry, I didn't have nothing. So. I think – I think he knew it wasn't right. I do.'

'Why?' I said.

''Cause he always apologized afterward,' Andray said. 'And give you extra money, more than he promised.'

I nodded.

'So when the storm comes,' Andray said, 'me and Peanut and Slim and some other boys – you ain't know 'em – we go to get food and water and shit, and we go to Vic's house. We broke right on in.'

'When was that?' I asked. 'Exactly?'

'Wednesday night,' Andray said. He swallowed. ''Bout ten, twelve. See, from over there, most people gone by then. Fucking open house over there. So I went over to see what I could get. And Vic, he ain't there. House totally empty – whole neighborhood empty, almost. That it. That the real story.'

I looked at him. 'You're sure,' I said. 'Wednesday night. You're absolutely sure?'

Andray nodded and held his right hand up like he was taking an oath, or proving he was unarmed. He looked me right in the eye. 'I lied to you, Miss

Claire. God's honest truth, I lied to you. That's why my prints all over that place. I was looking for shit.'

'Find anything?' I asked.

'Just beer and water,' he said. 'Just like I thought. But shit, we needed that. I remembered he had a whole closet of bottled water in there, so we went for that. People had kids, babies, with nothin' to drink. People need water out there, food for kids and shit. I took some beer, water, shit like that. Vic's house, lady next door. Both of 'em. I took whatever I could. Put out some birdseed.' He laughed a little and shook his head. 'I got a lot of shit to feel bad about. But not that. I broke into a lot of places those days. I ain't feel bad about one of 'em.'

I looked at him as it dawned on me what he was saying. 'Where else you break in?' I asked.

'Me and some boys,' he said, looking at his daiquiri. 'We got into that Walgreen's on Magazine. We got into Sav-a-Center, Whole Foods – that place *crazy*. We took water, juice, food, stuff for the babies, shit like that. We each took a shopping cart and bring it back downtown. One of the boys, he got a car, and we put stuff in there, too, but then he left town, and it was just carts. We could get cars, but ain't no gas. Then when that was all gone, we went to houses – houses we knew we could get into easy, like Vic's. People needed food – old people, babies. People was dyin' in there. We couldn't just . . .'

He shook his head and swallowed and didn't finish his sentence.

'You did that?' I said. 'Andray, that's not stealing, that's—'

I didn't know what to call it. Andray shrugged.

'Why'd you feed Vic's birds?' I asked.

Andray made a face like I'd said something stupid. 'They ain't *his* birds,' he said. 'They just birds. I mean, they gotta eat too.'

He was right. I had said something stupid.

'Who was the kid in the restaurant?' I said. 'Why'd those guys try and kill him?'

Andray shrugged. 'He wasn't no one. I mean, I know his name, but he got nothin' to do with you. Why they did him like that, I don't know. I *think* they think he was talkin' to the cops. I mean, that happens. Someone gets some fucking job and shit and they forget, you know. You think you out of it. But you ain't ever out of it.'

'So what about you?' I asked Andray. 'You want out of it?'

He nodded. 'For real,' he said. 'I'm sick of that shit. I just – you know.'

'You can take him with you, you know,' I said. 'Terrell. You don't have to leave him behind.'

Andray nodded. He didn't believe me and I didn't know if I did, either.

'Mick wants to help you,' I said. 'All you have to do is let him.'

Andray shrugged. I thought about explaining Mick's guilt, collective and individual, to him, but I figured he already knew about that.

'Look,' I said. 'Mick's kind of fucked up right

313

now. Depressed. But if you let him help you, that helps him. I mean, I don't know why. I never understood people like that. But if you can let him help you find some stupid job or whatever, you'd be doing a lot for him.'

'Yeah, okay,' Andray said, nodding. 'He's trying to get me in this GED program. I been thinking about it. Sometimes . . .' He stopped. 'Sometimes with Mr Mick I feel like – I don't know. Like maybe like I'm an experiment or some shit like that. Like he's got – like he's got something to prove or some shit like that. I mean, not that I don't appreciate—' he rushed to add.

'No, I know what you mean,' I said. 'But the thing about Mick is, you could tell him that. I mean, if you say it nicely, like you just told me. You could tell him that and he'd be okay with it.'

Andray nodded. 'Yeah. Okay.'

'You're smart,' I said. 'Getting a GED will be easy for you. You just need to work on your reading. The rest'll come easy after that.'

'I can read,' Andray said defensively. He could, I'd noticed that, but it was slow and laborious.

'How's that book Vic gave you?' I asked.

'It's okay,' he said. 'I mean, it ain't easy. I give you that. But I – I don't know. I like it.'

'Vic really gave it to you?' I asked, skeptically.

'Yeah,' he said. 'One night he caught me looking at it. I don't know. I liked the cover.' He took the copy of *Détection* out of his pocket and held it between his hands, bending it back and forth. I'd

314

noticed from the wear on his pants that he always carried it there.

'Anyway,' Andray went on, 'Mr Vic, he seen me with it, and he told me to go ahead and keep it. Said I'd do better with it than he did.' Andray shrugged. 'I don't know what *that* means.'

'What'd you think?' I asked. 'About the book.'

Andray smiled. 'I mean, honest, it don't make no sense to me,' he said. 'And it's hard. But I – I don't know. I kinda like it anyway. Like, there's this one little thing he says, it's kinda like my favorite. He says something like, if you hold on to a mystery, you never gonna succeed. You let it go through your fingers, and then it come to you, and it tell you everything. I don't know – I like that. Not that I got a lot of mysteries to solve,' he said, catching himself as if he'd said something foolish. 'It just. You know. Good advice, I guess.'

'Those who try to grasp on to the mystery will never succeed,' I quoted, astonished. 'Only those who let it slip their fingers will come to know it, and hear its secrets.'

That had been Tracy's favorite line from *Détection*.

'Talk to Mick,' I said. 'Let him help you.'

He nodded. We looked at each other.

'I'm sorry,' I said. 'I'm sorry I thought you killed Vic.'

He looked at me and nodded.

'I know,' Andray said. 'I'm sorry I lied to you.'

'It's okay,' I said. 'All that matters is that the truth comes out in the end.'

But the truth wasn't out yet.

Andray went to get us another round of daiquiris while I waited at the table. He'd told me a lot of truth. But he was lying about the most important thing.

He knew who killed Vic Willing. He wasn't in his apartment on Wednesday getting food. Why he was there, I still didn't know. But it wasn't the reason he was telling me.

No one looks you straight in the eye when they're telling the truth.

We had a few more daiquiris and at three or four me and Andray muttered some insincere protestations of friendship and exchanged a fake, manly, back-patting hug and wandered into the night.

CHAPTER 49

I lay in bed that night in a T-shirt and underwear and lit a joint, after a few attempts to get the lighter and the joint to line up just right. It was nearly four in the morning. I'd stayed in the bar drinking daiquiris with Andray until after three, pretending I believed his lies. I'd hoped something might slip out. Nothing did.

I'd cajoled, threatened, and held a gun to his head. If he hadn't told me the truth yet – and he hadn't – there was nothing I could do to make him. My bag of tricks was empty. I'd killed the last white rabbit.

Leon had fired me. One person had tried to have me killed and a few more were probably in line. Mick had had little faith in me to begin with and less now. No one was paying me and no one seemed to like me too much here in New Orleans. Or anywhere, for that matter.

In other words, a typical case.

I sat up and went back to the file I'd built on the Case of the Green Parrot. I started from the beginning, with the preliminary information I'd gotten on Vic, and read it through to the

317

end – every witness testimony, every fact, every figure, every omen, every sign. What I didn't have written on paper I went over in my mind.

By the time I dozed off at five, I only knew one thing for certain.

New Orleans was no town for happy endings.

CHAPTER 50

I was on the subway in New York City. It was night. Somehow you can always tell the time of day on the subway. Tracy sat next to me. Now she was fourteen again. On her lap she held her old tape player/radio, smaller than a boom box and bigger than a Walkman.

'You forgot the most important clue,' she said. 'I tried to show you.'

I reached out for her. But when I tried to touch her she slipped away.

'The most important clue,' she said. 'I tried to show you. But you weren't looking.'

Her blond bangs brushed the top of her eyebrows. She smelled like cigarettes and stale booze. We all used to smell like that.

'Can't you just come back?' I said. 'I miss you. We could go for a drink at Holiday. No one will—'

'I tried to show you,' she said, ignoring my question. 'Look up.'

I looked up. The entire ceiling of the car was painted with a street scene. It was New Orleans, water shining in the streets, drowned and peaceful. Above the buildings flew a flock of pigeons. The

319

pigeons flew out of the painting and settled around Tracy, landing on her shoulders and her lap. Now they weren't all pigeons; some were doves, some were cardinals, some were green parrots.

A pigeon settled on Tracy's shoulder.

'We tried to show you,' the pigeon said. 'The very first day. We gave you all the clues.'

'You wouldn't look,' a starling told me. 'We tried to show you, Claire. But you didn't want to see.'

'She never did,' Tracy said. 'She—'

My shrieking phone woke me up. I was in bed in my hotel room, the papers from the case file scattered around the bed. It was eleven o'clock.

I checked my phone. It was Mick.

'I need my car,' he said.

'And I need food,' I said. 'But first I need to take a shower. In coffee.'

I heard Mick roll his eyes over the phone. I told him I'd meet him at his place in an hour or two. We got off the phone. My head pounded and my neck felt like someone had tried to break it. I went to the lobby and got two cups of burnt coffee and drank them in a hot bath. When I'd finished the coffee I had a few hits of weed and three ibuprofens. This case involved far too much alcohol and not nearly enough sunshine.

I got to Mick's house at two. He came down and got in the car and we drove to Casamento's on Magazine Street. It had been my favorite restaurant when I'd lived here and it hadn't changed much. I got an oyster loaf and talked to the waitress about the price of shrimp and laughed when someone's little kid toddled over and offered me a bottle of hot sauce and played with two fat cats in the courtyard.

It didn't make me feel any better to see what New Orleans could have been. Just worse.

Our busboy was friendly and funny. He was about seventeen and I guessed he was in school. No one would work as a busboy if they weren't. Somehow he and Mick got started talking. Everyone knows everyone in New Orleans, even if it sometimes took them a while to remember exactly how and why they knew each other. His name was DeShawn.

'How's your mom?' Mick was asking.

'She's okay,' DeShawn said. 'Still struggling.'

'She get some therapy or something?' Mick asked.

DeShawn shook his head. 'She won't do it. Just goin' to church, prayin', all that.'

'She should give it a try,' Mick said. 'Helped me.'

'I know,' DeShawn said. 'I'm tryin'.'

As they talked I glanced up occasionally in between bites of oyster loaf. An oyster loaf is pretty all-consuming, and I wasn't paying much attention. A little bit at a time I took in the boy, lanky and big, still sizing up to a growth spurt. He had short hair and a diamond earring and a few tattoos, although less than most kids I'd seen. New

Orleans was the most heavily tattooed city I'd ever been in. On one forearm was a girl's name, typical and dull. On the other was a set of praying hands holding a crucifix, also dull.

Above the crucifix was a tattoo I'd never seen before. It was a tattoo of a parrot sitting on a branch of a live oak tree.

'That's one of the parrots from around here, isn't it?' I said. 'One of the green parrots?'

DeShawn smiled. 'Yeah,' he said. 'Got it when I was evacuated, out in California. Came out good, huh?'

'Really good,' I said. It wasn't really good, but I'd seen worse. I *had* worse. 'Most people never notice them,' I said. 'Why'd you get that?'

'I know!' he said. He smiled. 'Most people don't even know they live here. Never look up,' he said. 'Just reminded me of home, I guess. Remind me that I'd be back one day.'

'So you were here during the storm?' I asked. 'You and your mom?'

He nodded. 'Sure were. Up on our roof for three days.'

'Jesus,' I said. 'That's terrible. Listen, can I ask you something? You know a boy named Andray Fairview?'

'Claire,' Mick said, looking annoyed. 'Please.'

'Sorry,' I said to both of them. 'But—'

DeShawn shook his head. 'Don't think so,' he said.

'How about this guy,' I said quickly. Before Mick

could object I reached into my purse and pulled out the picture of Vic.

'You ever see him?'

'Claire!' Mick said. 'Totally inna—'

DeShawn took one look at the picture of Vic Willing and the blood drained from his face.

Mick may have thought it was totally inappropriate to ask DeShawn about Vic, and I suppose in a way it was. But it would have been worse to let a clue fly away without letting it tell me what it knew.

All you have to do is listen. All you have to do is not shut them up when they try to talk to you and the clues will tell you everything you need to know. And eventually, if you follow one to the next, wherever they fly, they'll lead you to the truth.

'Yeah,' DeShawn said. He grabbed the edge of the table as if he were dizzy. 'Jesus. Sorry, I got to—'

'Please,' I said, and pulled out a chair for him. The boy sat down.

'Sorry,' he said. 'That just brings back memories, you know?'

'Sure,' I said. 'Of course. I mean, Vic. Well.'

'*Vic,*' DeShawn said. 'I didn't know his name. You know him?'

Now I was confused.

'You don't?' I said.

'Yeah,' DeShawn said. 'I mean, no, not really. He, you know.'

'He –?' I said.

DeShawn looked from me to Mick and back again, confused.

'I'm sorry,' I said again. 'How do you know this guy?'

'He saved my life,' DeShawn said, his eyes welling up with tears. 'That man, he saved my life. Me and my mom too. He saved us off our rooftop in the Lower Ninth. He came for us.' DeShawn started to cry. 'He came and got us when the whole fucking world left us behind. *He* came for us. *Him.*'

'*Him?*' Mick said, face wrinkled up in confusion. 'Are you sure?'

'Him,' DeShawn said, pointing at the photograph. 'Yeah, I'm sure. *Him.*'

CHAPTER 51

DeShawn stopped crying and looked at the picture, hypnotized.

'Me and my mom,' he said. 'We was on that roof for three days. *Three fucking days*. No food, no water, nothing. We had all kinds of stuff in the kitchen. But it all got washed away. Helicopters went overhead, we were shouting like crazy. At *first*. Even a couple boats went by. But the boats was all full. And the helicopters never sent nothing down to us. I don't know what they were doing. But they weren't there to help.'

He shook his head.

'I still don't understand it,' he said, frowning. 'Why no one came. I mean, I read all the reports and all that. I *know* what happened. But I still don't understand. My mom, she's like – she just can't get over it. Can't get over that nobody came for us.'

He sat for a minute, his face wrinkled.

'Until him,' DeShawn said, pointing at the picture. 'Third day – third night, really. And when night fell – well, it was good 'cause it was cooler. That was good. But it was so dark. So dark, like nothing you ever seen. And that dark – that was scary. *Real* scary. People screamin' from their rooftops, shouting, cryin'. The sound was all around you. But you couldn't see them. You'd hear stuff splashing around in the water, but you couldn't see it. Didn't know if it was people or rats – and then every once in a while these, like, searchlights would kind of swoop down and you'd see everything all lit up, but just for a second. Like a strobe light in a club.

'And then, on that third night – we'd just about had it. My mom was prayin', I was prayin', but it's hard, you know. It's hard to keep faith. We thought the whole world left us alone. And then we see this little light. This tiny little light, way off in the distance. And then, just like a movie or a dream or something, this boat comes over. Someone on the boat's got a flashlight, and it's like – like this little cloud, like this cloud of light coming to us.'

DeShawn laughed. But his eyes were wet while he did it.

'It coulda been God, all we knew. I mean – being on the roof like that, it was like living in Bible times, you know? Like all that crazy stuff in the Bible or history or whatever you read about – it was like living then. Like you got trials and tests and anything could happen.

'Anyway,' he went on, 'in the boat there's a mother, her boy, and this guy. *This* guy. And the mother and her kid, they're shivering and freakin' out, almost like they was dying. Just totally fucked up. And the guy, *him* . . .' He looked at the picture of Vic. 'He was *smilin*'. Just smiling and happy like he was having the best day of his life. And he had a dog with him.'

'A dog?' I said. 'Are you sure?'

DeShawn nodded. 'A dog. I think it was the little boy's. Big German Shepherd type – my momma almost didn't get on the boat with him. I don't know how he knew we was there. Maybe he was one of the boats that passed us before, one of the boats that was too full. I don't know. I always wonder how he found us, but I don't know.

'Anyway. He helped us get in the boat. We wanted to get more – my neighbors was there, right next to us – but there was no more room. The man said the boat would tip if he put more in. So he just took us to the ground. Just dropped us off on dry ground like it was nothing. Me and Mom got off the boat first, 'cause we was in front, and there was people there with blankets and stuff. By the time we turned around, the rest of them, they was just gone.'

'Oh my God,' Mick said.

'Saved my life,' DeShawn said. 'For real. Me and my mom – we would've been dead. See, later, we went back to the house, and the roof was caved in. We don't know when it happened, but.'

He didn't finish his sentence.

'He saved your life,' I repeated.

DeShawn nodded. 'You know him?' he asked.

'No,' I said. 'He died not long after that. Sometime during the storm. We don't know exactly when. That's what we're trying to figure out.'

'Oh my God,' DeShawn said. He looked devastated. 'Jesus. That's so fucked up.'

'Did you see him again after that?' I asked after a while. 'Do you know what happened to him after he dropped you off?'

'Well,' he said. 'I think – I think he didn't make it back the next time. I think he drowned.'

'Because I saw my neighbor later,' DeShawn said. 'In Houston. And we talked about it, traded stories. And he told me that man never came back for him. No one came for them till the next day.'

We sat at the table and didn't look at each other.

'I always thought,' DeShawn said, 'thought I'd find him. I wanted to thank him or something.'

'You still can,' I said.

He looked at me. 'You think he hear me?'

'I don't know,' I said. 'But it's a no-lose bet.'

We sat for a minute and didn't say anything.

And then I remembered what Tracy had told me.

The very first clue.

Suddenly my hangover was gone.

Mick looked at me.

'What?' he said.

'Nothing,' I said.

'What?' DeShawn said.

'I gotta go,' I told them. 'I gotta go somewhere right now.'

I thanked DeShawn and paid the bill and Mick and DeShawn made promises to keep in touch and work on DeShawn's mother. Mick drove me back downtown. He still thought my truck was dead. He parked in front of my hotel.

'So I guess that's it,' he finally said. 'I guess we know what happened to Vic Willing.'

I looked at Mick. He looked almost kind of happy. If Vic could be redeemed, anyone could be redeemed – even Mick, with his survivor's guilt and imagined list of sins. Even the kids he worked with, with their misdemeanor murders and resolute uninterest in the future. Even me, with my bad habits and louche ways.

I knew he wanted that to be true. Maybe he needed it to be true.

But it wasn't.

Maybe we could all be redeemed. But it wouldn't happen today.

Mick looked at me. 'DeShawn just *said*,' he said. 'He just told us. Vic drowned. He went out rescuing people and he never came back.'

I didn't say anything.

'Claire,' Mick said. Disappointment spread across his face. '*Claire*. You can't be serious.'

I didn't say anything.

'This is the answer,' Mick said. 'This is the solution. The one you've been looking for. This is it.'

I still didn't know exactly what had happened to Vic Willing. But I had a pretty good idea, and I knew where I would find the rest of the story.

'Mick,' I began, gently, 'I know you think the clue is the story DeShawn just told. And that – that means a lot. It really does. But that's not the end. That's not the clue.'

'Then what is the clue?' Mick said, pissed off.

'The same clue it's always been,' I said. 'The same clue you didn't see from the beginning. That's the same clue you're not seeing now.'

We sat and didn't look at each other.

'Jesus, Claire,' Mick began. 'Can't you ever just—'

'No,' I said. 'Never.'

Mick shook his head and didn't look at me. I got out of the car.

'Of course, anyone may be saved,' Silette said in his 1978 *Interview* interview. 'No matter the crime. What they don't understand is that it is just like solving a crime; one must do it oneself, for one's own reasons, each on one's own time, and not for some stupid ideal of what the world can be or some childish notions of good and bad. The only way is to dive into oneself completely, which of course is the very last thing most of us will ever do. You must dive all the way to the bottom. Then, really, life can begin anew.'

In my room, on my bed, I turned up the heater and threw the I Ching.

Hexagram 4: Clouds over fire. The clouds surround the fire but do not put it out.

Some fires burn true and some burn false. True fire warms the hands. False fire burns but never warms. The best fires burn everything in their wake, and only leave behind perfect nothingness. The wise man knows this is best place.

I got in my truck and drove to the perfect nothingness.

CHAPTER 52

The streets of the Lower Ninth Ward were caked in grayish-brown dried mud. So was everything else. Nothing had been cleaned. Little bits of people's lives were scattered around in between the piles of rubble: a shoe, a book, a bra. The smell was bad: garbage and mold and death. Some houses had been pushed into each other, making indistinguishable piles of rubble. Some had boats or cars or trailers or pieces of other houses on top of them or stuck into them, forced into strange angles by the strength of the water. There were boats on top of roofs and cars on top of houses. Some houses had been pushed blocks from their foundations: you could tell because someone had spray-painted their former addresses on them, as if they were lost puppies someone could pick up and take back home. *Oh, look, here's our house. I was wondering where we left it.*

It would be a miracle if anyone lived around here.

I drove to the address on the card. The lots on either side were piles of broken wood. But the house at the address was still there. Two sides of it were blue plastic tarp, but it was definitely a house. It was a classic Creole cottage. The grass was high but the yard was picked up. The mud had been hosed off the remaining sides of the house. The sides were pink.

Sometimes miracles happen.

Jutting from one of the sides of the house was a metal plant hanger. Hanging from it by one broken chain and one slender intact one was a sign:

Ninth Ward Construction
We Can Do It!

Next to the letters was a poorly drawn sketch of a green parrot, wings outstretched.

That was the clue. That was the first clue and it would be the last.

'The detective who wishes a rapid conclusion to his case,' Silette wrote, 'need do no more than examine every thing he was absolutely sure would not lead to the truth, and need only connect those facts he was entirely sure had no relation at all. Because this, for better or worse, is exactly where the truth lies – at the intersection of the forgotten and the ignored, in the neighborhood of all we have tried to forget.'

I parked the car and walked up to the door and knocked.

And then I heard someone pump a shotgun

behind me and I thought maybe I had made a mistake.

I turned around slowly, hands up and open, face relaxed.

A man stood behind me, in between me and my truck. Next to him was a honey-colored pit bull standing at attention, eyes on my face. The man was holding a twelve-gauge shotgun pointed toward my head. He was about forty-five, thin, not tall. He wore a T-shirt tucked into neat blue jeans and white sneakers, sealed with a brown leather belt. He tried to look mean, or at least stern. It worked pretty well. Especially with the gun.

'If you from the CNN,' he said with a thick accent, 'you might as well tell me, so I can shoot you and get it over with.'

'I'm not,' I said. 'I'm—'

'And if you with the hippies, I'll shoot you faster,' he said. 'So whatever it is you want, you might as well go on and get the fuck away from here before I shoot you.'

Slowly I reached into my pocket and took out his card. I'd found it in Napoleon House on my first day back in New Orleans.

Ninth Ward Construction.
We can do it!
Frank
555-1111.
CALL ME I CAN HELP!

Frank frowned and looked at the little piece of paper I held out to him. When he saw what it was he shook his head like he'd seen a ghost.

'I tried to call you.' I said.

'Phone's been down,' Frank said. 'We had . . . we had a storm.'

'I know,' I said. 'But you can still do it. You can still help.'

He put down the gun. When he did, the dog settled down on the ground, sticking her legs in front of her and setting her head in between. She looked like a carpet.

I reached slowly into my purse and took out my picture of Vic Willing. I handed it to Frank.

Frank took the picture of Vic and looked at it. Then his face crumpled, every soft point closing in.

'Holy shit,' he said. He looked like I'd punched him. He stumbled over to the steps to his house and sat down.

The dog came and sat next to him and looked at him. Frank scratched the top of the dog's head.

'You come on in,' he said finally, 'I don't know if I can help you. I don't know if I can do it. But I'll try.'

Inside the house the walls were gone behind the blue tarp, but the supporting beams were in place. I heard the hum of a generator. A few shop lamps were hung up here and there, and a big TV was in the corner. The light coming through the tarp tinted everything blue.

Frank sat on a cable spool and gestured for me to sit on another. I did. The dog sat at Frank's feet. I explained that I was a private eye and I was investigating what had happened to the man in the picture.

'What do you need to know?' Frank asked.

'Everything,' I said. 'Everything you remember.'

Frank nodded his head and collected his thoughts before he began. I had the feeling he didn't get many guests.

'That man,' Frank began. 'He saved so many. I don't even know how many wouldn't be here if it wasn't for him. Boatload after boatload.'

I nodded. I didn't see any reason to tell Frank about the rest of Vic's life. I figured he'd seen more than enough vice and squalor for one lifetime.

'What happened after that?' I asked. 'After he rescued all those people?'

Frank looked at me. 'You don't know?'

'I don't know,' I said. I thought I knew, but I wasn't sure.

'I thought—' Frank said. 'I thought you knew. I thought you were here to find out who did it. Like a murder mystery on the TV.'

'Who did *what?*' I asked.

'Who shot him,' Frank said. 'That man was shot dead. Saw it with my own eyes. I thought you here to find out who shot him.'

'I am,' I said. 'That's exactly it. I'm here to find out who shot Vic Willing.'

I didn't tell him I had only just learned that myself.

Frank made us some tea – tea crystals mixed in bottled water – and he started from the beginning.

'It started with this woman, this fat lady. She gets off a boat – see, there was like this little kind of shoreline where we was getting people off boats and sending the boats back out. So this lady gets off a boat. And she's crying, "Claude, Claude, Claude." And this guy – *your* guy – he says, "Who's Claude? Who's Claude?" You know it's all dark, and it's just crazy out there. Just people all over the place. Just crazy. Like hell. So this guy, *your* guy, he says, "Who's Claude? Where'd you leave him?" I don't know where he came from, or how he got there. That, I can't tell you about. I mean, it was just chaos down there – dark, hot. People dropping like—

'Anyway. So this lady, she says' – Frank imitated the woman's voice – '"My bird. My bird, I left him on the roof in his cage. My little bird, I gotta go back for him. He's my baby. They forced me into the fucking boat without my baby, but I ain't going anywhere without him. I'm not leavin' him."

'And everyone else is just ignoring her. But *that* guy, he says, "A bird? You left your bird?" And she says, "Yeah, my bird. I had him for thirty years. I love him so much." She's crying and wailing. She says, "He needs me. He needs me. I can't leave him. I can't leave him like this." So your guy, he gets in a boat – there's boats all over, washed up from wherever – and he goes and then he comes back with that bird, a little parrot, and two people too. And dogs, two or three dogs.'

Frank stopped a minute and looked down.

'Some people,' he went on, 'they wouldn't take animals. They didn't mean—' He looked at the dog, as if he didn't want to discuss such things in front of her. 'They just didn't understand. They thought they was doing the right thing. They didn't mean nothing by it. But some people, they wouldn't leave without their animals. And I can understand that. I really can. Some of 'em got help and some of them didn't. Some stayed with their animals and, you know. And I got to say, I understand that. Because when you love something, well. You know. But a lot of people just didn't get it.

'So that guy. He goes out, and every boat he comes back with two or three people and a whole bunch of animals. Dogs, cats, whatever. He's taking all the ones everybody else left behind. He bring one boatload back, he go right out and get another. He ain't eat nothing, hardly even drink any water. Like a fucking machine,' Frank said. 'Boatload after boatload.

'Then one trip, he come back, and he got on out of the boat. And I heard – well, I thought I heard a gunshot. I heard *something*, but I wasn't sure what it was. I looked around and I didn't see anything. But then he, your guy – he'd just got off the boat and he had this kid in his arms, this boy. And he kind of like – I thought at first the kid was too heavy, and he couldn't hold him up, you know. The kid kind of fell out of his arms and he kind of like stumbled and then—' Frank waved his hand in the air, imitating a man falling down.

'He just like crumpled right down,' Frank said. 'It all happened fast, like—' He snapped. 'Like *that*. Of course, I knew what *that* was. I looked around and I seen a kid run off. Thug, long hair. Dreadlocks, kind of. White shirt, big pants. You know, like all of 'em wear. Didn't see his face. Didn't see much at all, you know, with the light. But one of the searchlights came down and I got a real good look for just, just about a split second. I didn't see his face, but I can tell you: thin, about five-seven, dark skin, hair like that, like all the thugs wear, tattoos. You know what they look like.'

Frank shook his head. He looked angry, and confused.

'These kids. Shootin' each other over nothing, shooting everyone they see. I mean, when does it end? When does it stop? A man like that, like some kind of a hero – and just this week, that musician, that mother with her baby just over there, and, what, seven, eight more. Ten? I mean, I seen a lot of people die. I went from Iraq to New Orleans and then they called me back again. But something like that – something like that, it sticks with you, you know? But I'll testify, sign an affidavit, whatever. I'd like to see whoever did this pay. I really would.'

Frank looked at me. I couldn't look at him.

'I don't know what's worse,' I finally said.

'Out of what?' Frank said, confused.

'I don't know if it's worse to tell you the truth,' I said. 'Or keep lying to you.'

Frank sat up and frowned.

'I'll take the truth,' he said.

I told Frank the truth. I told him who killed Vic Willing, and why.

'You still willing to testify against him?' I asked when I was done.

Frank's face darkened, like a shadow had fallen across it.

'I don't know,' he said. 'I'm gonna have to think about that one.'

I nodded. I hoped he wouldn't.

We sat and didn't look at each other.

'The thing about the truth,' Frank said after a while. 'It's never just what you want it to be, is it?'

'No,' I said. 'Doesn't seem that way.'

Frank made us some more tea. We drank it and talked about how he was rebuilding his house: a little bit at a time, with lumber 'borrowed' from houses nearby. For the first time I noticed that the walls, few as they were, were good old cypress, the joints fitted tight. The beams that I'd assumed to be leftovers were solid cypress too, and the floor was hard, finished heart pine.

'Gonna be some place,' I said.

Frank nodded, and stopped frowning.

'It is,' he said. 'It really is.'

'So,' I said when we finished our tea. 'Do you know what happened to Vic's – do you know what happened to his body?'

Frank looked away.

He nodded.

'The thing was,' he said, 'there was nowhere to put them. Not just him but a whole lot of people, *gone*.' He meant *dead*. 'Nowhere to put 'em. So one of the other rescue crews, these Indian guys, these black Indian guys – we gave him to them, we asked them to—'

He stopped and sighed and drank some tea.

'The Indians,' he began again. 'They put them in a boat and took them – well, I don't know where. They took them somewhere and, you know. Gave 'em, like, a burial. Each and every one, they promised me. Man I know from Central City. He's the Witch Doctor for the White Hawks. They know how to do it right. Put each one where they belong, someplace special. Like a burial at sea. They know chants, songs. How to do things right. And did something so, you know, they'd be okay. So they wouldn't keep floating back. So they'd just be gone. It wasn't for us,' he rushed to add. 'Not for us. For them. To do the right thing.'

I nodded.

We were done. I tried to give Frank some money,

but he wouldn't take it. I thanked him and then he thanked me in return.

'What for?' I said.

'For telling me the truth,' he said. 'I know it ain't easy.'

He stopped and deepened his frown.

'People like you and me,' he said. 'We can take it. Not everyone can. But I'd rather have the truth, ugly as it is, over every beautiful lie in the world. Because I seen too many times where the lies end up. Here. There. And sometimes I think people like us, people like you and me – we holding on to it for everyone else. Holding on to it so when everyone is ready, it's there. And it ain't easy, holding on to it. Not with all the good-looking lies all over the place. Not with everyone goin' around with their *have a nice day and thanks for calling* and *don't worry about the levees* and all that. It ain't always easy.'

'But it's worth it,' I said.

'Yeah,' Frank said. 'It's worth it.'

On the way out, before I got into my car, I saw a copy of *Détection* poking out from under a bucket of plaster on what was left of the porch.

CHAPTER 53

By the time I'd finished with Ninth Ward Construction it was after seven. I called Mick. We met at a different Middle Eastern restaurant on Magazine Street for dinner.

I told him I'd solved the case. He wasn't too happy with my solution.

'That could have been anyone,' he said. 'That description could be one of a thousand boys.'

'But it wasn't *anyone*,' I said. 'It wasn't a thousand boys. It was one person. You know that.'

'I don't know anything,' Mick said, scowling.

'There's a difference between not knowing,' I said, 'and not wanting to know.'

Mick frowned. We finished our meal quietly. We were like people grabbing a bite to eat after a funeral. But it was something worse than a funeral for Mick. It wasn't someone he knew who had died. Everyone knows that's gonna happen someday. You prepare for it, even expect it.

But Mick had lost something he hadn't even known he had. He'd been counting on a happy ending. But there is no such thing. Nothing ever really ends. The fat lady never really sings her last song. She only changes costumes and goes on to the next show. It's just a matter of when you stop watching.

The hard part was waiting for the next show to start after everyone was lying on stage with their heads chopped off. But he'd make it.

'Promise me you won't do anything until tomorrow,' Mick said when we left. 'Just sleep on it. Think about it, okay? Promise me.'

I promised.

Then I went and did something.

CHAPTER 54

I found Andray on his regular corner. The sun was just going down. He and some other boys were in various stages of lounging on the steps of the abandoned lavender Victorian behind them. A slow day in the world of low finance.

Andray came over to my truck. He had a tight, forced smile on his face. I rolled down the window and he stepped up and leaned inside.

'What up, lady,' Andray said with his forced smile. 'What you still doing here?'

'You did good,' I said. 'Really, really good.'

He didn't say anything. He dropped the fake smile. From the look on his face I guessed he was hoping I was talking about something else.

He shook his head and turned, ready to run. I put my hand on my gun.

'Don't even think about it,' I said. 'You know I'll catch you. It's over.'

'Fuck,' Andray said, twisting and turning as if he were fighting the very air around him. 'Fuck, fuck, fuck.'

'You almost had me beat,' I said. 'First you drew the attention on you. You left your prints in Vic's house. Made sure I knew you knew him. Did everything you could to make me look at you and not the real killer.'

Andray stopped twisting and turning and looked angry and didn't say anything.

'And that was,' I said. 'Wow. Kind of brilliant actually. Because who would think, huh? You were betting that there wouldn't be enough evidence to arrest. And this being New Orleans, even if you were arrested, you'd be out in, what, thirty days? This town can't convict a murder case with ten eyewitnesses. You sure didn't have to worry about leaving your fingerprints at the scene. It was just enough to distract everyone from the real killer.

'But then I showed up,' I said. 'And you didn't know people like me – people who actually *solve* mysteries – really exist, did you?'

Andray looked furious.

'You told everyone you knew not to talk to me,' I went on. 'You led me wrong every chance I gave you, and you weren't really out getting diapers that night, were you?'

Andray shook his head.

'That ain't me,' he said bitterly. 'Risking my life to help some other person – that ain't me.'

'No,' I said. 'You would *never* do that.'

If he could tell I was being sarcastic, he didn't let on.

'You tried to drive me out of town,' I continued. 'Maybe you even set up that shooting at the restaurant. I don't know. But that's my guess. Did you even really know Vic?' I asked. 'Or was that all bullshit too?'

Andray didn't answer.

'My guess is you really did know him,' I said. 'That at least that part of the story was true. But I don't need to know. I know one thing, though.'

Andray tried to pretend he wasn't interested. He wasn't good at it.

'You really did feed his birds.'

Andray's face softened a little, and he nodded.

'We'll get him a lawyer,' I said. 'I don't blame him at all.'

'*You* don't,' Andray said. 'You think the lawyers, the cops, all them – you think *they* ain't gonna blame him? Killing – shit, kill-ing a DA. A fucking white, rich DA. You know that boy hardly ever even use his piece before? He play tough, but shit – he can't even shoot. Can't shoot for nothing. One lucky shot.' Andray laughed bitterly. '*Once*. Fuck. I used to take the nigga out for target practice, he ain't hit one fucking bottle, not one, but this time he gotta—' Andray let out a sound of exasperation. He stomped one foot on the ground.

'Here's how you can help now,' I said. 'Find people to testify that Vic did the same thing to them. Document how he was totally let down by the system – abuse, neglect, all that stuff. I'm gonna get him a good lawyer, I think we can build a good case. And I think we can get him a federal trial too, or at least a change of venue, considering the conflict of interests here – the DA's office can't

347

really prosecute someone who killed one of their own. That's a good thing. Pretty much every place else is less corrupt than here. And considering that he killed an actual ADA, the system might not be a real safe place for him. I mean, I doubt he'd get convicted. But he might get pretty banged up in jail.'

Andray nodded, but his eyes filled with tears. 'He could get the chair,' he said, trying not to cry. 'Oh, God. Life in Angola – shit.'

'I'll do everything I can to make sure that doesn't happen,' I said. 'I swear to you.'

Andray looked at me.

'I swear it,' I said again.

Andray looked at me and blinked his tears away. My swearing didn't mean much to him, but he knew he would get through this anyway. Just like he always had. With his friends.

'There's one thing you have to tell me,' I said. 'Where'd you really get that copy of *Détection*? Vic Willing never read that book in his life.'

An almost-nearly smile pulled at Andray's mouth, but he forced it down.

'If I told you,' he said gruffly, 'you wouldn't believe me.'

'I'll believe you,' I said.

Andray looked around. He kicked the ground with his expensive boot. From the look on his face I knew that even if he did deign to tell me the story, it didn't mean I was forgiven for solving the mystery he had worked so hard to hide.

'Once,' Andray began, still looking at the ground, 'my Uncle John – I told you about him?' I nodded. Andray went on: 'My Uncle John – once he took me to see this friend of his. This lady – she a little like you, actually. Somehow, some way, you remind me of her a little. Lived in this big house Uptown. White lady, real rich. She was . . . she wasn't exactly an Indian herself, but she was, like, a friend. Like a friend to the tribes. Knew all the songs, knew all the big chiefs. Anyway, we went up to see her, John and some of us kids – I was maybe seven, eight. And it was this big house, and I, somehow I got away from everyone else and I got kinda lost. I was in the library – house had its own library, if you believe that.'

I nodded. I missed that library every day.

'And that book,' Andray went on. 'I don't know. It was like, like it was a light or something. Like I – I don't know. I mean, Mr John told us not to touch anything, but it was like – like I *had* to take it off the shelf. Like it *wanted* me to take it.' Andray looked at me. 'You ever feel that way?'

I nodded. I had felt the same way when I saw the book in my parents' dumbwaiter, so many years ago.

'Anyway, just then, the lady, she come in. I was – shit, I thought I was gonna be in real trouble. I thought Uncle John would . . . But that lady, she seen me with the book, and she *smiled*. She was like – like she was *glad* about it or something. You know things happen, when you a kid, and they

349

don't seem so strange, 'cause you don't know better? And then when you think about them later, they don't make no sense at all? It was like that. So then, it didn't seem so strange. She asked me about my name and where I stayed and who my parents were, normal stuff. Real nice. Real nice lady. And she took me in the kitchen and made us tea. And after, she read the leaves leftover in the cup. And then she took the book and she gave it to me. And she told me . . .'

Andray stopped and looked around. He sighed.

'She told you that you'd know the right time to show someone the book,' I finished for him. 'And she told you to remember this. To remember. And you did.'

We looked at each other. Andray's face wrinkled in confusion.

'Sometimes,' Andray said, tears streaming down his face, 'sometimes the world seem so fucked up, like nothing make any sense at all. Like there's no sense at all. Just – just vicious like that. Just vicious. But then sometimes, sometimes, it's like – like it all fit together perfect, like a puzzle. Like you find this little piece, maybe five years ago, maybe ten years ago. And then years and years later, you see where it fits. And you see it made sense all along. Only you was too blind to see it. Too small to see it all at once.'

He sniffed. 'Don't seem like that now, though.'

I wanted to hug him but I figured he might shoot me.

'But maybe someday,' I said carefully, 'you'll look back and the pieces you have now, all the little bits that seem so awful – maybe they'll all fit together just right, and it'll all make sense.'

I didn't know if I believed that myself. Andray shrugged. The door slammed shut; he stopped crying and our moment of friendship was over. He turned around to his friends behind him.

'Terrell,' he called out. Terrell, who'd been sitting on the steps of the abandoned house with the other kids, looked up. Andray gestured him over. He came over with his usual big open smile, dreadlocks flowing around his face, white T-shirt reflecting the moonlight.

But when he saw the look on Andray's face, he stopped smiling.

When he reached the truck, Andray nodded at him.

'She know,' Andray said.

Terrell's face crumpled. 'Fuck,' he said.

'Come on,' I said to Terrell. 'Get in.'

Andray looked sore as hell at me when we drove away. I figured he'd get over it. If he was going to be the detective he was clearly meant to be, he was gonna need help, training, and an education you couldn't get in any school. And even as good as he was to begin with, there weren't too many places he could go to get it. Mick would teach him everything he knew – that would take about three months. After that, he'd need me. There was no one else.

For the first time I knew how Constance felt when she found me.

Like I'd spent a lifetime sifting through dirt and shit and finally, at the bottom of the pile, found a bright, beautiful piece of gold.

CHAPTER 55

I drove Terrell to a parking lot and stopped. After we parked I realized it was the same lot where Andray had almost killed me. COMMUNITY COFFEE! the old mural shouted. NEW ORLEANS COMES TO LIFE WITH COMMUNITY COFFEE!

Terrell sat silently while I drove, looking out the window, leaning as far away from me as possible. When we parked he looked straight ahead. We sat in silence.

'You gonna tell the police?' Terrell said after a while.

'No,' I said. 'I'm going to talk you into turning yourself in to the feds.'

He didn't say anything, just set his face and stared straight ahead.

'It's the best way,' I said. 'You can't go on like this forever. You can't live just hoping you'll never get caught. It'll drive you crazy. I've seen it happen.'

'I can't go to Angola,' he said. 'No fucking way.'

'I'm gonna get you a lawyer,' I said. 'A good one. Mick's gonna help, Andray's gonna help, I'm gonna help. You're not going to be alone.'

'Yeah,' he said bitterly. 'I know who's gonna be there.'

I looked at him. He looked out the window. We sat for a while until he was ready to talk.

'It only happened like, like six times,' he said. 'I was – shit, I was twelve years old. It was this mentoring thing. Like a Big Brother thing? We were supposed to – it was a long time ago. I don't know why I couldn't just forget it. I don't know why I couldn't just forget. I wanted to. But it was always with me. All the nasty things we did, it was always in the back of my mind, like just sitting there. Just waiting to come out and ruin everything, fuck everything up. Like sometimes when I'm with a girl and, you know, everything's going good, and then *that* shit's got to come in my head and fuck it all up.

'So that night. Shit. I went down to try to *help*,' Terrell said bitterly. 'I wasn't even thinking about – about *him*. He was like, not even on my mind, not at all. Shooting someone, that wasn't – I wasn't even thinking about that. Me and some other boys, we were up at this girl's house. Shonda. And people is coming in to see us, other people we knew. People with no way to get out, like us. Stuck here. And they start telling these stories – each one crazier and crazier. About the water bein' so high, about people stranded, about no one helpin' them. People left all alone with no one to help.

'So I make up my mind. All the rest of those niggas, they can sit around and smoke weed all day if they want. Me, I'm not sittin' around doin' nothing when kids dyin' out there. People stranded on rooftops and shit. I'm not sitting around doing nothing while that's going on.

'So I go down to the water. I go down and it's a fucking mess down there. I mean, really a mess, because garbage and shit is washing up from everywhere. And it's hot, and people is acting crazy, screaming and crying. And there's – fuck. There's *bodies* everywhere. I hadn't thought – I mean, I thought I'd go down there and it'd be like some sailor shit, pulling people out of the ocean. But it was – people was crying, people was hungry, people was all sunburned, being on their roofs for days. People was looking through the dead people looking for their kids and shit. It was like when in church, when they talk about hell? Like it being hot and dead people all over and shit? Like your worst nightmare, but it ain't a dream anymore. *That's* what it was like.

'I went down there to *help*. To try to *save* people. I mean . . .' Terrell's voice trailed off, as if he couldn't quite believe himself how it all turned out.

'Anyway,' he began again. 'I started feeling like, you know, this was a mistake. A *real* mistake. I was like – I didn't even know where to begin. So I just went to the water, went up toward there and figured I just pitch in. And then—'

He stopped, and turned toward the window. Tears were running down his beautiful face.

355

'And then you saw him?' I guessed.

'And then I saw him,' Terrell repeated softly. 'I saw him up at the water, right at the edge. Just a few feet away. He didn't see me. He was getting out of a boat with this kid, this boy – little kid about twelve. Real dark kid, all wet, shaking. So *him*, he picks the kid up, out of the boat. And he just *held* him, held him like—' Terrell shook his head. 'Like he was gonna carry him away,' he said. 'Just take that boy and, you know. And I started to sweat – I was already sweating, but really sweat – and I was shaking. It was like, like that kid was.' He started to cry. 'Fuck. Like it was happening all over again. Like it was *still happening*. Like it never stopped. Like everything I done since then, everything I am, all my friends, my brothers – it was all just gone and it was just, just that fucked-up time forever, that tiny little fucked-up time *forever*. Like I was in that room with him, over and over again, and I wasn't getting out.'

He stopped talking and cried.

'But this time,' I said. 'You could protect yourself.'

He nodded.

'Andray and Trey,' he went on. 'They always telling me, you got your piece, use it. I always carry, ever since I was a kid. But I ain't never – I mean, I could shoot, and I *did* shoot. But I never killed no one before. But this time, this time. They always telling me, that once you do it a lot, it becomes automatic, like you don't even think about it no more. It was like that. I was in that room with him, in that fucking hell, in that room, dead bodies everywhere, everyone screaming and crying, and him going and getting another boy. *Another boy.* I couldn't let that – it was like automatic. I hardly even thought about it. I just – I wasn't even thinking. It was just this mess in my head. Just all this shit. And then I remembered my protection. And it was like – like a way for it to be over, you know? I didn't think about murder or nothing like that. It was just like, make it end. Make it over. Finally. Not just that minute, that one time. All of it. Like if I shot him here, in real life, I could get him out of my head once and for all.

'And I did it. I took out my gun and I shot him. I don't know how, but somehow I got him, *pow*, right in the heart.'

He stopped, hypnotized by his own memory.

They tell you it's going to be easy. Automatic. They tell you you'll forget about it soon. But you never do. Some people just do a better job of pretending than others.

'Then what happened?' I asked gently.

Terrell shook his head. 'I don't know. I don't remember. I mean – I just ran. I don't know where, I don't really remember. I just got the fuck outta there. I ran 'cross the whole fucking city. When I stopped, I was up in Audubon Park. I found a little spot, kind of like hidden, under a tree. This big tree, branches coming down to the ground. A little spot I knew. Used to sleep there sometimes. I just stayed there. Just stayed there, tryin' to catch my breath.'

'And then Andray found you,' I said.

Terrell nodded. 'He knew me. Knew that spot. Knew I used to go there when I was a kid. Andray, he wouldn't leave town without me. And then once he saw me, and I told him everything – shit. He jumped right up to action. First thing we do is, we go to Vic Willing's house and leave his prints all over. Andray's. 'Cause he know he didn't do it. He know that gonna throw everyone off. But it ain't enough to convict on. Then he tell me my story – *our* story. That we was together the whole time, went here, went there. All these details – he knew, nobody doubt a story like that. Not for that time, not with all the little things he put in there. Then we go, we get a car, and we get the hell out of town. Get goin' to Houston. The whole time, I was like – like I been hypnotized or some shit. But Andray, he took care of everything. Always take care of me. When we got back, he made sure no one knew. Not no one saw me, at least not my face. And when you started lookin' around, he did every-thing he could to get rid of you. Told people not to talk to you, tried to scare you off, out of town.'

'He risked going to prison for you,' I said.

Terrell nodded.

'I know it,' he said. He took a deep breath. 'So what happens now?'

'Now,' I said. 'I talk you into turning yourself

in. I'll make bail right away. You won't spend more than a night or two locked up, not until the trial.'

He shook his head. 'No way,' he said.

'You been sleeping much lately?' I asked.

Terrell didn't answer.

'Eating?'

I'd noticed Terrell was rail thin. He didn't say anything.

'This is how you get your life back,' I said. 'I know it's awful. I know you're terrified. But this is how you start again.'

He nodded. We sat still for a while. Some could have eaten and slept just fine. Some people could have pretended much better than him. But not Terrell.

'That night,' Terrell said. 'It was like – like before that happened? When I was going down to the water, on my way there? Walking through the city? It was like – like I thought I was gonna be a hero or some shit. Like I was gonna be savin' people. I saw this, like a picture of myself, like a picture in my head. Like a movie, you know? And I was on a boat. Just like he was. And I was savin' these kids, these boys, from the water. And it seemed *so real*. Like I was seeing the future.' Tears poured down his face. 'And it was – shit.'

He stopped and turned away.

'And you were happy?' I guessed.

Terrell turned back and nodded, still crying. 'I felt like I was really – it really felt good, you know? Like I'd already done it. Like the movie, the thing I was seeing in my head, me saving all those kids, I'd already done it. So I don't understand how . . .'

He broke off, crying. For the first time I saw how Vic felt in his last moments. Proud. Good. At home with himself. Probably for the first time.

But that didn't help Terrell.

It was cold in the truck. I turned the heat up. I looked at Terrell, crying, his head hanging down. All defenses were gone. All pride was lost.

A door was open. But Terrell needed the right clue to lead him through it.

There are no coincidences. Only opportunities.

'"Consider the possibility,"' I said, quoting Silette, "that what we perceive as the future has already happened, and intuition is only a very good memory."

Terrell didn't say anything. But I could tell he was listening, and his crying quieted a little.

'There will never be any shortage of floods,' I told him, reaching over to take his cold, rough hand. 'There will always be people who need to be rescued. And there will never, ever be enough people to save them all.'

Terrell nodded, still crying. He knew that was true. He knew it because he had needed rescuing over and over again, and he had drowned over and over again, and no one had ever come to save him. No one except Andray.

I called Mick. Mick met us in the parking lot and together we took Terrell to a federal agent Mick knew at their headquarters out in Metairie. We didn't turn him over until we got a promise of protective custody right away – not from the other inmates, but from the local cops. The feds disliked the locals as much as Mick and I did, and they promised to keep him safe.

When they took Terrell away he looked scared. Terrified. That's not always a bad thing. Now he could face his terrifying thing and finish it once and for all. He'd come out the better for it. *If* he came out. But this was his best hope of becoming the person he was meant to be – the man who saved children from drowning.

One of the feds had known Vic Willing.

'Vic Willing?' he said incredulously. 'That guy? He . . . you know?'

'He sure did,' I said. 'Terrell's not the only one.'

'Jesus,' he said. 'You just never know with people.'

'No,' I said. 'You never do.'

By the time we were done with Terrell and the paperwork and explaining everything to the feds, it was noon the next day. Mick and I left our cars in the federal parking lot and walked down the street – if you can call anything in Metairie a *street* – to a little sandwich shop and got po'boys. I got shrimp and Mick got oyster and we shared both, and they were, maybe, the most delicious thing in the world. We didn't talk much. After we ate we walked back to the parking lot where our cars were. We looked at each other. Mick was okay. It wasn't the happy ending he'd wanted, but then again, it wasn't an ending at all. Just a break while the fat lady changed costume. There was plenty of time to get Terrell back on track before the next show.

'Well,' Mick said, grudgingly. 'I guess you were right. I guess your way worked after all.'

'My way always works,' I said. 'But next time, you won't believe me all over again, It'll be just like this never happened.'

'You think there'll be a next time?' Mick asked. I couldn't tell if it was hope or dread in his voice.

I shrugged. 'Yeah,' I said. 'I think there'll be a next time.' We hugged goodbye.

'Call me sometime, okay?' I said. 'You could e-mail too, you know.'

'Yeah,' Mick said. 'Okay.'

When we broke apart I saw that he was smiling.

We got in our cars and left.

CHAPTER 56

On my way back to my hotel I called a law office in New York where I knew someone I could ask for a favor.

'MacGowen, MacGowen and MacGowen,' the bright receptionist said.

'Give me the middle MacGowen, please,' I said. 'And tell him it's Claire DeWitt.'

In a minute MacGowen got on the phone.

'Claire DeWitt,' he said, pretending to be happy to hear from me. 'What can I do for you?'

'It's what I can do for *you*,' I said. 'Because I have got the pro bono case of a lifetime for you, my friend.'

'Jesus, Claire,' MacGowen said. 'I got three kids going to college next year, I got a wife who eats money for breakfast, I got a mortgage—'

'But wait,' I said. 'There's more.'

I told him about the case. I told him about the storm. I told him about Terrell and the abuse he'd lived with. I told him about how much his friends loved him, about how he was a kid born in the worst circumstances, a kid who no one had loved and no one looked out for, a kid who raised himself

363

from nothing and turned out pretty fucking good. I told MacGowen that Terrell was kind and smart and if he went to prison it would be a fucking shame. A fucking shame for everyone.

MacGowen didn't say anything for a long time. I heard him sigh.

'Okay,' he said. 'I'll do it.'

We went over all the details. Before we got off the phone I said:

'Listen. There's this young detective, just starting out – he knows the kid, knows the victim, knows about the case, and he'll work for free, or close to it. He will be an invaluable asset. Name's Andray Fairview. I'll e-mail you all his information.'

'He's good?' MacGowen said. 'He'll really help?'

'Oh, he's good,' I said. 'Almost as good as me.'

'Wow,' MacGowen said. 'I've never heard you say *that* before.'

'Well, it's true,' I said. 'And someday, he'll be better.'

When we hung up I made another phone call.

'Claire DeWitt,' a woman hissed in a thick Bhutanese accent. 'You never to call here again. Very clear with you. Never call again.'

'Just get the lama on the phone,' I said.

'Lama never talk to you,' the woman insisted. 'Lama not talk to Claire DeWitt ever again.'

'He'll talk to me,' I said. 'You'll see.'

After a few minutes of arguing she relented and got the lama on the phone. Constance had sent me to study with him years ago. Some of it took. Most of it didn't.

'Claire DeWitt,' the lama said in his California accent, betraying his origins as a Santa Cruz surfer. 'My biggest failure. How the hell are you?'

'I'm okay,' I said. 'And thanks, I'm flattered.'

'I had high hopes for you, Claire,' he said.

'Well, I aim to disappoint,' I said. 'But listen. You still doing that prison ministry?'

'Sure,' he said. 'What's up?'

'I got this kid,' I said. 'I mean, I know this kid. And he really could use someone like you.'

'Someone like me?' the lama said. He sounded amused. 'Gee, Claire, if I remember right you called me a useless, pathetic, creepy piece of—'

'Well, I'm not saying I was wrong,' I said. 'But you're probably better than nothing, and if anyone ever needed that shit, it's this kid. He . . . he got dealt a bad hand. That's the short version. And he's got friends, but he needs to learn some things. He needs to learn to live with some really heavy shit, and I don't think they can help him do that. And the stuff you taught me – he could use that. He could really, really use that.'

The lama was quiet for a minute. I felt something in my skull – like a headache, but without the pain. I held back the urge to curse the lama.

'Claire DeWitt,' he finally said. 'There might be hope for you yet.'

'Don't bet on it,' I said.

'Oh, I'm not,' he said with a laugh. 'Believe me. But yeah, of course. Of course I'll work with the kid. Hook it up.'

CHAPTER 57

That night I wandered around the city. I
wondered if it would be the last time.
I couldn't imagine ever coming here again.
But I'd thought that before. I drove out to the
park where on my last last night in New Orleans
I'd seen an Indian gang chanting. There was no
Indian gang tonight. Instead there were about a
dozen kids on these little toy cars and motor-
cycles – they looked like the little cars the Shriners
drive in parades, powered by electricity or gas,
making little put-put vroom-vroom sounds as they
drove around the park. The projects across the
street were closed but someone had wired some
lights up for the park, probably taking power from
the city, so the kids could play at night. There
were a dozen kids or more between maybe eight
and thirteen years old, mostly boys. They rode
their little cars and bikes around in circles and
figure eights, hitting each other and getting up
again, racing to a dead tree and back, shrieking
and laughing, all under the jury-rigged lights.

I wanted to go home.

On the way back to my hotel, on an empty block,

I saw a man sitting on the curb, drunk and crying. I didn't think twice. It was a pretty common sight in any city, let alone here. But as I got closer I realized I recognized his white jumpsuit.

It was the Wildlife and Game man. The man who eliminated parrots.

I parked the truck and went over to him and sat next to him.

'Come on, buddy,' I said. 'Let's get you home.'

If he recognized me he didn't give any sign of it. He just kept crying. His face was wet with snot and tears. He looked at me like I'd been sitting next to him the whole time.

'He was looking at me,' he said in between sobs. 'Just looking at me like, *Jorge*. Like he was saying my name. Just looking at me like he was so sad.'

'It's okay,' I said. 'It's all gonna be okay. Where are you staying?'

But he wouldn't budge. 'He was *looking* at me,' he said. 'He wouldn't stop looking at me. And I held him in my hand—'

'Okay, pal,' I said. 'Come on. Time to go home.'

'I held him,' the ugly man went on, still crying. 'I felt his little heart beating and his blood – his blood was all over my hands. His heart didn't know to stop beating, that his blood was just all—'

'We all have blood on our hands,' I said. 'But it's time to go home now.'

'I realized,' he went on, sobbing, 'I realized what I had done. It only wanted to live. It just wanted to live and be left alone. Just like they all did. I couldn't do it again.'

'Okay,' I said. 'Let's—'

'I couldn't do it again,' he went on. 'I promised him that he would be the last. Now I don't know what to do with them all.'

I felt a little sick. 'All?'

I looked at him. I realized he wasn't drunk. Just miserable.

'I don't know what to do,' he said. 'I need help.'

His ugly face pleaded with me.

'Take me,' I said. 'Let's see.'

He kept crying.

'I won't hurt them,' I said. 'Come on.'

He stood up, wobbly, and we walked to his car. It wasn't locked. We got in and he drove, still crying, out toward the Industrial Canal. At the bridge he kept going. In the Lower Ninth we stopped in front of a house that was, impossibly, standing, upright. It was a run-down pink cottage.

He got out of the car and I followed. He'd stopped crying now. We slipped through the driveway to the back of the house. I noticed the front lawn was overgrown with weeds almost as high as my head. No one lived here.

'Shhh,' he said to me. 'Don't scare them.'

He was smiling now. Slowly and quietly we crept around to the back door. From the pocket of his jumpsuit he took a little scrap of steel wire and stuck it in the keyhole. He twisted it this way and that until the lock clicked open.

'Babies,' he cooed softly as he opened the door. 'Hey, babies. Hey, birds. Daddy's home. He brought a friend but she's okay. We can trust her.'

I smelled them first; the clean-dirty smell of earth and seeds I'd first smelled in Vic Willing's terrace. Then I heard them, a thousand little coos at once. Then the man in the jumpsuit flicked on the light and I saw them.

Parrots. Everywhere.

The house was furnished and we'd come in through the kitchen. It was an ordinary poor person's kitchen – cheap vinyl tile on the floor, Formica kitchen table, empty wood boxes stacked as shelves – except on every available perch there was a green parrot. There must have been fifty in this room alone. And every one of them seemed happy to see the ugly man. They squawked and flapped their wings and did little dances in place. Two couldn't wait and flew right toward him, landing on each shoulder.

The man looked like a different man now. He smiled. He wasn't so ugly.

'Babies,' he said indulgently. 'Naughty babies, be quiet. No one can know you're here.'

He reached into his pocket and took out a handful of sunflower seeds and fed them to the two on his shoulders.

'Silly birds,' he said.

One flew over and landed on my shoulder. I laughed. The man laughed too, and we smiled at each other.

The bird's feet scratched and tickled my shoulder. He gently pushed his beak into my hair.

'Erk,' he said into my ear. 'ERK.'

'I never knew who I was before,' the man said. But now he was Vic Willing.

'Erk! Erk!'

'You'll see, Claire,' he said, smiling, in his mellifluous southern voice, 'when you open your eyes.'

'Erk!'

'The blood just washes off.' He looked down at his hands, clean and white.

'It's like,' he said, and I got the idea that he was telling me something very important, 'it's not like it never happened at all,' he said, the birds preening his white hair. 'That wouldn't mean anything. It's like it all happened, every last bit of it. But somehow, you can go on anyway. Somehow, you can know every last bit of it and still go on.'

Vic looked happy but I was overcome by a sour feeling. Jealousy.

I looked down, and my own hands were covered in blood.

'Your time is coming,' Vic said. 'Ain't no one forgotten about you, girl. But you got to be patient. Maybe the most patient of them all. But at the end, I promise you, is something glorious.'

When I woke up, I knew the Case of the Green Parrot was closed.

And I knew that, like Jack Murray, I would go to hell and back before I solved the rest of my mysteries.

CHAPTER 58

After some coffee I drove out to the Industrial Canal and dropped in the gun I'd bought and the weapons I'd taken from Andray. Back in my room I put together a little package explaining who'd done it and why with a bill for my services and put it in an express mail envelope for Leon.

When I was packed and ready to go I sat on the bed and made a call to Washington, D.C.

I'd missed my flight into New Orleans because of a case I solved that involved a Homeland Security officer and a girl who wasn't his wife.

But I wasn't going to miss my flight out. I had a favor I'd been saving for a rainy day, and today it was pouring. I wanted to get out of here and back home to California as soon as possible.

'I'm sorry,' the man who answered the phone said brightly. 'The senator really can't talk to anyone without an appointment.'

I hadn't talked to the senator in three years, not since I'd solved a mystery no one else could fix for her. She didn't want to owe me. But she owed me all the same.

'Could you tell her?' I asked. 'You could just tell her I'm on the phone.'

'I'm sorry, I—'

'You could try,' I said. 'Because she'll want to talk to me. Just write it down. Write it down on a little slip of paper and—'

'The senator really can't—'

'She can.'

'She won't—'

'She will,' I said.

Less than a minute later the senator picked up the phone.

'Sorry about that, Claire,' she said. 'He's an aide – he didn't know.'

'It's okay,' I said. 'But listen. I could use a favor.'

'Name it,' she said, all business.

I told her about the trouble I'd been having flying.

'So I was hoping you could help me out with that,' I said. 'I was hoping I could just get on the airplane from now on, you know, like a normal person.'

'Of course,' she said. 'Absolutely. It's done.'

'Thank you,' I said. 'Thanks a lot. I really appreciate that. But the thing is, I've got a flight tonight. A flight home from New Orleans. Louis Armstrong Airport. And I really, really don't want to miss this flight.'

The senator had come to me when no one else would help her, when there was no one else she could trust. It's funny how people forget those times. You'd think I was the one who put her daughter in that opium den.

She paused for a second too long before she answered. But it was the right answer. 'Of course,' she said. 'I'll take care of it. I'll call the airport myself. I'll do it as soon as we're off the phone.'

We thanked each other again and I hung up.

I picked up my suitcase. I felt like my bones had been replaced by lead, my blood by oil.

That's the thing about being a private eye. The job will bleed you dry. No one ever says, Hey, maybe the PI needs a break. Hey, let's buy the PI a drink. No thank-you cards, no flowers, no singing telegrams, and half the time you don't even get paid.

CHAPTER 59

A few days before Constance died we stayed up late one night talking in her parlor, each of us on one of her long velvet sofas. Of course, I didn't know she was going to die soon. But I knew change was coming. I felt it in my blood, I saw it when I slept. That night she was in a rare mood. Usually she taught by example and metaphor, dream and command, but tonight we drank wine and talked and she answered a few of my questions directly. Her white hair was piled on her head and she wore black silk pajamas from Hong Kong. She smelled like violets always, and sometimes like a special shampoo she used from Paris, and the old-fashioned makeup she bought on Canal Street.

Not many good things had happened to me before I met Constance. But after I met her I knew how to recognize the good parts of life and stay with them for a minute or two before they flew away, joining the dead wherever the dead go. This was one of the good moments: her hair, her smell, her house, Mick sleeping in the spare room, all of us a family.

I loved New Orleans. I thought I was finally home. I loved the city so much, it hurt sometimes.

'The truth is a funny thing,' Constance said. 'Just when you think you've got a hold on it, it slips away.'

'Then why do it?' I asked. 'Why bother to solve mysteries? Don't they ever end?'

Constance laughed. 'Oh, no,' she said. 'No. Mysteries never end. And I always thought maybe none of them really get solved, either. We only pretend we understand when we can't bear it anymore. We close the file and close the case, but that doesn't mean we've found the truth, Claire.'

'Then what does it mean?' I asked.

'It only means that we've given up on this mystery,' Constance explained. 'And decided to look for the truth someplace else.' She yawned. 'That's enough for now, dear. You go on and get some sleep. I'll see you in the morning.'

'Good night,' I said. I stood up and turned around. But then a strange feeling overcame me and I turned back around. Suddenly tears were streaming down my face.

'I . . .' I began.

'Yes?' Constance said. It was dark, and she couldn't see I was crying.

'I . . . Thank you,' I said. I realized I had never said it before. 'For everything. Thank you.'

Constance looked at me and smiled.

'You're welcome, my dear,' she said. 'You are very, very welcome.'

I nodded. Then I turned and started toward the door. I would never see her alive again.

'And yes,' Constance called out behind me. 'I love you too, Claire.'